C000056377

THE VELVET RIBBON
CLUB AEGIS

Christie Adams

Blue Topaz Books

UNITED KINGDOM

Copyright © 2015-2018 by **Christie Adams**

All rights reserved. No part of this publication may be reproduced, distributed or transmitted in any form or by any means, without prior written permission.

Blue Topaz Books
Suite 12678, PO Box 4336
Manchester, United Kingdom, M61 0BW
www.bluetopazbooks.com

Publisher's Note: This is a work of fiction. Names, characters, places, and incidents are a product of the author's imagination. Locales and public names are sometimes used for atmospheric purposes. Any resemblance to actual people, living or dead, or to businesses, companies, events, institutions, or locales is completely coincidental.

Edited by **Julie Naughton**
Cover by **Syneca Featherstone**
Book Layout © 2017 **BookDesignTemplates.com**

The Velvet Ribbon / Christie Adams—5th ed.
ISBN 978-1-910791-51-6

CLUB AEGIS

Aegis—the shield of Zeus, and by extension, a means of protection. The men and women who are members of Club Aegis have all played their part in protecting their country. They work hard... and they play hard. Their lives are not always easy—and sometimes they have to put their lives on the line, not just for their country but for those they love.

Available now
The Velvet Ribbon
A Wanting Heart
Love Is Danger
Passion's Last Promise
Winter's Fire

Next in series
No Going Back

CHAPTER ONE

The sound of heels on hardwood provided the metronomic fanfare that alerted Alex to the imminent arrival of Beth Harrison—his executive assistant, right-hand woman and, of late, source of growing frustration. He looked up from the correspondence in his hand, eyes narrowing at her approaching reflection in the tinted window that gave him a panoramic view over London.

Those damn fuck-me shoes! A muscle tensed in his tightly clenched jaw. While her working wardrobe went from black to white, with every shade of grey between, her footwear was downright rebellious—immaculate heels, never less than four inches in height, in a myriad selection of styles and eye-catching colours.

Which ones today? It was a question that crossed Alex's mind every morning. He'd never considered himself to have any kind of shoe fetish until Beth came to work for him. Every morning it was the same, and the

litany of colours was ever-expanding. As for today—
would it be the peacock blue? Or the metallic purple, perhaps? He was rather fond of the latter.

No, today it was a new pair... new to the office, at any
rate. The vivid red patent leather heels, with an ankle
strap adorned with an eye-catching bow, were incredibly
flattering to her slender feet and shapely ankles... and
those gorgeous legs clad in sheer black nylon with seams
straighter than an arrow. Oh, the fantasies he'd had about
having those legs wrapped around his hips while he sank
his cock into her lush body, felt her contract hard around
him, heard her panting cries as he spilled inside her at the
moment of her climax...

His eyes continued upward, taking in the flannel-grey
pencil skirt, the way the fabric clung to her curves, so fitted that it gave her hips an ultra-feminine sway as she
walked. He experienced a sharp, momentary twinge of
disappointment; for the lines to be that smooth, there was
no way she was wearing stockings. He tried to curb his
disappointment that beneath the skirt, there would be no
tantalising exposure of creamy skin at the top of her
thighs.

She wore the crisp, snow-white cotton blouse with the
top buttons undone, hinting at a delicious cleavage. The
long sleeves were fastened at her delicate wrists with
mock cufflinks. French-manicured nails tipped elegant
fingers that clasped a notebook and pen.

And then there was her face: heart-shaped, lightly
made-up, alluring green eyes behind unremarkable spec-

tacles, all crowned by luxuriant, upswept brown hair threaded with gold, and not one strand out of place. In the three years that she'd been his assistant, he'd never seen her anything less than cool, calm and utterly professional.

What he'd give to see her come apart under the force of the orgasms he could give her.

He really shouldn't harbour such thoughts. Ten years his junior, Beth had never, as far as Alex knew, been married. He, on the other hand, had an unpleasant, expensive and thankfully long-distant divorce behind him, which made him too old and too cynical for someone as lovely as his assistant.

"Yes, Mr. Lombard?" Her voice was as composed as ever.

Three bloody years, and she still wouldn't call him by his given name—it was always *Mr. Lombard* or *Sir*. His thoughts lingered on the second option and what it brought with it—the prospect of her calling him that as her Dom, along with the equally enticing prospect of his collar adorning her elegant neck.

None of which was ever going to happen, for so damn many fucking reasons. She was the best executive assistant he'd ever had—in light of his strictly hands-off approach when it came to his staff, there was no way he'd date her. He was also pretty sure she wasn't a sub, but even if she had been, he knew he couldn't give her everything she'd need from her true Master.

And if Beth had been a sub, she would have deserved so much more than a training arrangement with a broken

Dom or an emotionally meaningless scene at the club. He could never give any sub more than that. Not now, not for a long time in the past... and not for the foreseeable future.

"Mr. Lombard?" There was a frisson of concern in her soft, clear voice now—it shattered his obsessive train of thought and brought him back to cold, hard reality. He shifted his focus to the present and tried to ignore how he was turned on by the thought of stripping her of everything except those heels and having her kneel before him.

"I'm sorry, Beth," he found himself saying absently. "Have we had any more information about the Robertson-Wolfe contract yet?"

"Nothing yet, sir. I'm keeping a look out for incoming emails."

Shit, shit, fucking shit, damn! Why the hell did she have to call him that now? "Thanks, Beth," he growled, trying to ignore the fresh images in his head. "Let me know as soon as anything comes in."

For a moment, Beth debated whether or not she should enquire about her boss's wellbeing; she decided to err on the side of caution and beat a hasty retreat.

The strangest look had flickered across Alexander Lombard's face when she'd answered his question about Robertson-Wolfe, but her sense of self-preservation prevented her from pursuing it with her panty-droppingly attractive, six-foot-three, man-mountain ex-military boss. Gossip among the staff insisted that he'd served in the

Special Forces, and that after he'd left the military he'd spent some time working in "private security"—whatever that really meant.

Beth wasn't sure about the Special Forces part of it, but he still carried his military experience in his bearing. And although the details remained elusive, she did know he shared a history in security with his best friend, Cameron Fraser, who came into the office on a regular basis and was due to call in that very morning.

She kept the sigh to herself until she returned to the outer sanctum that was her office. Whatever was riding Alex these days, it wasn't getting any better.

Sex. It had to be sex, she realised a few minutes later, seated once again at her desk. Or, more accurately, a lack of sex. He hadn't asked her to order flowers, or book tables for two at his favourite restaurants for about six months, all told—if he wasn't dating, he wasn't getting laid, and not getting laid was bound to make such a virile alpha male grouchy.

Beth almost snorted. Grouchy? A bear with a sore head, toothache and rampant haemorrhoids would be less grouchy than Alex Lombard had been at times recently. She looked at the clock; it was just after eight-thirty, and she knew he would have been in the office since before seven. He hadn't had any coffee yet; she eyed the pristine espresso coffee maker in the corner of her office, next to the grinder, wondering if he'd notice if she switched to decaffeinated beans in an attempt to make him less tetchy. She shook her head. What was that saying again? *The road to hell is paved with good intentions…*

He was on the phone when Beth went in with the small cup of liquid dynamite; she had learned early on that hot coffee took precedence over everything else. He was in the middle of an animated conversation in fluent Italian, his voice deep and bone-meltingly sexy. How could a voice have her hormones leaping to attention so easily? It didn't seem possible, but the spear of need that ripped through her body appeared to indicate otherwise.

That was why she always maintained an air of formality when she addressed him; if she started calling him by his given name, it would be the beginning of the end. *Mr. Lombard* kept her from getting all dewy-eyed and moon-struck about *Alex*.

Beth loved her job. She'd gone along to the interview expecting it to be for a regular executive assistant's role, but it had turned out to be so much more—leaving aside the calls to florists and restaurants, which she made for him as a favour. Right from the start, Alex had made it clear that he didn't expect her to waste her talent or her intelligence on simply providing refreshments, dealing with the mail and running errands.

Instead, he'd given her a list of clients of her own—a subset of his own exclusive portfolio—and after an initial period of intensive training and mentoring, he'd allowed her to run with it. He trusted her judgement in all things. She valued that trust, and well… making an extra cup of coffee or the odd phone call wasn't such a hardship, was it?

The last six months aside, Beth was uncomfortably aware of a steady stream of women who had paraded briefly through her employer's life—all quite a bit younger than her, judging by the voices on the other end of the phone calls she'd fielded, and none of them had lasted much longer than about three months, if she recalled correctly. She'd heard the gossip about Alex having been married, and that the marriage had supposedly gone spectacularly sour; ever since then, she'd been fighting her natural impulse to "fix" him—her Fairy Godmother instinct.

"Good morning, angel! And how are you this fine day? Is the brute in?"

Wrapped up in her work, Beth hadn't realised how quickly the morning was going until the cheerful male voice greeted her. She recognised it instantly; it belonged to Cameron Fraser, another walking mountain of testosterone. He swept into the office like a force of nature, straight to her desk, and lifted her hand to his mouth to place a gallant kiss to the back of it—she couldn't help but smile at the old-world charm.

And where Alex was dark, moody and could be downright scary, Cam was all blond hair, blue eyes and muscular charm by the bucketload, packed into six feet and one inch of immaculately attired masculinity. Attractive, yes, but as far as Beth was concerned, he didn't quite have the same charisma as her employer.

"I'm fine, thank you, Mr. Fraser," she smiled up at him, rising from her seat. "Yes, Mr. Lombard's expecting you—can I get you some coffee?"

"Don't go to any trouble on my account, Beth—I'll see myself in."

Had Beth been a fly on the wall, she would have seen a completely different man lean his hip on the corner of Alex's desk; Cam, another former Special Forces operative, could be every bit as cold and ruthless as his friend if the need arose. When it came to business, they meant business, and like Alex, Cam too was a Dom.

"So have you taken her as your sub yet?" Cam asked the question seriously, knowing full well what the answer would be—one of the first things he'd done on entering the outer office had been to check for the presence of a collar.

"Don't go there," Alex growled without even turning around.

Cam gave an exasperated sigh. "Are you going to give me that crap again? About just training them because that's all you have to offer them? Alex—"

"I can't and you fucking well know why!"

Cam swore under his breath. The tightly controlled anger was getting old now. For years he'd witnessed his friend settling for perfunctory scenes with subs or just training them, instead of finding the one with whom he could have a true emotional connection. Yes, he knew why Alex was acting this way, could even understand it after a fashion, but Cam knew that Alex needed more, even if the man shied away from it like a virgin confronted with a St. Andrew's Cross. Going back to the counsellor was the answer, but that would mean Alex actually confronting the fucking question…

"Why the hell not? Hasn't it occurred to you that she might just be—"

"I don't date my employees!"

"Then maybe it's time you started. Beth's perfect sub material—always so eager to please, moves like a dream, she's classy and elegant. If you don't, I will."

That made Alex swivel his executive chair around to face the other man. "Like hell you will, Fraser." The statement came out just short of a snarl.

Cam raised a speculative eyebrow to go with the slightly crooked, smug grin; his ex-military buddy only used his surname when Cam had put a particularly large burr under his saddle. "I thought that would get a rise out of you, old man." From time to time, he liked to remind Alex of his seniority, in terms of both age—all of two years—and former rank. "So when are you going to do something about it?"

Any response the other man might have made to that challenge was put on hold when the subject of their animated conversation came in with two steaming mugs of coffee. As she turned to leave, Cam fired an "I-told-you-so" look at her employer.

Alex waited long enough for the door to close behind her. "Your point?" he demanded, his tone more than a touch acerbic.

"You didn't even have to ask her. Cheers!" Cam raised

his mug before downing a hearty swig of the steaming brew. "And she makes bloody good coffee as well."

The conversation turned to business, the original reason for Cam's visit. Before Alex had started Paduan Ventures—named for St. Anthony of Padua, the patron saint of lost articles and those who seek them—he and Cam had been partners in a security consultancy. After the incident that still cast a long shadow over him, Alex had walked away from the company, leaving Cam in sole charge; since then, Cam had developed the business into a substantial concern with clients located all over the world.

Given the nature of the business Alex was in now, security was a major concern. Some projects had been going awry lately, so he'd called Cam in to conduct a full investigation.

Once all the arrangements were made, Cam turned the conversation back to the woman in the outer office—or tried to.

Alex scowled; he'd been doing that a lot lately. "Don't you have work to do, Fraser?"

"Nothing that can't wait five minutes. It's Friday—are you going to the club tonight?"

Cam was referring to Aegis, the discreet private club where he and Alex could let the dominant sides of their personalities out to play. While Alex had still been a regular visitor over the last six months, indulgence in terms of taking part in the scene was something that he had avoided, preferring instead to nurse a Scotch or two before disappearing back to his city-centre apartment.

"Maybe." His tone was as noncommittal as his response.

"I'll see you there." Cam's voice was determined. "And for fuck's sake, will you play with at least one sub tonight? You'll be losing your touch."

"Will you get the hell out of here?"

Cam grinned wickedly as he opened the door. "Okay, I get the message—see you later!"

After saying goodbye to her employer's friend, Beth checked the time—lunchtime at last. She could switch off from work for a while and jot down the ideas that had been flitting through the back of her mind. She had just enough time before she went to the coffee shop for lunch with some of the girls from the office.

The ideas were for her latest attempt at breaking into the writing business. Realistically she knew the odds were against her, but for Beth writing was almost a form of therapy, a way of exorcising a longing that, on more than one occasion, she'd been told was downright perverted.

She wanted to know what it was like to submit to a Dom.

Books and the internet were as close as she'd got; writing was her way of taking part in that intriguing world. She read novels, of course, and at times her imagination was prone to running away with her, but she wasn't kidding anyone. If she were that brave, she'd be living the lifestyle instead of just writing about it. Where she was and where she thought she wanted to be were two entirely different places, and in between them was the massive wall she'd built to protect the very part of her that wanted to be on the other side of that wall. It scared her to death, but at the same time she wanted it so much.

And she knew exactly who she'd want for her Dom— that was yet another reason to address him as *Mr. Lombard*. There wasn't a cat in hell's chance that he was ever going to assume that role for real. Even if he had a tendency towards that sort of thing, she was the last woman he'd take for his sub. Without her glasses, she was as blind as a bat, and while she wasn't out and out overweight, her curves were a little more ample than the media tended to prefer. Over the years, she'd learned well how to dress to impress. And to camouflage.

Feeling badgered by the pop-up reminder about her monthly lunch date on her computer screen, Beth quickly scribbled down the few lines her imagination had just come up with, and in the rush not to be late, she completely forgot to slip the notebook back into her desk drawer.

A few minutes later, Alex emerged from his office, a brief frown marring his brow at his assistant's unexpected absence. A glance at the wall clock clarified the matter; she was probably downstairs at the coffee shop, buying her usual salad lunch and a skinny latte with sugar-free vanilla syrup. As a devotee of the double espresso, he wondered briefly how she could stomach such a concoction. Irritated by the distracting thought, he focused on the matter that had brought him out of his office in the first place—perhaps the contract he wanted was on her desk.

He scanned the neatly set-out documents she was dealing with. His visual sweep came to a screeching halt at the small, brightly coloured notebook. He'd seen her scribbling in it during her lunch hour on several occasions, but she'd always put it out of sight as he approached, with a grace and economy of movement that the Dom in him appreciated. It was obviously something private, but with barely a qualm he flipped the book open, expecting to see nothing more remarkable than a shopping list.

The precise cursive script was instantly recognisable as Beth's; feminine, eminently legible, and executed with a fountain pen. Alex liked that—so few people used fountain pens these days. His eyes narrowed as he scanned the lines, and it didn't take long for what she'd written to send the blood surging to his dick. This was no shopping list. *What in the name of heaven…?*

Strait-laced Miss Harrison was describing—in elegant detail, no less—a scene that could have come straight from the club where he fully intended to drink away most of the forthcoming evening. And judging by the description of the sub who was being disciplined so deliciously, she was painting herself in that role.

There was more. He flicked through the notebook and found disjointed snippets of prose—descriptions and conversations that looked as if they belonged in a somewhat larger work; a short story, or perhaps even a novel. Either way, she wrote beautifully, and he didn't just mean her refined handwriting—she wrote about the act of submission as the truly exquisite gift that it was.

Holy crap.

She knew about his world. Not only that, she appeared to understand it too. How had he got her so wrong?

She wasn't a collared sub; of that much Alex was certain. She wore no jewellery of any kind that might indicate ownership. That led him to conclude that she was probably untrained, possibly even only just beginning to explore that side of her sexuality, perhaps undecided about whether it was for her or not. Whether she *needed* it or not.

After replacing the book precisely where he'd found it, Alex located the document he wanted and returned to his office. His mind, however, was far from being on work. Instead it was on Beth, her writing, and what lay beneath.

She let precious little of the non-work Beth out of the bag. Professional in the office, not especially given to socialising with her colleagues beyond the odd lunch and attending the office Christmas party, she maintained an almost aloof distance. Occasionally, though, she'd slip up and reveal a very keen wit. There was no doubt she was intelligent.

So how did a smart, gorgeous woman with a cutting sense of humour spend her evenings and weekends? It would seem that she used at least some of the time to indulge in erotic fantasies and write about them.

Having left the door to his office ajar, he was immediately aware when she returned, looking relaxed and happy. She'd been away a while—maybe she'd lunched with a friend. Alex found himself wondering about that mysterious companion. A female companion, he hoped, because no other man was going to lay a finger on her.

The fierce sense of possession in the thought startled him—though Beth was often in his thoughts, this was the first time he'd felt something so visceral and primitive screaming that she was his.

He continued to watch her moving around the outer office, admiring her customary grace and efficiency. He imagined slowly removing her clothing, until only the heels and stockings remained—her legs were made for them, and they'd draw attention to a pussy he would ensure she kept deliciously smooth.

Sideswiped by his thoughts, Alex suddenly felt like he was making his way through an unmarked minefield. What the fucking hell was going on with him? Was this the result of the conversation with Cam melding with the impact of his insight into the secret thoughts of Beth Harrison? Did he dare hope that this might be the first sign of the past loosening its hold on him?

Those events still had the power to make his blood run cold. They'd also left him unable to function as a Dom within a loving relationship. For years, instead of being open to the possibility of finding the sub who could be his soul mate, he'd played out scenes or taken subs into his protection as trainees and nothing more. He'd derived no real pleasure from the scenes, just the satisfaction of giving the subs what they needed; those training contracts had specifically stipulated that there was to be no sex between Dom and sub. When he needed physical intimacy, it was—or had been until six months ago—strictly on his terms within vanilla relationships, which, by their very nature, were time-limited. Domination was as much a part of him as the blood in his veins—he couldn't endure even the thought of living completely without it. Consequently, each of those relationships was doomed to end even before it started.

And then Beth had come along, the best assistant he'd ever had and as vanilla as the day was long, a combination of factors that had enabled him to keep his desire for her in check. Until now. He could kid himself no longer. In many ways she was his ideal woman, he'd known that for a while, but he'd countered that with the certainty that any little signs of natural submissiveness were simply wishful thinking on his part. That game was now up.

For too long he'd been a gutless coward, too scared even to try having a real relationship with a sub. A decade after the event, he was still letting those bastards rule his life. Was he going to let this situation carry on and risk finding himself watching Beth develop her submissive side with another Dom? Could he once again be the Dom he used to be? For Beth?

Maybe Cam was right. She was everything he wanted. Was he going to let the fact that she worked for him get in the way of finding out if there could be something real, something meaningful between them? Was he really going to let this chance pass him by, the chance to have a real relationship with the first woman he'd really wanted in years… the woman he never thought he'd have?

The remainder of the afternoon passed well enough—apart from the fact that by four o'clock, it was getting really difficult for Alex to conceal the hard-on he was getting every time Beth came into his office. Or, more to the point, when she left it; he found himself lusting after that gorgeous, curvaceous rear as it swayed out of the room, contemplating which implements he might use to bring a rosy hue to her skin. The genie was well and truly out of the bottle now, even if he hadn't yet made a final decision about taking things forward.

The end of his day brought a particularly tense teleconference. Once it was over, Alex sat back in his executive chair, closing his eyes to try to relieve the tension that was building in his temples. Ever since the explosion that had left its mark on his back fifteen years earlier, he'd been prone to getting these almost unbearable headaches. Still, it was well after five-thirty; the office would be silent and empty when he left to make his way to the club.

"Mr. Lombard, is there anything you need before I go?"

You. On your knees, between my legs, and hold my cock in your lovely mouth. Don't suck—if you do, your beautiful backside will get twenty.

He pushed aside the errant thought—right now, it was the last thing he needed. "Thanks, Beth, but I'm fine—you go and enjoy your weekend."

Uncharacteristically, he missed the fact that she didn't

say goodbye; what he didn't miss was the cool fingers suddenly massaging his temples. *Dear God, don't let this be a dream.*

"Keep your eyes closed," came her soft voice. "Is there any medication you take for these?"

She'd evidently noticed his damn headaches before. So what else had she noticed about him? He shook his head briefly, unwilling to shatter the moment by speaking, even though the abrupt movement did nothing to help the pain that sent a skewer through his brain. Her touch was gentle but insistent; it was all he could do not to let out a moan of both pleasure and relief.

Silence stretched out; time stopped. In an alternate universe, she was wearing his collar and those wonderful fuck-me heels, and he was going to show her what a gloriously sexual animal she was. As sensual fantasies went, he couldn't think of anything better.

And then reality thudded firmly back into place.

"I hope your head's starting to feel better, Mr. Lombard."

Her voice came from somewhere in the direction of the door; he opened his eyes and saw her standing there, jacket on, bag at her feet, and knew that if he were taking her back to his place tonight, she'd get well and truly fucked, whether his headache had gone or not.

"It is." How was his voice so steady? "Thank you, Beth—you have a healing touch."

She glanced briefly towards the floor, clearly embarrassed by the compliment—he'd have to do something about that during the course of her training. Lowering her gaze like that, as part of her submission, was one thing; being embarrassed by compliments—especially from him—was something he would not permit.

And there he went, off on the runaway train again. Had it been inevitable all along? He needed to think—he sure as hell wasn't going to charge into this without considering it from all angles.

"You're welcome, Mr. Lombard. I'm sorry, but I have to go now—my bus is due."

What on earth had come over her?

Beth felt her face flame with colour as she waited for the lift. She prodded the call button again, even though she knew damn well it would have no effect. Having fantasies about the man was one thing, but actually touching him like that, when he was vulnerable, was about the worst idea she'd ever had, and she'd had some doozies in her time. What had happened to her determination not to fling herself at a man who would never be interested in catching her? Thank God it was the weekend and she wouldn't have to face him tomorrow.

Years of wanting the man had finally overwhelmed her good sense. She'd seen him every working day in that time, witnessed the number of women who had passed through his life, and nothing had diminished the feelings that had grown for him, in spite of her best intentions.

The sigh she gave held more than a hint of longing. She couldn't help but wonder what he would be doing that evening—and with whom he might be doing it. He might not have dated for six months, but the drought could end at any time.

The journey home seemed to take longer than usual. When she finally arrived there, she closed the door of the one-bedroom apartment behind her and made a beeline for the shower. It was only when she was standing under the hot, soothing cascade that she gave way to the mortified tears of embarrassment that had been threatening ever since she left the office.

It had felt so good to finally touch him when she gave in to that stupid impulse to ease away his pain. She'd seen him go through that before, and her tender heart had ached through not being able to do anything to help— today, she could bear it no longer and had rushed in where angels would fear to tread.

When she had no more tears left to cry, she emerged from the shower. Drying herself quickly, she wrapped a towel around her sodden hair and pulled on her soft, fleecy dressing gown. She wasn't going anywhere tonight—no change there, then—so she poured herself a glass of wine, switched on the TV and channel-surfed, trying to find something half-decent to watch, to take her mind off the lonely weekend that stretched ahead of her… and the humiliating memory of that stupid episode with Alex.

Her mind, though, had other ideas. It kept tantalising her with way his skin felt, the heady masculine scent of him… and fantasies of what it would be like to be the woman who shared his bed.

A couple of hours after he left the office, Alex was propping up the bar at Aegis, slowly sipping his way through his third Scotch of the evening.

The black leathers and boots were straight out of the Dom handbook, but for reasons he didn't care to dwell on, Alex wore them with a flowing white shirt that he kept unbuttoned. The subs tended to love the swashbuckling pirate look; tonight, however, he had no desire to play out a scene, hence the whisky. And the reason for the lack of interest was that he had a lot to think about.

Cam, on the other hand, was indulging in a session in one of the private rooms. Alex hadn't seen him since he arrived, but had been told that his friend had taken one of the unattached subs for a little bondage and discipline.

He looked around the club. The usual Friday night crowd was there—the place was thronged with people in various states of dress and undress, milling around the lounge, bar and public rooms. The private rooms were fully booked too. He wondered what effect the recent change of ownership would end up having on the place. Minimal, he hoped. Word was that the new owner was one of their own, a former member of the armed forces or intelligence services like the vast majority of club members, but he—or she—hadn't seen fit to introduce him or herself yet.

Out of the corner of his eye, he watched a Dom he

didn't know leading his sub around on a leash. The sub was collared, naked and barefoot. If he brought Beth here, she'd be dressed, albeit provocatively. She'd be here to be shown off, and he'd love every minute of it, knowing he was the envy of every unattached Dom in the room. As he realised the implications of that thought, Cam's voice drew him back to the present.

"Well?"

Alex watched the sub his friend had just brought back from the private rooms make her way to join a couple of her giggling friends. If the pink glow of her backside was anything to go by, she was clearly very satisfied by the time spent with Master Cameron.

"Well what?" Alex feigned more interest in his glass of Scotch than was strictly warranted.

"Have you decided what you're going to do about Beth?"

"How did you know I was thinking about her?"

Cam sighed and rolled his eyes. "How long have we known each other? Exactly. It's in your face, Alex. And I hope that *that*," he shot a pointed glance in the direction of Alex's drink, "means you've already played?"

Alex shook his head. "Cam, something happened today, and I need to work out the best way to take things forward."

His friend took a step back, eyebrows raised. "Now you're intriguing me. Is this to do with Beth?"

This time Alex nodded, although a part of his mind was occupied elsewhere, fascinated by how the amber fluid in the glass he held reminded him of the highlights in Beth's hair.

"Wanna talk?"

The darker of the two men raised an amused eyebrow—Cam getting all touchy-feely? No wonder the former SAS staff sergeant was looking in the opposite direction, as if pretending that someone else had uttered the two words. "Shut the fuck up, Cam," Alex said without a hint of animosity. "I'll deal with it."

"So are you going to fire her, or man up and take her?" The persistent bastard's voice was deadly serious, and so was Alex's when he responded. His decision was made— so much for thinking things through.

"I'm going to do the only thing I can to resolve this."

It was after two in the morning when Alex returned to his apartment; he'd left Cam at the club, enjoying yet another scene with another eager sub. He went straight to the bedroom, shed his clothes and headed for the shower.

The hot water felt good hammering down on his tired body. It had been a long day. He'd been in the office earlier than usual for the conference call with Japan, spent another day around the woman who gave him a hard-on just by breathing, and found out that there was a chance that she was a sub-in-waiting. And to top it all, he was preparing to leave his comfort zone.

More than enough for one day.

He dropped the towel in the laundry hamper and padded back into the dark bedroom, to look out over the city from his refuge on one of the upper floors of the exclusive block. She was out there, somewhere, in all those twinkling lights—he wondered what she was doing. Sleeping, probably. Alone, he hoped. If she'd been in his bed, sleeping was the last thing she'd be doing.

He put a hand around his uncomfortably hard erection and began to masturbate, the other hand on the wall, braced for support. This had been his only release for the last six months, and it looked like tonight was going to be no different.

Then his hand stilled. Were the mechanics of a physical orgasm going to do it for him this time, given the revelation about Beth's interests?

Alex found himself thinking back to the time when life was considerably less complicated and he'd discovered that he was a natural Dominant. He and Cam had been in the States, on a training mission with their US counterparts. It was while they were on a forty-eight-hour leave that they'd discovered the club that had changed their lives. Gone were their preconceptions of BDSM being all about kinky sex—it didn't even have to include sex at all, yet it could also be a whole lifestyle.

Over time, he and Cam had completed the training and become masters of the art. Alex learned that he wasn't into the lifestyle aspects of D/s—his preference was for sexual Domination when it came to his personal life, although he had also found a great deal of satisfaction in training subs who were looking to lead a submissive lifestyle 24/7.

Alex loved women, the way they smelled, the way they tasted, the way they felt—all the glorious textures of the human female body—and he could say with confidence that every woman with whom he'd enjoyed any kind of D/s relationship, be it a scene at the club or a training contract, he'd left happy and fulfilled... except one, and she had been his ex-wife.

By the time she'd got around to yelling at him about his filthy perversion, the love had long gone and her words hadn't been able to wound the way she'd intended. He blamed himself; he should have told her about his preferences when it looked like their relationship was getting serious, long before marriage was on the radar. He'd thought that somehow he could navigate a safe passage through those choppy waters, but it wasn't to be.

With such a disparity between their sexual needs, the only thing Alex could do was let her go. It hadn't stopped her taking everything she could get her claws on, but the divorce, once declared absolute, was just that—absolute. He had no idea where she'd gone, or with whom, and by then he hadn't cared about either.

Alex dropped onto the massive bed. *Beth. His.* Something primitive stirred inside him. He pictured her lying face down on this bed, pillows under her belly and hips so that she was in the perfect position for him to take her. She was restrained, of course, and begging her Dom to fuck her.

Christ, Cam *was* right—she was perfect sub material.

His perfect sub.

And if she did see herself as the green-eyed female protagonist she'd written about—if she had a secret desire to submit to a Dom—would she really want to make that fantasy a reality? Fantasising about D/s relationships was one thing, but the reality of them was a whole different prospect. Hell, even he was still learning—not just about Domination and submission, but also about himself.

Alex rolled over onto his stomach, trapping his erection between his belly and the bed. He grimaced at the discomfort, but Christ, it felt good, reminded him that he was still alive and still capable. His muscular buttocks clenched, fighting the urge to move as if she were under him.

How could he get her to the apartment? Wine her and dine her, bring her back here, and—"Oh, by the way, Beth, I'm a Dom and I want to own you, body and soul."

Yeah, that'd work. The thought dripped sarcasm. Even if she really had submissive tendencies, an approach like that would probably still scare her half to death. With his thoughts going in unproductive circles that left him mentally exhausted, Alex eventually fell asleep.

It was a pity it wouldn't last.

CHAPTER TWO

On Monday morning, after a weekend that felt much shorter than usual, Beth arrived in the office to find a message from her employer, informing her that he was going to be in Antwerp for a few days and would be back in the office on Thursday. Part of her was relieved, but it was really just delaying the inevitable—she'd still have to face him on his return.

The next part of the message caused her eyebrows to rise in disbelief. She was to close the office for three days, give everyone paid time off, and hand the office keys to Cam Fraser so that he could perform a thorough security check.

By ten o'clock the offices were deserted, save for Beth. She was just waiting for Cam and his crew to arrive, so that she could hand over the keys as instructed, and then she too could go and make the most of the unexpected break.

"Good morning, Beth!" Cam breezed into the office. His usual tsunami-like charm offensive would have swept all before him, had there been an all to sweep. "Good weekend?"

"Yes, thank you, Mr. Fraser. I certainly wasn't expecting Mr. Lombard's message when I arrived this morning."

Cam perched a hip on the corner of her desk, looking very masculine and, it had to be said, extremely attractive in his formal business suit. Clearly tailored to a very high standard, it fitted him to perfection. He gave a sarcastic snort. "You know what the old man's like. Once he gets an idea in his head, he has to do something about it and we all have to jump."

She had to agree—her employer did like getting his own way. That was one of the traits that made him an ideal model for her fantasy Dom.

For her own peace of mind, Beth made one more sweep of the office to make sure there were no stragglers, and then returned to Reception where Cam was waiting for her.

"Do we have the all-clear, angel?"

"I believe so, Mr. Fraser," Beth replied, almost on a sigh. She held up her hand. In her palm rested the keys to the offices, the safes and the climate-controlled strongroom—the vault that held the most environmentally sensitive of the treasures sourced for their clients. All of a sudden her expression became very serious. "I've been responsible for these keys for three years. It's not a responsibility I give up lightly."

"Worry not, light of my life," Cam assured her with an insouciance she found vaguely disturbing. He plucked the bunch of keys from her hand. "You can leave everything in my hands. Go and treat yourself to some retail therapy," he suggested with a playful wink.

Beth shot him a look, one eyebrow raised. *Men!* They never did grow up. Even Alex had been known to throw his toys out of the pram occasionally, in the adult male version of a tantrum that would have done a four-year-old proud.

"Thank you, Mr. Fraser." She fixed her gaze on the face that was far too handsome for any woman's good, trying to make that gaze as steely as possible. "Just you make sure you look after this place, or I'll—"

"You'll what, dear Beth?" he prompted, not bothering to hide his amusement at the prospect of a threat from a woman around three inches shorter than him—and that was with the monstrous heels she habitually wore—and conservatively, a hundred pounds lighter.

"I'm not sure, but I'll do my best to make it dire!" she promised. "Good day, Mr. Fraser."

Cam watched her leave, admiring the feminine grace she displayed so naturally. She was a prize, all right, and just what Alex needed, even if he was having difficulty recognising the fact.

With a thoughtful look on his face, Cam checked the time. His crew would be arriving in a few minutes, but there was time for a quick phone call, to a man who wasn't in Antwerp as everyone believed—he was at home in Hampshire.

"Alex? Beth's just gone. You know, she really is too lovely to take her responsibilities so seriously all the time—you need to do something about it. What? You are? About fucking time! I'd ask you if you were planning to share her, but I'm kind of attached to my family jewels."

Cam ended the call with his friend's expletives still ringing in his ears, and pocketed his phone. He grinned, thinking about what else Alex had told him. A long time ago they'd set up the playroom together at Alex's country pile in Hampshire—if only Beth knew what was awaiting her.

More than that, though, Alex was finally getting his shit together again. And while that was good, Cam knew the man and the baggage he still carried well enough to be aware that the road ahead was unlikely to be without its problems. Still, with Cam and soon Beth in his corner, Alex wouldn't face that journey alone.

His expression one of deep thought, the man in question took a few minutes to digest what his closest friend had told him.

Having made his decision, he'd spent the weekend concentrating on Beth and how best to take their relationship from a purely business footing to a more personal one. By midnight on Sunday, he had come to the conclusion that he needed a few days' distance from his assistant to ensure that he came to a sensible and workable decision. The fictitious trip to Antwerp presented the ideal camouflage.

As he'd told Cam, he also needed to make sure that the playroom was ready for her. When he'd put the playroom together years ago, he'd wanted something modern and clean, where the dark intimacy was created not by the theme but by the lighting, the drapes and the equipment. With Cam's input, he'd achieved that.

The playroom was conveniently situated right next to his bedroom, and while a very small number of specially selected subs had been honoured with sessions in there, none had ever found their way to the sacrosanct domain of his bedroom. His ex had been the last woman in there, and she'd left enough bad memories to last a lifetime.

Then maybe it's time you made new memories.

The voice was soft and gentle; the voice was Beth's.

It took very little effort on Alex's part to picture her on the well-padded spanking bench, her hair streaming towards the floor while he got intimately acquainted with her luscious behind.

Alex had to laugh at himself then. Talk about zero to sixty in three point four seconds. He'd had years of avoiding anything remotely meaningful with a sub, and now here he was, readying the playroom at his home for Beth, of all people, a woman who was a complete novice... if his assumptions about her were correct, of course.

The picture in his mind changed, became a slideshow of different images. Beth, on her knees in front of him, her body gracefully posed in the first position, with her long hair draped over the swell of her breasts; Beth, bound to the bed in the playroom, while he taught her body a lesson in sensual pleasure; Beth, nurtured by the aftercare that had aided her return from subspace; Beth, curled up beside him while she slept, exhausted from wave after wave of orgasms that would be his gift to her.

And there was no denying it; he opened the bedroom door and stared at the huge bed—Beth was the only woman he'd wanted in it for a long, long time.

The weekend had been something of an epiphany. Alex now knew why he had become so dissatisfied with his life of late—why he'd developed a new habit of going into the office early even when there was no purpose, and why he stayed late unless he had a compelling reason to be elsewhere. The emptiness of his apartment reflected the emptiness of his life.

And at least the office had Beth.

This weekend could signal a major change in his life, but Alex was uncomfortably aware that he was dealing with the symptoms, not the disease. The events in his past were still the real demons that plagued him, and he'd let them have the upper hand for too long. The doctors had advised professional assistance to help him overcome what they'd chosen to label PTSD, but for Alex that would be an admission of weakness, an acknowledgement that the darkest period of his life had got the better of him. As such, that was simply not acceptable. He could handle the disease alone.

Needing to steer his thoughts in a happier direction, Alex let his imagination run away with him: Beth as his sub, in his life 24/7, both at home and in the office. Not only would he have her there beside him at work, she'd also be coming home with him. A leisurely dinner together, some time to relax, and then he would lead her to the bedroom and take ownership of her—everything she was, everything she thought, everything she felt. But only when it came to sex.

The best thing he could do now was get down to some work. He closed the bedroom door and went downstairs, heading for his well-equipped office.

In Beth's opinion, Thursday morning came around far too quickly. Cam Fraser had agreed to meet her at the office at a ridiculously early hour so that she could take back possession of her keys. He'd given nothing away regarding the exercise, and it was impossible to read anything into his usual breezy attitude. They'd chatted briefly and then he'd taken his leave of her, one hand in his trouser pocket, a tuneless whistle accompanying his leisurely departure. Sometimes the man was so laid back, he was almost horizontal.

Beth really needed to focus on something work-related. Writing rather than retail therapy had been her indulgence of choice, so now she was hoping that she could face her employer without blushing, given his role as the blueprint for her Dom—*the Dom in my book*, she corrected herself sternly.

"Beth, what the hell are you doing here so early?"

Caught off guard, she floundered for a moment but then grabbed the lifeline of her sense of composure—it had always served her well during the time she'd worked for Alex. She looked up at his handsome, if somewhat annoyed face.

"Good morning, Mr. Lombard," she greeted him in her usual open, friendly manner. "Thank you for the last few days—it was most… unexpected."

He made a dismissive gesture. "You didn't answer my question. It's six-thirty in the bloody morning."

Her hand indicated the stack of mail she'd picked up on the way in. "The office has been closed for three days. Emails and phone messages have piled up, too. I wanted to make an early start on the backlog."

His steely gaze moved from the pile of envelopes back to Beth. "That isn't your job. I pay clerical staff to look after that crap, so you can take it all back to their office. *Now*."

Beth's breath caught in her throat. She'd never heard that tone in his voice before. It was a tone that was intended to intimidate, and it sent a delicious ripple up and down her spine.

"I said *now*, Beth." His commanding voice drew her mind sharply back into focus. "And when you're done, you can come into my office."

With that, he strode off into said office without a backward glance, leaving Beth to deal with an instinctive compulsion to obey. Almost as if she had no control over her own legs, she stood and headed for the office shared by the three secretaries.

On her return, she went straight in to see Alex. His jacket and tie had been dumped in a heap on the sofa and the man himself was seated at his desk, his forehead resting in his hand while he studied a document. Without thinking, she rolled up his tie and placed it on the coffee table, and took his jacket to hang it in the small closet.

She had no idea that Alex was watching her keenly from under his hand—and even if she had been aware, there was no way she would have guessed that her graceful movements were sending all sorts of decadent, lustful thoughts through his mind. He wondered how she'd react to the impact those thoughts had on his body.

Today she was wearing a smartly tailored black skirt, teamed with a silk blouse in dove grey, the ever-present black, sheer, fully fashioned hosiery with a Cuban heel—and today's fuck-me shoes were in iridescent peacock blue, with a narrow ankle strap that was attached to the shoe at the back of her heel. Four-inch heels on the shoes, of course. When she reached to hang his jacket in the closet, her almost-balletic grace threatened to give him a hard-on that would last the rest of the week.

"You wanted to see me, Mr. Lombard?"

She had taken up a position on the other side of the desk, directly opposite him. Her hands were clasped together in front of her—no fidgeting, he was pleased to see. He came out from under the screen of his hand and looked up at her.

"Sit down, Beth. This won't take long." He paused while she obeyed, crossing those incredible legs at the ankles and tucking them under the chair. *Always the lady.* Her hands remained clasped on her lap. For a brief moment, he thought about her training. The training itself wouldn't be the problem—no, the problem would be getting her to accept what she was...

The sub who belonged in his bed, and the woman who belonged in his life. He wasn't sure he'd succeed, but he sure as hell was going to try.

"Do you have a valid passport?"

Beth raised her eyebrows. He got the distinct feeling that she wasn't expecting that question. "Yes, sir—it's good for the next four years."

"Excellent. Clear your calendar and mine for next week. Can you book us on the first flight to Antwerp next Monday? We'll be returning on Thursday, so can you also book us a suite each at... damn it." He extracted a business card from his wallet, glanced at it briefly, and then passed it to Beth. "Here."

She scanned the card. "Is this where you stayed this week?"

"No, I thought we'd give this one a try. If you have any trouble booking the suites, ask to speak to the manager—his name's on the back of the card—and mention my name. Everything okay, Beth?"

"Sir, I'm a little confused about why you need me to go with you?"

"Career development," he replied, his tone somewhat

curt due to the spontaneous nature of his improvised response. "Unless there's some reason—"

"Oh, no, not at all—I'm looking forward to it."

Beth normally relished the thought of the bus ride home on a Friday, but this time all she could think about was that it was another day nearer to Antwerp—and spending time alone with Alex without the distractions of the office.

And that was why her mind wasn't on her surroundings, when she left the building and became another crime statistic for the Metropolitan Police. The mugger came from nowhere, sent her flying into an awkward heap, and made off with her bag before she knew what happened.

Stunned and in shock, she looked around, her mind in total denial of what had just happened. The dirty, grazed palms and knees belonged to someone else, as did the ankle that hurt like hell when she stood up. Instinct more than anything drove her to limp barefoot back to the office, shoes dangling from one hand, knowing that there was at least one person still there.

The door to Alex's office was closed when she finally made it to her own desk. The sliver of light spilling from under that door was the only indication that its occupant was still in residence. Now that she was here, Beth realised that the last thing she wanted was for her employer to see her in this state. Blinking back the tears that threatened to overwhelm her at any moment, she picked up the phone and dialled the non-emergency number for the police. Maybe she could get this done and disappear before he even realised she was there.

Summoning every last ounce of control she possessed, Beth reported the crime. She held out absolutely no hope of getting her belongings back, but making the call was the only thing she could do. The dam finally broke when she replaced the receiver; tears stung her eyes, her vision blurred, and then the icing on the cake appeared before her—Alex, and he was frowning at her. *Again.*

Getting changed to go to Aegis, Alex had just unfastened his shirt prior to shaving when he heard noises outside in Beth's office. *What the...?* The office was closed for the weekend, so who the hell was that he could hear? He tensed, ready to take on whoever was out there, and opened the door a crack, so as not to alert the intruder.

No, not an intruder, but Beth, who must have left a good fifteen minutes earlier. What on earth had brought her back to the office? He was about to go to her when it dawned on him that she was on the phone. She finished the call and promptly burst into tears—not great dramatic floods but heartbreakingly stifled, half-swallowed sobs that spoke volumes about loneliness and despair. He hated the thought of her knowing first-hand what those emotions felt like.

Something ugly twisted in his gut. "Beth, what's happened?" He moved swiftly to confront her, his state of semi-undress forgotten.

She looked at him, and he was struck immediately by her valiant attempt to regain her composure. "Nothing. I… I—" Her lovely mouth trembled for a moment. "I'm sorry. I know I shouldn't be here. My bag was snatched, he pushed me and I fell. My shoes…" She looked down at the scuffed heels, sitting untidily to one side. "I'm sorry. I didn't know what else to do."

It was then that he saw the torn nylons and the grazes to her knees—her palms were probably skinned too. "Let me see," he commanded gently, hating seeing his so-capable assistant looking so bewildered and at a loss—so vulnerable.

And trusting. She offered her hands to him. He pushed aside the mental image of those wrists enclosed in soft leather cuffs, disgusted with himself for thinking such a thing at a time like this. Her injuries needed to be cleaned and cared for, and in his office he had just what he required for the job.

Her hands were one thing—her legs were a different matter entirely. There was no point in starting while the ruined nylons still adorned her far-too-tempting limbs, but when she stood to remove them at his request, her gasp of pain snagged his attention immediately. "What is it?"

"My ankle." She pointed to the offending limb. "I think it might be sprained." Her teeth bit into her lower lip.

"Here." He stood in front of her, holding out his hands, palms up. "Let me help you up, and then put your hands on my shoulders."

He'd undressed women before—more times than he could count—but this time was sorely going to test his self-control. He tried not to think about where he was going to have to put his hands, how she'd feel beneath his touch—there was a time and a place for that, and this wasn't it.

"Tights or stockings?" His gaze held hers as he asked the question. Surely the rising tide of intimacy was just a figment of his imagination?

"Tights." Her voice was little more than an embarrassed whisper.

She gasped as he lifted her skirt. Focused on his mission now, he hooked his thumbs in the waistband of her tights and gently pulled them down over her hips, crouching so that he could ease the nylons over her injured knees. There was an intimacy to the task that caught him off guard; the warm, feminine scent of her was weaving a spell around him, even like this. He smoothed her skirt back into place.

"Sit."

Her instant obedience zinged through his bloodstream. Any other time and—*No! Time and place, Lombard! Time and place—remember that!* With the utmost care he finished removing the hosiery, trying to ignore the alabaster perfection of her skin and how smooth it looked, and failing miserably.

However, kneeling before her, he could get a proper look at the injuries she'd sustained in the assault and it made him seethe anew at the thought of some low-life causing her such anguish and pain.

"I'm sorry, Beth, but this is going to sting."

Even though he'd warned her, he still heard the sharp intake of breath when the pad, soaked in hot water and antiseptic, made contact with her raw flesh. "Are you all right?"

Although she nodded, Beth was biting her lower lip; Alex suspected that she was hurting more than she was prepared to admit. Although they looked as if they'd smart like hell, the grazes were relatively minor. Her ankle, however, was a greater cause for concern. She could barely put any weight on her right foot. Nor could he rule out the possibility of shock from the mugging itself. There was no way he was letting her out of his sight tonight.

"At least he didn't get the office keys," she murmured, her hand closing on the bunch of keys she'd left on her desk.

Alex made an impatient noise. "Sod the bloody office keys! What about your own keys? And your credit and debit cards? What else did you have in your bag?"

No cards—she'd left her purse at home by accident this morning, and her keys were still in her coat pocket. "My mobile phone."

After the theft was reported to the mobile phone company, Alex continued with his questioning. "Was there anything with your address on?"

She thought for a moment, and when she told him that there was, it sealed the deal for Alex. She was going home with him, whether she liked it or not. Furthermore, he was going to get Cam to check her place and make sure that everything was all right.

Beth listened with more than a touch of disbelief as her employer called his friend to ask him to check her home. With the robbery already reported to the police, all of a sudden *home* was the exact place she wanted to be.

"Not just yet, love," Alex said absently, concentrating on cleansing her hands. "I need to finish getting you cleaned up and comfortable first. I'll get dressed again, and then you're coming home with me."

No! She couldn't possibly do that. "Mr. Lombard, please." Beth tried to regain her composure and some sense of control. "I'm perfectly capable of taking care of myself—"

"Normally, of that I would have no doubt, *Miss Harrison*," he agreed, with additional emphasis on her name. "However, would you care to explain why you're shaking like the proverbial leaf?" He took her hand in a firm but gentle grasp, carefully avoiding the grazed area.

All of a sudden, Beth was close to tears again. He was being so nice to her, but her knees were hurting, as were her hands, her ankle was giving her hell, and all she wanted was warmth, comfort and familiarity.

Her employer's chest wasn't helping, either. She knew he worked out and it showed in the hard, sculpted muscles that moved so enticingly as he worked on her injuries. Then she remembered something he'd said earlier in the day.

"You were going out this evening," she recalled, quietly appalled that she'd ruined his plans. "I'm sorry. Look, I can get myself home—"

"And then what?" His voice was neutral. "You can't walk. You need someone to take care of you."

He straightened up. "Stay here, I won't be long." And with that, he disappeared back into his office once more.

Beth sighed. She wasn't used to being taken care of like this. A solitary tear trickled down her cheek; she swiped it away with the back of her hand. Now she was just feeling sorry for herself. She had her Transport for London smartcard, it was in the same pocket as her keys, and she was sure she could get to the bus stop under her own steam, if she was careful and watched where she was putting her feet.

She slipped her feet back into her shoes, wincing when it came to the right one. Somewhat gingerly she stood up, braced herself and took her weight on her left foot. Now for the first step...

Her brief cry of pain and collapse back onto her chair were timed beautifully for Alex emerging from his office. He was pulling on his suit jacket; the shirt was buttoned now, although he had left it undone at the collar, and his tie was looped loosely around his neck.

"What the hell...? Beth, for once in your life, will you stop being so bloody stubborn and independent, and let me take care of you? You're staying with me tonight, and that's final! And stop bloody apologising!"

The words died on her lips—how had he known what

she was about to do? Was she *so* predictable? *Predictable* as in *boring*?

"Take these." He held out his keys—office, car and, she presumed, the keys to his apartment. "I need you to lock up—I'll have my hands full." And with that, he slipped one arm under her legs and the other around her back. Automatically, her arms went around his neck.

Her face inches from his, Beth almost stopped breathing. Her senses were overwhelmed: the feel of his arms around her, holding her effortlessly to his chest, the clean, masculine scent of him... and then all the visuals. She was mesmerised by his dark eyes, framed by thick black lashes that women would kill for; the clear skin stretched taut over cheekbones that would challenge the skill of a master sculptor, and the rugged hint of five o'clock shadow clinging to the firm lines of his jaw.

And his mouth. What she wouldn't give to be the woman entitled to place a gentle kiss to those lips...

The office secured for the weekend, they took the lift to the underground car park. Beth expected Alex to let her down while they were in the lift, but no—she remained securely in his arms. Although neither of them spoke, she felt that there was a whole subtext going on. It had to be her imagination working overtime, painting Alex into the role of the Dom in her manuscript again.

At this time on a Friday night, it wasn't surprising to see only a handful of cars in the underground lot. Alex installed her in the passenger seat of his black Aston Martin and moments later the car's powerful engine roared into life, taking them out of the subterranean cavern and into the busy streets of London.

CHAPTER THREE

There was something surreal about travelling through the bright lights of the city, in a breathtaking car driven by an equally breathtaking man. That being the case, it was hardly surprising that Beth's mind was a million miles away, in a secret place that was warm, dark and intimate—and she'd taken that man to that place with her.

In the darkness, her imagination was in danger of running wild. No one could see the way she moistened her suddenly dry lips, or the subtle changes in her expression that reflected what was going on in her mind, the visions of a wild interplay of a male body and a female one, tasting, touching, exploring… fucking.

Thankfully the journey didn't last long. An expert driver, Alex guided the expensive car through the traffic with cool confidence, heading for an equally expensive part of town. Beth stole the occasional glance at his hands on the steering wheel and the gear stick; flying in the face of good sense, she couldn't help but picture those hands on her own body, his touch arousing her and giving her pleasure such as she'd never experienced. The effort to drag herself out of the fantasy required a huge intake of breath that finally broke the silence.

"Are you all right, Beth?"

Not trusting herself to speak coherently, she nodded, then realised he probably wouldn't be able to register such a response in the darkness—she had to speak. "Fine, thanks." How she managed to sound so relatively normal, she had no idea.

"How's your ankle?"

She flexed the offending joint, wincing as pain shot up her leg. "Still sore," she muttered, at the back of her mind more than a little relieved to find that speech was getting easier.

"It'll probably get worse before it gets better. When you've had a shower, I'll get an ice pack on it and strap it up for you."

Shower? Who said she was having a shower? Obviously his perception of her visit to his apartment was vastly at odds with her own. But Lord, she thought as she flexed her stiffening shoulders, she could really do with standing under a cascade of hot water to ease the aches that were setting in—when the bag thief had sent her flying, parts of her body had moved in ways they just weren't designed to.

She got to Alex's apartment the same way she'd got from the office to his car—in his arms. And whatever she'd imagined that apartment to be like, it was nothing like the masculine statement of the reality—wide open space, decorated in black, brown and cream with the odd rich, dark-red accent, all ultra-modern in style.

The largely open-plan apartment was on two levels. The central sunken area—Beth remembered an article in a design magazine that referred to such a feature as a conversation pit—provided a focal point, with comfortable seating arranged around a large chunky coffee table that could almost have been a piece of modern art.

The raised outer area was almost like a wide walkway around the perimeter of the apartment. Straight ahead of her there were two doors to the left, while on the opposite side to the doors, the walkway was wide enough to accommodate an open-plan kitchen and dining area.

Alex carried her down to one of the huge, comfortable-looking sofas and gently lowered her to it. She quickly took in other features around the room: the modern flame-effect fire on the wall, the bookcases, the impressive-looking sound system, all very masculine. There were only two other doors, one of which had to lead to Alex's bedroom.

The man himself looked down at her, his expression unreadable. "Right—first things first. The guided tour can wait. There's not that much to see. Can you tolerate aspirin? Good; stay there and I'll bring you some."

She watched him covertly as he moved around the kitchen. He'd divested himself of his jacket and tie, and in the fitted white shirt she could appreciate the play of his powerful muscles. With a slight shiver, she remembered how it had felt to be in his arms, cradled carefully against that broad chest. When he turned to bring her the medication and a glass of water, she saw that he was also carrying a plate of crackers and cheese.

"You need to eat," he said, his expression unyielding. "You can't take aspirin on an empty stomach, and since we haven't had dinner yet, you have to have something."

Beth waited for him to leave the plate on the coffee table so she could help herself; the last thing she expected was for him to sit beside her and actually feed her the snack. Was he really sitting there, large as life, presenting the cracker and Brie as if he were feeding a child? Wide-eyed, she looked at him, and in return received a raised eyebrow and a stern look.

"Eat."

Her eyes never left his as she took a bite, chewed and swallowed. If she'd thought that that would satisfy him, she'd have been sadly mistaken. He let her take a sip of water, and then watched as she took a second bite. When she went to take the cracker from him, the look in his eyes was enough to stay her hand. The process continued until both crackers were finished. He then dropped the aspirin into her hand.

"And make sure you have all the water. Good girl." He took the glass from her when she'd finished it. "I think we could do with a drink. Tea or coffee?"

"Coffee—thank you." Again, she was unable to meet his gaze—why did the image of a sub thanking her Dom for attending to her needs come so easily to mind? Beth took a deep breath—she really was getting far too involved in her writing. Then again, given her intense personal interest in the subject...

Trying not to stare, she watched Alex again while he made the coffee. He truly was irresistible as a spectator sport. Seeing him in his home environment was... educational. Try as she might, she was finding it more difficult to remember that he was her employer and that was the beginning and end of their relationship. She was only human, and the part of her that acknowledged he was a highly attractive man clamoured to be heard.

Highly attractive. The words simply didn't do him justice, now more so than ever. She'd seen him with a day's worth of stubble before, in the office, but here, in the informal environment of his home... Beth couldn't really explain it, she just knew that she was responding to his more rugged appearance in a way that had always lurked beneath the surface at work, but wasn't so easy to hold in check here. Here he was dangerous, his military past somehow more visible... or maybe she was just more aware of it without the camouflage of mundane business activity to conceal the truth.

She gave herself a mental shake. Trying to dissect her responses wouldn't help anyone. What would help was remaining in control until the current situation passed. Which it would. Tomorrow at the latest. *Not. A. Problem.*

The distinctive ringtone of Alex's smartphone caught her attention. Beth couldn't hear his side of the conversation, but something made her think it was connected with her predicament, a feeling that Alex confirmed when he returned, bearing a tray laden with elegant white mugs, sugar, cream and a large pot of coffee.

"That was Cam. He's checked your place out himself. Everything looks okay at the moment, but he's going to have someone keep an eye on things for you over the weekend."

Beth's eyes widened. Suddenly a thought occurred to her—how could Cam Fraser have checked her home when she still had her keys?

"Beth, my sweetheart, he's an expert in his field—you'll never even know he was there."

Stunned, she stammered out her thanks. Even so, she was still taken aback by the watch being put on her humble apartment.

"Cam said it's the least he can do for all the fantastic cups of coffee you've made for him over the last few years, quote, unquote," Alex cut in. "Beth? Are you all right?"

No. No, she wasn't. All of a sudden, the way Alex was taking care of her, the way his friend was making sure everything was all right... it all combined to make her hands tremble and her eyes fill with tears again. Even though it was only a temporary situation, it had been so long since her life had included someone with whom she could share the burden of responsibility.

Alex's arms around her pulled her into the shelter of his body, his hand busy freeing her hair from the barrette she wore to keep it tidy for the office so that he could thread his fingers through the tumbling waves.

"Shh, love, it's all right," he comforted her, his low, rich voice making things worse as well as better. "You're safe. I'll protect you. I'll always protect you."

That voice and the words it spoke were her undoing. Suddenly, all she could do was howl noisy tears, when all she wanted was some stability and for the feeling that her world was being pulled out from under her feet to stop.

And for Alex to carry on holding her as if he'd never let her go.

Sometime later, while he was contemplating the world through a generous measure of his favourite whisky, Alex's thoughts ran through the events of the evening. While Beth had showered—without his assistance, it must have been down to sheer determination on her part, a fact that surprised him not in the slightest—he'd rustled up a simple pasta dish and then waited for her to reappear.

He'd left his robe for her to wear, and as soon as he saw her standing at the bedroom doorway wearing it, he'd had to fight down the urge to strip it off her and take her to bed. Instead, he'd carried her back to the sofa, where he'd applied an ice pack to her bruised ankle before strapping it up. After dinner—where he hadn't pushed his luck by feeding her that, as well—he'd given her an hour or so before ushering her off to bed.

A low growl vibrated in his throat. He could really do

without the image that filled his mind at *that* memory. He had Beth precisely where he wanted her and couldn't do a thing about it. The mental torture was every bit as excruciating as—

No! He wasn't going to think about that, not now, not ever. And he certainly wasn't going to think of it in any way that might connect it to Beth. She was pure and innocent, not to be defiled by the festering darkness that lay in his past. Was he really doing the right thing? Not for himself but for her?

Yes. It had to be right. If she wanted to explore submission, she needed a Dom she could trust. Moreover, *he* needed her to be with a Dom he trusted, and that narrowed down the field significantly. He'd grudgingly consider Cam... or maybe not, given the surge of feral jealousy he experienced at the thought.

Now clad in jeans and a faded T-shirt, Alex slouched on one of the sofas, his bare feet up on the coffee table as he continued to share his thoughts with the glass of whisky and the classical music that softly wound its way around the apartment. So much to think about. The way she'd allowed him to carry her, the way she'd accepted him feeding her the cheese and biscuits... the way she'd cried in his arms.

He really did want to protect her—for the rest of his life. There was no point in denying it. And if he didn't even want Cam to be the Dom she went with, there was only one option left. Just as well he'd already decided to take it.

The sound of the entry phone muscled in on his meditative mood—that would be Cam, coming around for a drink and a discussion after his visit to the club, where he'd gone after leaving Beth's apartment.

"How is she?" Cam's voice was uncharacteristically serious, devoid of its usual levity.

Alex nodded in the direction of the bedroom. "Asleep now."

The two men went to the bedroom door. Alex pushed it further open, and the sight that met him almost stopped his heart.

He'd given Beth one of his T-shirts to sleep in, but she must have got too warm—it was lying in a pool at the bottom of the bed. She was resting on her side, her back towards the door with the duvet bunched around her waist, revealing magical curves cast in shadow and light. A sleeping goddess, he thought somewhat whimsically, with the power to turn him into a primitive creature of full of need, compelling him to worship at the altar of her glorious femininity. Sheer, raw want flooded through his body all over again.

"Christ, Alex, she's beautiful."

He wasn't about to argue with Cam's assessment, although Alex was fleetingly tempted to punch him for it. Recognising the instinctive possessive reaction for the nonsense it was, he gestured for both of them to leave, so as not to disturb her. Once away from the bedroom, he knocked back the last of his Scotch. "Drink? I need a refill."

His glass replenished and matched by the one he gave his friend, Alex sprawled on one of the two sofas arranged around the coffee table. Cam took up a similar relaxed position opposite.

"I was going to take her to Antwerp on Monday," Alex began, gazing into the distance. "Told her it was a business trip to look at some diamonds, otherwise she'd never have agreed to go."

"And now?"

Alex hoped his shrug looked more casual than it felt. "Trip's off, obviously. I've cancelled the flights and the hotel, for now, at any rate. She'll be staying here for the weekend, maybe longer—depends on how her ankle heals. What the hell are you grinning at, Cam?"

The other man allowed his grin to become a brief chuckle. "You have got it bad, old man. And on the evidence in there," he nodded towards the bedroom "I can't say I blame you. There's something about her, and the way she looks right now? It's there in spades."

A sober, thoughtful look settled on Alex's features. "She writes, you know."

"Let me guess—romance?" Almost rolling his eyes, Cam had the air of a man confident in his prediction.

Alex laid his head back on the sofa, his gaze fixed on the ceiling. "Not exactly—not the way you mean." He closed his eyes, remembering what he'd read and how it had made him feel. "Romance with a D/s twist, and from the way she described the sub, I think she sees herself in that role."

The other man gave a low whistle. "You say that like it's a bad thing. What's the problem?"

Alex's short laugh was lacking in humour. "The problem is, does she want to submit, or does she just want to write about it? You know as well as I do how many women walk into Aegis thinking that they're submissive and end up all but running out screaming. She doesn't know I've read her notes, but if they're part of a larger work, I'd sure as hell like to read it."

"You're overanalysing this, Alex." Cam took an appreciative sip of the twenty-five-year-old Scotch, unadulterated by ice, water or any other pollutant, conventional or otherwise. "You've seen how she is in the office—how she's been since the day she started working for you. She serves. Were you planning on making a move on her in Antwerp?"

"Something like that. I wanted her to start getting used to the idea that we don't just have to have a business relationship and that if she's a sub, she can explore that safely with me."

Cam nodded, his expression contemplative. "She needs looking after—she's special. We both know that while she may be this strong, capable woman in the office, she's also kind, considerate, honest to the point of being her own worst enemy—"

"Will you shut the fuck up? You don't need to sell her to me."

"That's good to hear. Have you thought how far you're going to take this? Further than just training her—if indeed that's what she wants? She might just be—"

"Cam, don't." Alex didn't have to be a genius or a mind-reader to know what his friend was about to say. "One step at a time, okay? She may not want to take it any further than writing about it." He wasn't sure what he'd do if that were the case. Offer his services as a technical advisor, maybe.

"Good point." Cam's agreement was surprisingly sober. "Anyway, when and if you do decide to take this further, you know I've got your back."

It was gone midnight by the time Cam left, taking with him the spare set of keys for the office so that he could let the staff in if Alex and Beth didn't make it into work on Monday. Now that that was taken care of, it was high time for Alex to make himself comfortable on the sofa for the night. Over the years, he'd slept in far worse places—one in particular being the most putrid, terrifying shit-hole imaginable. The question was, with Beth there, even a room away, would his nightmares make their regular visit?

Alex finished the last of his Scotch, troubled once again by the thought of how much alcohol he'd been going through lately. There were several contributing factors—one was in his bed right now—but she was only a small part of the full picture. A lot of it was how he spent his nights: the erratic sleep patterns, the wakefulness… the just-not-wanting-to-go-to-sleep in the first place.

With the lights dimmed, he stretched out on the sofa.

As he tried to relax, he took long, slow breaths, counting each one in and out, focusing inwards. Sometimes it worked and he managed to get some sleep. Sometimes it didn't, and then he'd pace the apartment for a while, or just look out over the city, or there was always some work to be done—his business stretched around the world.

When sleep came, it didn't last long—it never did. Cold and sweating, Alex sat bolt upright in his makeshift bed. The horrific nightmares that still haunted him had struck again, sending him back to that hell-hole of ten years ago. He concentrated on his breathing again, taking deep, measured breaths that gradually began to slow his racing heart rate. Controlling his respiration like that was about the only piece of advice he'd taken on board when they'd tried to tell him how to deal with the root cause of the bloody nightmares.

His thoughts swung back to Beth, his true north in so many ways. Unable to resist the temptation, he rose and padded silently to the doorway of his bedroom, just to check that she was all right and he hadn't woken her up.

She was still fast asleep in his bed, lying on her front this time, her hair an unruly cloud. The thought of curving his body around hers was so tempting. Cam was right— submissive or not, she was special.

And she was naked in his bed, and he couldn't do a thing about it. Jaw rigid with frustration, he turned to leave; the last thing she needed was to wake up and find she was the victim of a priapismic Peeping Tom. Where the hell was that double whisky that had his name on it?

Jeans pulled back on, he was back on the sofa, nursing that Scotch and absorbed in thought, until he heard the sharp intake of breath behind him.

Beth wasn't sure what woke her. She never slept well in strange beds anyway, and when the strange bed belonged to her employer—for whom she still harboured distinctly non-business-like thoughts—there was no chance she was going to sleep soundly.

This wasn't the first time she'd woken up. Too hot to sleep, she'd finally resorted to removing the T-shirt Alex had put out for her—only to find that being naked in his bed was just as disturbing.

Beth didn't know what to do with herself. Had she been unable to sleep at home, she'd have dug out her notebook and started writing, but that was impossible in the present circumstances, so the next best thing was reading. There were no books around in the bedroom, so that meant braving the room where Alex was sleeping—there were plenty of bookcases out there and maybe, if she were quick enough and quiet enough, she could grab a novel.

But not like this. Even if her body had been perfect, she still wouldn't be prancing around naked out there, it simply wasn't her style. Her legs were probably the best part of her; she'd been blessed with long legs, and even though she was her own worst critic, she knew that they were in pretty good shape. Beyond that, though, the appendectomy scar was old and faded, but still visible and thankfully her breasts were still adequately defying gravity. However, without the camouflage of her clothing, anyone could see the tricky areas where no amount of dieting and exercise had ever been able to shift the few extra pounds she carried. And if a man she was seeing was disappointed by that... well, that was his problem, not hers. Not that she was seeing Alex. *Nope. Not her. No, siree.*

Beth reached for her glasses and then the discarded T-shirt, a garment long enough to cover what needed to be covered. Unbidden, a hot shiver scurried down her spine as the soft fabric that usually covered his skin caressed hers. The sensation triggered the memory of Alex deftly bandaging her damaged ankle, or more specifically, the gentle touch of his firm, capable hands. At the same time she'd wanted it both to stop and to last forever.

Enough. She'd procrastinated for long enough. It was time to put all those silly fancies out of her head and do something about trying to get some sleep. The first step with her right foot was painful but manageable—perhaps there was something to that ice pack treatment after all. She might just get away with this.

There was still a glimmer of light coming under the door. Alex couldn't possibly still be awake—he'd probably just fallen asleep and left the lights dimmed. Beth didn't even want to think of facing him in such a skimpy outfit. There was only so much embarrassment she could take in one day.

As she left the bedroom, her focus was on the bookcase straight ahead of her. It was only as she drew level with the end of the sofa that she realised that, far from being asleep, Alex was still awake, half-naked, and nursing a glass of something alcoholic between his knees as he leaned forward, staring into the middle distance.

The sight of him was perturbing enough, but when she saw the crisscross of old, ragged scars, emphasised by the way what little light there was fell across his back, the gasp left her lips before she could stop it. When he turned in her direction, she felt like the proverbial deer caught in the headlights of a car.

"Beth." He rose in one smooth movement, depositing the glass on the coffee table before taking the most direct route to her, straight over the back of the sofa and up to her level. The sheer grace of it made her breath catch in her throat. "What are you doing out of bed? Can't you sleep? Is it your ankle?"

The volley of concerned questions couldn't initially get past the impact of what she'd seen. She looked up at his face, the question plain for anyone to see in her eyes. What had happened to him to cause those scars?

Alex met her troubled gaze. Even in the subdued lighting, he could see the threat of tears in her eyes—she must have seen the long-healed wounds that stretched from his shoulders to the small of his back.

"It's all right, Beth," he said softly, knowing that he needed to reassure her. "It was a long time ago."

She found her voice. "What was it?"

"IED. I was lucky; others, not so much. Now, what's

up? You should be asleep."

The IED was only part of the story. He'd been left with the rest of the scarring after the incident that still had a terrifying night-time hold on him, and he'd see hell freeze over before she'd hear one word about that from him.

Beth was shaking her head. She still had that troubled look in her eyes, and he found himself wishing he could kiss it away. A Dom's job didn't always mean administering a sound spanking. It meant taking care of his sub's worries and problems too. It meant protecting her.

"Come with me. I think some warm milk may be in order."

Damn, but she felt good in his arms, as if she'd always belonged there—he'd carry her anywhere. Somehow, she made his incredibly sexless T-shirt look incredibly sexy. Her mouth, with its perfect, pink Cupid's bow, was just inches away from his and begging to be crushed in a kiss that she'd feel all the way down to her toes.

He deposited her carefully on the sofa, and then tucked the supersized lightweight blanket that had covered him around her. "Stay there, love. I'll be right back."

While he worked in the kitchen, Alex kept a surreptitious eye on his houseguest. At least she wasn't in any hurry to move from where he'd deposited her. He was also remembering her reaction to his scarred back—gentle concern rather than pity, and something else that he was hesitant to name.

He poured the warm milk into a glass, then added a little honey and a touch of vanilla extract—warm milk on its own might do the trick, but it didn't taste very interesting.

"There you go, try that," he said when he returned to her side. She accepted the glass and took a delicate sip, followed by a slightly less ladylike one that left her with a subtle but visible milk moustache. Before she could do anything about it, he produced a clean handkerchief and did the honours. "Like it?"

She nodded. "Delicious—thank you very much, Mr. Lombard."

They were both half-naked, and she was still addressing him formally. For a potential sub, she was exhibiting some very strong-minded tendencies. He liked it. "You're most welcome, Miss Harrison," he replied with a slight incline of his head, formality masking the hint of unexpected amusement.

He watched her finish the milk, a glimmer of a smile appearing in his eyes as her eyelids began to droop. She didn't react when he took the almost-empty glass from her. He wished he could say the same for himself when she leaned against him with a sigh, her breathing relaxing into the easy rhythm of sleep when his arm went around her. If he could get a hard-on when she was just around him in the office, he stood no chance with her snuggled against him like a sleepy kitten… and there was the evidence, pushing against the fly of his jeans.

He should have taken her back to bed immediately, but now that she was settled there was no sense in waking her up. He just hoped that the nightmares wouldn't come again—once in a night was enough, but his main concern was that Beth shouldn't witness their effect on him. She didn't need that.

And neither did he.

Most nights, Alex was reluctant to close his eyes—but not tonight. Beth felt too good beside him. She felt right. He pulled the huge blanket over both of them, and then let himself relax, his feet up on the coffee table. Whether her ankle was better or not, she was spending the weekend here, with him. Tomorrow he'd talk her into letting him collect some clothes and anything else she needed from her apartment. For tonight at least, he could pretend that she was his.

CHAPTER FOUR

A slow stretch shouldn't have had her wincing, but the shaft of pain across Beth's shoulders caused an explosion of memories that had her sitting bolt upright and staring wide-eyed at the man sitting beside her. She could still feel the comfort of the arm that had been wrapped around her and the heat from the body she'd been curled against all night.

Oh. Dear. God.

Alex was looking at her with a totally inscrutable expression. She wished she could say the same for herself. Nerves dried her mouth at the sight of him, all sleep-tousled hair and stubble-shadowed jaw... and that chest, which she really wished he'd put away. That chest was stopping her from thinking about anything other than the way he looked—potently male and way too dangerous for a woman who had been without a man's company for far too long.

Beth couldn't have said how long they just looked at one another—she was focusing her efforts on not letting herself give in to the very real urge to kiss him good morning. It was Alex who finally broke the silence.

"Good morning, Miss Harrison." There was a smile in his voice as he spoke her name. "How do you feel? Stiff and achy?"

Oh shit, no! Please tell me I didn't look straight at his crotch when he said that! Beth felt colour blaze into her cheeks as she forced herself to look up... and saw the wry grin and raised eyebrow that told her that betraying glance hadn't gone unnoticed. "A little," she muttered.

"Ankle still sore too? If you need more aspirin for it, I'll get you some toast and coffee for now, and then we'll see about lunch later. What about your hands and knees?"

As she offered her palms for inspection, Alex swung his feet off the coffee table and sat forward. He cradled her hands with his as he checked the grazes, frowning slightly when his gaze travelled to her knees. They'd borne the brunt of her fall, but were starting to recover as well.

"You were pretty shaken up yesterday," he commented. Beth wondered why he was still holding on to her hands. She wondered even more why she suddenly felt so wobbly when one hand moved to curl a stray lock of hair around her ear. Why was he looking at her so intently?

She found her voice. "Yes, I'm sorry about that, Mr. Lombard. I don't know what came over me. Thank you for looking after me, and I need to call Mr. Fraser to thank him for checking my apartment. I should really be getting back home."

"Dressed like that?"

The way he looked her up and down made Beth's cheeks burn. It also reminded her that she hadn't given a thought to her clothes, which seemed to have miraculously disappeared without a trace. How could she forget something as basic as clothing? What was being around this man away from the office doing to her?

"I need to get dressed. Where are my clothes?"

"In with the dry cleaning and due to be picked up," he glanced at his wrist watch, "any time now." He checked the time again. "It's nearly ten o'clock."

"Is there something wrong with that?" She was puzzled by his odd reaction to the time, almost as if he couldn't quite believe what his watch was telling him.

Alex frowned. "I haven't slept this late at the weekend since... I don't know when."

She was still confused. "Is that a good or bad thing?"

"It's nothing for you to worry about. You take the bathroom first, while I dig out another T-shirt for you. There's a hairdryer somewhere around here too. Unless you need the aspirin?"

Beth flexed the joint. Although it was still painful, she was happy to report that she didn't require any medication for it.

"Good. Then I suggest you get your behind under that shower, because I can't until you have, and when we're both done you can tell me what I need to collect from your apartment for the rest of the weekend."

Beth blinked. She couldn't possibly have heard what she thought she heard. "Excuse me?"

"You're staying here, with me," he directed, in a tone that brooked no argument. "Then we'll see how you're doing on Monday morning. If necessary, we can both work from here. Cam can open the office for the staff."

She'd clearly missed the memo—the one where he'd informed her that he was taking over her life. She was still trying to think of a suitable rejoinder when he spoke again.

"Beth, adorable as you are, and as much as I could sit here looking at you all day, I need you to get in that shower now, and if you don't move in three seconds, I will put you under the shower myself."

Adorable. He thought she was adorable? She had no time to process the statement, because four seconds later, she was being dumped rather unceremoniously on the bed, so that he could remove the bandage from her ankle.

"Will you be all right on your own now?"

Stunned into silence, she managed a jerky nod and watched the human whirlwind disappear.

Fifteen minutes later she was all freshened up, wearing the clean T-shirt Alex had left for her. Aware that he was just a few feet away in the bathroom, she sat on the edge of the bed while she dried her hair.

And oh, she shouldn't have had that thought about him under the shower. She should *not* have had that thought. Not when her imagination was busy filling in the details of the rest of the body that went with that chest.

Rivulets of warm water flowing over hard muscle. Foaming suds following the smooth curves of biceps and deltoids, pecs and abs and—

Don't go any lower. Beth licked her lips. No, she wasn't wondering what he'd taste like. Nor was she standing behind him in the shower, her arms weren't going around his waist, and she wasn't resting her cheek against his back…

Get a grip! Beth gave a suppressed shriek in a combination of frustration and impatience with herself. She really had her head in the clouds this time. She needed to concentrate on what she was doing and get her hair into some semblance of order, rather than the damp bird's nest it currently appeared to be. Without a brush or a comb, the best she could do was run her fingers through it, and there was no way she was rummaging around Alex's personal space.

She was so wrapped up in what she was doing that she didn't notice when the sound of the shower stopped. What she did notice was movement on the bed behind her, the sudden heat of Alex's body at her back, and his strong, muscular—naked—legs on either side of hers. *Oh Lord.*

"Give that to me."

It was that tone of voice again, the one that wouldn't take no for an answer. The hairdryer was taken from her, and with infinite gentleness Alex began to dry her hair. The sensations he created immediately started to cause another internal riot. Beth bit her lower lip; it would be so easy to lean back against his strength, but instead she focused on the powerful thighs that framed her more slender ones, the way the muscles moved… and more scars. Without thinking, she touched the long-healed, puckered scar on the left one.

"I was lucky with that one," he said, his tone matter-of-fact. "Half an inch to the right and it would have been the bullet with my name on it."

Her fingers involuntarily squeezed his thigh. "Oh God!" she sighed softly.

It was the most natural thing in the world to slip his arm around her waist and draw her back against his body to offer comfort. When she turned slightly, to lay her head on his shoulder and cling to his arm as if it were the only safe haven in a storm-tossed ocean, Alex set the hairdryer aside and wrapped her in his embrace… and experienced a sense of homecoming the like of which he'd never felt before. A new calm flowed through his body—she might not know it yet, she might even take some persuading, but Beth was his.

"Don't fight it, love," he urged softly, his voice as tender as his touch. "Let me take care of you."

She lifted her face to him. His heart twisted at what he saw in her eyes. Tears? For him? Cupping the back of her head so she couldn't turn away, he lowered his head and pressed his mouth to her soft lips. His self-control had been tested to the limit and beyond. It was time to let something go.

"I told you, it was all a long time ago, in another life," he murmured, stroking her hair to reassure her, his urge to protect her almost overwhelming.

As if she suddenly realised what she was doing and whom she was doing it with, Beth jumped up, dashing treacherous tears from her eyes. "I'm sorry, Alex—Mr. Lombard, I don't know what I was thinking."

In one swift movement, a muscular arm around her waist captured her and returned her to her former position, seated between his thighs. "Hallelujah!" he breathed into her hair. "She finally called me Alex."

He swore he could feel the radiating heat of her embarrassment. "I'm sorry, sir, it won't happen again."

Alex groaned. *Sir.* Dear God, didn't she realise she'd just made it a thousand times worse? No, she wouldn't—how could she? "Why not?" he demanded, using the same tone of compulsion that he would with a recalcitrant sub.

"I can't." Her voice was barely more than a whisper, as if saying the two little syllables of his name were the worst thing she could ever do.

"Say my name, Beth," he commanded. His voice was quiet, but it held a core of steel.

She shook her head slowly. The way her lips were pressed together filled him with a fierce need to release her from whatever thought or memory or fear was making her doubt him. "Say it!" he urged again.

This time she couldn't resist it, that something in his voice that subs responded to every time. "Alex…"

"Again." He had to hear it once more—no, not once.

Like a man lost in the desert, who suddenly came upon an oasis, he had to drink his fill over and over again.

"Alex…"

How could something as simple as a name be so potent? The way she said it sent a bolt of lightning through every cell in his body. "See, it's not so hard, is it?" *Unlike a certain part of my anatomy.* He fought down the urge to divest her of her clothing, tie her to his bed and give her a first lesson in submission. "How about if we finish drying your hair, then I get dressed, and we talk?"

The talk happened over an early lunch. At first, Alex just watched Beth pick over her food; she was clearly deeply troubled. This talk was going to be pivotal to their future. He had to coax her out of her comfort zone and show her that life outside it wasn't so scary.

"Now then, Miss Harrison, we have something of a mystery to solve. I've let this slide for far too long. Why are you using my name to maintain this distance between us? You and I are a team, we work well together—I have friends who aren't as close to their wives as I am to you— so please, tell me what's going through that formidable mind of yours?"

Keeping a close eye on her as he spoke, Alex frowned a little as he sensed her withdraw from him even more. She was as taut as a bowstring. He could have sworn he could actually see her pulling together her courage, moulding it into a shield. There would be none of that nonsense if she were his sub. In time, he told himself. *In time.*

"I can't," she murmured at length, refusing to look at him. "You're my employer, I can't... Please."

"No one else I employ seems to have a problem calling me by my given name, Beth. Why is it so difficult for you to do it, I wonder? Could it be that there's the potential for more to our relationship than just work? Is that what has you running scared?"

"Mixing business and pleasure never works. Never."

"Calling me by my given name in the office hardly constitutes a blazing affair, Beth. Is that really such an awful thought? You and me, in a relationship that isn't just about work?" His gaze narrowed, assessing her reaction.

Her eyes went wide, her voice little more than a hoarse whisper when she spoke. "We can't."

"Why not?"

"Alex, I'm not stupid, I've seen the way women go through your life—I don't want to be one of them. I can't risk getting into that situation. I need my job."

Alex stiffened. What was the best way to deal with that brace of assumptions? How could he tell her that the vast majority of those women had been subs under his care for training and no more? That could easily be too much for her to handle right now. All he could do for now was reassure her that her employment was secure, no matter what happened between them.

"This has nothing to do with your job, Beth. And those women? They have nothing to do with what's happening between us. I may have dated a couple of them, but that's it."

"What about the others?"

"Mentoring, through a club I belong to." Maybe it was stretching the truth a little... a lot. Even so, Alex wasn't entirely sure his woman was buying it as an explanation. "Beth, you mean a great deal to me. I'm not going to do anything to hurt you. I'll take care of you."

He was waiting for the objections, but none came. She did, however, look scared to death, which might explain the lack of a response. He knew he'd taken her way out of her depth, but he wanted her to learn that she could trust him in all things.

"Why me?" Her eyes lifted to meet his at last. "Why do you want me?"

"A man would be crazy not to want you, Beth. What man wouldn't want an intelligent, sensual, beautiful woman in his life and in his bed?"

After lunch, still dazed by the turn of events, Beth handed Alex the keys to her apartment. The situation she now found herself in was even more surreal—she still wasn't quite sure how she'd come to be Alex Lombard's girl-friend.

Such a bland way to describe what Alex had said she was to him. He'd left her in no doubt that she was his woman, a declaration that held a possessive edge that sent a shiver down her spine. There must have been a point somewhere in the conversation where she could have said no to him... mustn't there? Even though she racked her brains, Beth couldn't actually remember where that point might have been.

Of course, even if such a point had existed, she had the strongest feeling she wouldn't have said no anyway.

"I don't know how long I'll be, love. Once I've picked your belongings up, I have another meeting with Cam about the security inspection, but I'll be back as soon as I can. In the meantime, make yourself at home, help yourself to anything, but try not to use that ankle too much. And if you do need to take any aspirin, don't have it on an empty stomach." He nodded in the direction of the packet of medication sitting next to the glass of water and plate of biscuits on the coffee table.

And with that, the bossy so-and-so was gone. The apartment fell silent and Beth was left alone with her thoughts.

It hardly seemed possible that so much could have happened in so short a time. All her determination to keep Alex at arm's length had been rendered futile in the space of a few moments. She'd fought so hard not to fall into the trap of letting herself get close to a man who couldn't possibly be interested in her, only for him to sweep her efforts aside as easily as if they were a house of cards.

Events had overtaken her and overwhelmed her. Alex had completely dismantled the boundaries of their employer-employee relationship, and was building in its stead something that could give her everything she'd ever desired.

Almost everything.

Beth felt as if she were standing on the edge of a cliff, about to dive headlong off it. The strangest thing was, she felt like she wanted to make the dive, but she couldn't shake the feeling that she was heading for shark-infested waters.

At last he was on his way back to the apartment. Beth's belongings, including her precious laptop, were safely stowed in the boot of his car, along with a few extra bits and pieces he'd purchased for her at an exclusive boutique owned by one of his trusted female counterparts from Aegis.

However, Alex's good mood was somewhat tempered by what he'd heard from Cam. The security sweep had revealed the existence of an extensive covert surveillance operation—several bugs had been planted through the office, along with a handful of concealed cameras. The good news was that there was nothing to incriminate any members of the staff.

It was a fact that gave Alex no small measure of relief, but still left the question of exactly *who* was responsible. His gut was telling him that it wasn't as simple as plain old industrial espionage, even though he could name a good half-dozen possible guilty parties—but until Cam came back with more information, confirmation of that would remain elusive.

Putting those thoughts out of his mind, Alex found it quite amusing that all of a sudden, for the first time in forever, he was in a hurry to get home. There was only one thing better than going home to Beth, and that would be going home to Beth wearing nothing but his collar. She was truly gorgeous. He had a preference for tall women, but unlike many men, skinny model types didn't turn him on. Beth, with her curves, her smile, her intelligence and her wit, did.

And he knew, more than ever, that she was a woman of warmth and passion who just needed a secure environment in which she could come out and play. Anyone who wrote about submission the way Beth had wasn't just interested in writing about it—she wanted it, he was sure. Once the subject was broached, she'd then understand why the women she'd seen pass through his life had been such a brief part of it.

With Beth, though, he'd discovered he loved just talking to her as well, found out from their conversations a little more about what made her tick, and now he carried with him a much more three-dimensional view of the woman he'd wanted to claim for so long.

When he entered the apartment, he was greeted by music playing on the sound system. Of Beth there was no sign, until he realised that in addition to the music, he could hear the soft but distinctive sounds of a woman pleasuring herself. His eyebrows rose and a smile of roguish pleasure teased his mouth into a curve. As he went further into the room, the sounds became a little louder.

Although he couldn't see her, he was pretty sure she was lounging on one of the sofas. Alex took another couple of silent steps, and there she was… well, her toes, at any rate. Another step, and her feet came into view. Finally, he saw her gorgeous legs, twisting and writhing in the throes of intense arousal. He advanced a little more, and at the sight of the hand working between her thighs, his body responded of its own accord. With the T-shirt hiked up around her waist, the sight of her smooth, delicious pussy fucking her hand took his breath away.

He'd give anything to know what she was thinking right now, what fantasies she was creating in that fertile imagination—and if, by any chance, he figured in any of them. Had she ever picked up on the Dominant traits he'd shown around the office?

The enchanting little sounds she was making were becoming slightly wilder now, less controlled as she began to approach the point of orgasm, and the erection he was sporting was correspondingly growing more uncomfortable.

Alex had always prided himself on being a good Dom, taking care of his subs' needs, respecting their limits while at the same time testing those limits within reason—and trying to teach his subs self-control, among other things. Perhaps Miss Harrison would benefit from one such lesson.

As stealthily as he'd entered—wasn't it strange how military training could come in handy in civilian life?—he moved slowly backwards, to the point where he could make out that he'd only just arrived. In silence he opened the front door again, then slammed it shut, at the same time yelling out, "Beth, I'm back—you'd better be decent!" with a wickedly playful tone to his voice.

And lo and behold, there she was, sitting up and looking as if butter wouldn't melt in her mouth. Even if butter wouldn't, he thought ruefully, he very well might. He decided not to make any comment about the warm, delightful scent of aroused woman that he detected in the air. He'd put money on the fact that he'd managed to prevent her achieving her climax, and if he had, then she would be one deliciously frustrated female.

"I've got your laptop, so that should keep you out of mischief for a while," he said, feigning complete innocence as he placed the computer bag beside her on the sofa. "I'll just take your clothes into the bedroom. Would you like me to clear some drawer space for you?"

The play of emotions across her face when she looked around at that comment was interesting. She was a little flushed, which was hardly surprising, and her expression spoke volumes about trying to work out what her answer should be.

"Um, no, it's okay, thanks. I mean, it's not like I'll be here long, is it?"

If she wanted to think that, he wasn't going to argue the point—for the time being. She'd need time to adjust to her new position in his life, as well as his position in hers. "Give me a few minutes, and then you can get changed into something less comfortable—if you really want to."

When Alex emerged from the bedroom, his guest was busily typing away. From the speed at which she was typing and the lack of any apparent pauses for thought, she was clearly deep in concentration. He hoped she was working on her manuscript. Sneaking up behind her for a look over her shoulder would be easy.

His eyes narrowed as he scanned the screen. She really did write very well. Her prose was both fluid and descriptive, and clearly came from the heart, even if it wasn't entirely factually accurate. Now facts *were* something with which he could help.

"You write beautifully, Beth, and while what you've written could happen, owned subs would never indulge like that without their Doms' permission—not unless they were bratting and actively seeking to be disciplined. And depending on their Doms' moods, the form of that discipline may end up not being what they were hoping for."

As he stepped down over the back of the sofa to slide into position by her side, Beth slammed down the lid of her laptop, her face drained of colour. The waves of tension emanating from her body were off the scale.

"Beth," he said quietly, "don't shut me out, and don't be ashamed. Talk to me."

"There's nothing to talk about." Her knuckles were white, where she was gripping the laptop. "It's rubbish, just… stupid rubbish."

"It isn't." Very carefully, Alex sat back, his posture as non-threatening as he could make it. Now was as good a time as any. "Do you know what I am?"

"Of course I do. My employer, and now…" Her voice trailed off and she was staring straight ahead; even the least observant person in the world would see her stress levels were rising with each passing second. At any moment she could bolt for the refuge of the bedroom with its lockable door.

"Beth. My woman. Am I going to have to put you over my knee and give you a good spanking? I know I'd enjoy it, but the question is, would you?"

Now that got her attention—and the colour flooding back into her cheeks. Her eyes were wide, her mouth frozen with the sharp intake of breath. Even so, Alex could see the truth dawning in her eyes. Now she knew.

"Yes, Beth," he said, with the gentle authority he wanted her to accept. "I'm a Dom, and when I call you my woman, I mean it. I can teach you all about the beauty of submission to your Master, and you're going to teach me all about you."

While her stomach performed Olympic-standard gymnastics, Beth digested the confirmation of what her subconscious mind had always suspected, right from the very first day she'd gone to work for him—that Alex wasn't just a dominant personality, and that was why he'd provided the perfect model for the central male character in her book.

"Beth? Look at me. I know this is a daunting conversation to have. I've already thrown a lot at you today, but if you'll let me, I can help you to accept what I see in your eyes. Don't be afraid."

She couldn't help herself—she had to obey him. The

look she saw in his eyes was like a laser beam searing the depths of her soul, laying bare all the things she knew were there but had shied away from for so long.

"You can't be a Dom." There was a hint of desperation in the denial. If it wasn't true, then she could retreat back into the safety of her ordinary little world. Her fantasies could remain just that. "You can't be."

"Why not, Beth? You've clearly done your research. You know D/s exists. And for it to exist, there must be practitioners of it. Is it so difficult to believe that I'm one of them?"

Beth set her laptop down on the coffee table. She really needed to go and get dressed properly. If she did that, sanity would surely return to this conversation.

"Where are you going, sweetheart? Don't run away." He caught hold of her wrist. "Tell me what you want."

She closed her eyes, trying to shut out that insistent but gentle, understanding voice. But it wasn't just his voice, nor was it just his words—there was an additional element in his tone that was communicating with her in a way that she felt rather than heard. He was weaving a hypnotic spell around her that was nearly impossible to resist. Standing in front of him, she had to try just one more time to stop the juggernaut, even if it meant their personal relationship was over before it had a chance to begin.

"Alex, I'm not what you want," she said, not sure who she was trying to convince more, him or herself. "I'm not glamorous, I'm not skinny and I'm not beautiful."

A solid lump of grief settled in her stomach. "Look at

me, Alex—look at me for what I really am."

CHAPTER FIVE

"Since you insist."

With that, Alex pulled Beth towards him so that she straddled his lap, grasped the hem of her T-shirt and in one swift movement, before she could work out what he was up to, removed it from her body and flung it to one side.

He looked, just as she'd asked him to, and he saw what she really was—she was incredible. Her body was as gloriously, gorgeously imperfect as he could have hoped for. Her breasts were soft, natural curves, just like the gentle swells of her belly and hips; her nipples, hard and tight, invited a man's mouth to take them. It didn't take much to imagine how she'd look with the adornments of bondage.

Glamorous, skinny and beautiful—she seemed to think that they were the attributes a man sought in a woman. How wrong she was. Glamour could be bought from any department store, in women's wear and cosmetics—it was nothing more than a shallow quality that had nothing to do with the woman beneath the clothes and make-up. As for skinny—so overrated. No man in his right mind wanted a woman who looked like she'd break in two if they tried anything other than gentle, missionary-position sex.

And not beautiful? She was so wrong—she was the most beautiful woman he'd ever known, because her beauty was inside as well as out. And he would find great pleasure in teaching her just how beautiful she was. He'd been a fool to fear this connection for so long.

Right now, though, her face told a different story, one that broke Alex's heart and gave him his first goal. Her expression was stricken as she tried to cover her breasts and pussy as if they were something to be ashamed of. He was going to make sure that one day, she would be in a place where that expression was consigned to the past. With the utmost care, he took hold of her wrists and held her arms away from her body. Her head fell forward, a lustrous brown cascade covering her shoulders and breasts.

"Don't, please. I should be—"

"You should be who you are, no more, no less," Alex cut in, his voice calm but firm. He pressed a kiss against the inside of each pale wrist. "Do you know what I see when I look at you, Beth? I see femininity, I see loveliness—and I see a woman who has been in conflict with herself for a very long time."

He studied her face for a moment. "I can take that conflict away and give you something that will let you be at ease with who you really are. The woman you've always been but have been too scared to acknowledge. I would consider it a privilege if you would allow me to do that. I know what a sensual, sexual being you are already. It's there in your writing, in the way you were enjoying your body before I came back—"

"Oh, God, no!" Clearly horrified, she struggled against the hold he had on her.

"Beth, stop it." His voice held a warning he knew she couldn't ignore. "What I saw was exquisite. I wanted to watch you bring yourself to orgasm, and one day, I will."

Her pussy was still wet when he grasped both of her slender wrists in one hand, so that he could slip the other between her legs, his gaze never leaving her face as he eased his fingers between her folds to stroke her still-swollen clit. Her response was a soft little grunt of reaction that sent a new shaft of desire through his body.

The play of emotions that she was experiencing was plain to see. She was torn between wanting what he was doing to her, wanting to listen to him, and wanting to fight everything. Alex had met more conflicted subs in his time than he could shake a stick at, so he knew exactly what was going through her mind—nice girls weren't supposed to let strangers do things like this to them, nice girls weren't supposed to actually want or even like sex at all. He'd seen it all before, heard it all before, but this time, because it was Beth, it was different. He wanted so much more for her... for both of them.

"Why are you doing this to me, Alex?" she whispered,

trying to move her pussy away from his hand.

The answer to that was simple. "Because you're mine. Tell me how you feel. Right now, Beth—tell me. No filters."

Her eyes were haunted in the moment before she turned away from him. "Ashamed. I feel ashamed."

Alex swore under his breath. Shame was the last thing he'd intended her to feel. "That stops right now. No one should be ashamed of their desires, their needs. I can teach you never to be ashamed again. Will you let me teach you?"

"Train me, you mean?" Now she was prickly and defensive. Oh, he was going to love learning all about this woman. She'd keep him on his toes, all right.

"I've used that word, yes, but it's not the way I work. Some Doms do, but I prefer to think of it as teaching, because it's as much about you teaching me as it is about me teaching you. For example, I would need to learn your limits, both soft and hard—the things you won't do now but might do in the future, and the things you'll never do."

And the first thing he needed to teach her was the necessity for clear communication in their relationship. It was something a lot of subs knew about, but confronting them with it often came as a shock.

"Now—when was the last time you had a lover? When did you last have a man do this to you?" He tapped her clit, felt her body tremble in response.

She reacted much as he expected. Eyes wide and with colour blooming in her cheeks, she was clearly lost for words. Alex felt almost primitively pleased that there was no instant response. He was even more pleased when she somewhat hesitantly admitted that the brief relationship had both started and ended in the two months before she'd come to work for him.

"And you dumped him, didn't you?"

She went still. Alex could tell by her expression that he was right. His Beth needed a strong man to give her what she really needed from a relationship. He wanted to be that man for her.

"And no lovers since," he concluded thoughtfully. "A woman like you is made for sex, Beth. You need to be fucked hard and often." *How she blushed even more delightfully at that!* "Does masturbation really satisfy you, or do you miss having a flesh-and-blood cock inside you?"

He could see that the bluntness of the question shocked her. While he wanted her to reach the point where they could both talk so frankly with ease, there was a small part of him that took delight in verbally headbutting her sensibilities. He started to stroke her pussy again, noting with approval that she was considerably wetter than she had been a moment or two earlier. On the face of it, it would appear that she *did* need a cock—*his* cock—to satisfy her need for sex.

So where did he go from here? He could take her into the bedroom, begin to prove to her that she was a natural sub and scare her to death, or he could keep her by… letting her go. In one fluid movement, he released her wrists and stood up, carefully setting her back on her feet as he did so. Without giving her a chance to speak, he replaced the T-shirt, but before he spoke there was one more thing he had to do—he lowered his mouth to hers to place a gentle kiss on her lips, the kind of kiss a man gave to the woman he cherished above all others.

"Go and have a shower now, love, and dress up—I'm taking you out for dinner. Think about what I said, and we'll talk about it again tomorrow."

Standing under the shower, Beth was a bundle of nerves. This wasn't her life; there'd been a terrible mistake, and somehow she'd been transported into someone else's life by accident. Otherwise, she'd have to consider all the things Alex had just said and done to her, and none of that could possibly be true.

After a leisurely shower—leisurely to give her time to think—Beth returned to the bedroom and delved into the bags Alex had left for her. She was expecting to find the clothes she'd asked him to collect from her apartment. They were there all right, along with some things she didn't recognise: a cocktail dress in teal satin and black lace, with a pair of stylish peep-toe black patent heels and a matching evening bag.

This must be what he meant her to wear for their dinner date.

I'm going out to dinner with Alex Lombard. Beth rolled the phrase around in her mind but it was still difficult to relate it to herself. She wondered how long it was going to take her to get used to the idea that she was his latest conquest.

"Now you're getting silly!" she muttered under her breath. Conquest, indeed. More like charity case.

She could be stubborn and uncooperative about it, she supposed, and put on the jeans and baggy top that she'd also found in the bag. The truth, though, was somewhat different—she didn't want to be stubborn and uncooperative. Now that she'd calmed down a bit, she found herself wanting to please him. And the dress was very beautiful.

It was just a pity he hadn't thought about underwear as well.

"You don't need it, Beth," came his amused voice in response to her murmured comment. He was leaning against the doorframe, arms folded and legs crossed at the ankles. "The bodice will support your breasts and the knickers stay off—as my woman, you'll only wear underwear when I give you permission to do so. Now get ready. You'll wear the dress, the nylons and the shoes. And don't overdo the make-up."

And with that, he walked past her without a backward glance, on his way to the bathroom.

Simmering with affront, Beth stared after him. As if she *would* overdo the make-up! All of a sudden, a strange feeling came over her, as if her skin didn't quite fit right any more. This was the Alex who'd taken charge of the situation back at the office, but somehow… intensified. Was this the side of him that all his previous girlfriends had seen? Was this a glimpse of Master Alex? She suspected it was—and the shiver that went through her then was one of excitement, rather than fear.

She wasn't used to going without underwear; the feel of the fine fabric on her skin was downright sinful. And Alex was right about the bodice. It was almost like a corset, while the skirt had just enough material in it to allow her to walk comfortably. Well, comfortably enough—she certainly wouldn't be going anywhere in a hurry in this dress.

With just a touch of lipstick and a quick flick of mascara, she ran the brush through her hair and took in her appearance in the full-length mirror. It was like looking at a total stranger, but instead of being shocked by the transition, Beth felt completed by it, as if she were looking at someone she was always meant to be.

Having left the bedroom to Alex, she was in the main living area, standing at the huge windows so she could take in the awesome view of the city, when she heard movement behind her. That would be Alex—and if she were dressed up to the nines, would he be similarly attired? He'd scrubbed up quite well for the office Christmas parties, she recalled, even though he'd only stayed long enough to make sure everyone was having a good time.

Talk about suited and booted. Quite simply, he was stunning. All of a sudden her ideas about this dinner date ratcheted up several notches on the casual to formal scale. The man could surely make simple black and white look like the sexiest fashion combo on the planet. He was clad in an immaculate black dinner suit, the quality unmistakable, with a dazzling snow-white shirt, a black tie, and gleaming black leather shoes. With his height and build, and the commanding air that he wore like a second skin, he couldn't help but attract attention. He certainly had hers as he made his way towards her.

"So, where are you taking me?" Beth asked, trying not to stare too much—not an easy thing to do when her eyes just wanted to devour him from head to foot and then start all over again.

"A little place I know."

She shook her head. "Alex, you might as well tell me, I've booked tables for you at all your favourite restaurants for the last three years."

"Not this one, you haven't." She could hear the superior smile in his voice, as well as see it on his face. "Turn around."

"Why?"

One stern look was all it took to make her obey him. She'd have asked herself why, but she had a feeling that it would take all night to find an adequate answer to that question.

"I have something for you."

It was metal and it was cold—and it had the close fit of a choker rather than the easy drape of a necklace. "What is it?"

His hands were warm on her shoulders. "Not what you're thinking, sweetheart. We're a long way from that. And when it happens, if it happens, you'll know exactly what I'm doing to you." She felt his lips brush her temple. "Now, let me look at you."

Beth performed a slow pivot in front of him, coming to a stop when she faced him. Close up, he was even more beautiful and overwhelmingly masculine. She leaned towards him and inhaled deeply, letting the clean, intoxicating scent of him soak into every cell of her body. God, she was burning for the touch of those lips on hers! "Well? Will I do?"

He looked at her in silence, and with each passing moment Beth felt her level of anxiety rise. It went off the scale when he spoke, his tone affecting her every bit as much as his words.

"Raise your skirt and stand with your legs apart."

With nervous hands, she lifted the hem of her dress to mid-thigh, her stance as wide as she dared. Her heart was racing as she met his gaze and she thought it might stop altogether when she saw the dark disapproval there.

"All the way, Beth," he said gravely. "I want to see that you've obeyed me. And keep your eyes open."

Her face flamed even more as she exposed herself to him; her breath hitched when he swiped a determined finger through her moist folds, raised it to his mouth, and very deliberately tasted it. Tasted *her*.

"Aroused already, Beth?" His smile was that of a hunter whose prey was firmly in his sights. A slow burn started in his dark eyes. "You probably want to know the reason for this. It's quite simple really—I decided that tonight, while we're out, I want to know that you're avail-

able for sex. Don't look so scandalised, sweetheart—
knowing isn't *doing.* I also want you to be aware with
every movement that you belong to me and you've given
me your obedience. And," he added in a somewhat lighter
tone, "you'll do very nicely. You can cover yourself up
now. How are the shoes? Can you walk all right, or shall I
carry you down to the car?"

The sudden return to relative normality threw her for a
second, but as she smoothed the dress down over her
thighs, Beth regained her composure enough to react as if
what had happened was nothing out of the ordinary. She
should want to slap that attitude out of him—she would
with any other man—but with Alex it turned her on. God,
was she in trouble.

"In that suit?" It had to be Savile Row's finest. "Thank
you, but I can manage to walk in these silly little heels."

He looked pointedly at her feet. "You call those silly
little heels? No wonder you damn near broke your ankle."

"They are little, compared to what I usually wear.
What I usually have to wear to have any chance of not
having a permanent crick in my neck when I'm in the office. Although I would need stilts to avoid the risk
completely," she added with a hint of mischief in her
eyes. From being scared and nervous mere seconds ago,
she'd somehow found her sense of humour again. She
might be a sub in his eyes, but that didn't mean she was a
doormat. Beth took a step closer, and, in a clearly exaggerated manner, lifted her chin to look him in the face. To
issue a challenge.

With his finger and thumb he took hold of her chin. The flame glinting in his eyes matched the fire that suddenly burst to life in her heart. One side of his mouth lifted slowly. "If we didn't have a reservation waiting for us, you can rest assured that we would be discussing this further."

His fingers extended, the tips stroked her cheek, and then with the middle finger alone, he tilted her chin up and branded her lips with his mouth. "Let's get your coat."

Beth expected them to go down to the basement car park, but instead they exited the lift in the lobby. It was all glass and marble and chrome, and like Alex's apartment, it screamed wealth. Not to mention security—CCTV cameras occupied strategic positions to cover the entire area and the main doors, and then there was the concierge, who looked more ex-Army than a concierge probably should.

"Alex? I thought we were going in your car?"

"We were," he agreed amiably, "but then I decided I wasn't going to let you have all the fun tonight. Your carriage awaits, milady."

He opened the door for her. Right in front of her, looking sleek and hideously expensive, was a gleaming Rolls Royce, complete with an immaculately turned-out chauffeur who was coming around the car to open the rear passenger door for them.

"Alex, you're insane!" she whispered hoarsely, trying to climb as elegantly as she could into the back of the

Rolls, while holding on to her companion's hand.

"Only occasionally, Beth, only occasionally!"

And always around you.

The back of the Rolls Royce, though spacious, was warm and intimate. And dressed in the clothes he'd bought for her, wearing the diamond collar he'd had made almost three years ago, Beth took his breath away. She made his heart race as if he were a teenager on his first date.

He'd lied when he'd implied that it wasn't a collar—in an uncharacteristic moment of weakness, he'd removed it from the safe but had deliberately not let her look in a mirror. She might catch a glimpse of it in a reflection here or there, but he was determined that she would only see how beautiful she looked in it once she fully accepted her place as his sub.

A vivid image came to mind: Beth, in his bed, wearing nothing but the diamond collar, waiting for him—for her Master—to accept the gift of control over her body and her pleasure. He was almost getting a hard-on just thinking about it. Probably best not to think of it too much, then—it would ruin the line of his trousers.

Their destination was his favourite restaurant, his bolt-hole of serenity when he needed time away from day-to-day life. Wanting to keep it for that special someone, to date he'd only ever gone there alone. He hadn't wanted to sully it with memories of time spent there with other women who had passed through his life. The fact that he was taking Beth there now, and that it felt so right to do so, just confirmed her place in his life.

Though in the heart of Mayfair, the restaurant itself was well off the beaten track—the mews location ensured that only those in the know would be aware of its existence. Alex had been a regular customer for more than five years now, and was greeted warmly by a member of the front-of-house team.

"Mr. Lombard, it's a pleasure to see you, as always. Would you and your guest like to follow me, please? Your usual table is ready."

With her coat safely hanging in the cloakroom, Beth was extremely conscious of the heat of Alex's hand on her back as they followed the host through the restaurant. Once again she was thrown off balance by the fact that not only was there a whole side to Alex's life of which she was completely unaware, he had now chosen to share it with her.

So this was his favourite place to dine in style. She already knew Alex had taste, but this place was in a different league—and it suited him perfectly. He looked completely at home in this cocoon of refinement and elegance. The décor was an impressive blend of natural tones and shades, modern but timeless, and it offered a distinctive sense of tranquillity.

Once seated at the table, located in a secluded part of the restaurant, Beth covertly studied her companion while she was perusing the menu. Alex was sipping a Scotch on the rocks, and although the menu was open in front of him, she had a feeling his mind was elsewhere. Whatever she'd thought she'd known about him, something was telling her that the way she viewed him was about to change beyond all recognition.

And how well did she know herself? Here she was, in a public place, dressed up to the nines and without a shred of underwear, so maybe not as well as she might have thought. Forty-eight hours earlier, she would never have imagined herself capable of doing something so risky. Yet, with Alex seated opposite her, that risk faded into insignificance.

Lost in thought, Beth didn't even realise that the waiter had arrived to take their order, and she couldn't believe it when Alex ordered for her.

"And please let Mark know that we'll have a bottle of whatever he recommends to complement the food."

Beth waited until the waiter left before turning her attention to the man opposite her.

"Tell me you would have chosen anything different, Beth," he challenged her before she could say a word. His expression was intense, daring her to argue. "I know your choices from the last three office Christmas parties, and you are nothing if not a woman of habit. But don't worry, I'll teach you to be more adventurous outside the bedroom, as well as inside it."

She deliberately ignored the provocative comment. "Who's Mark?"

"The sommelier. What he doesn't know about wine

isn't worth knowing. Nothing else to say, love?"

She took a slow, deep breath. "I suppose you do know that these days, women are perfectly capable of making their own choices when it comes to eating out? Lots of other things too."

He raised his eyebrows, his expression one of consideration of her statement. "It doesn't alter the fact that you're here, in the outfit I chose for you, and while you are making the politically correct point every woman should, you haven't exactly screamed blue murder about it."

She couldn't argue with that, but that didn't mean she was letting him get away with it. "There's time yet. What I will say is that you've given me a lot to think about today, including why you brought me here," she gestured towards their surroundings. "It's not every day your boss tells you he's a Dom and he thinks you'd make a good sub."

Smiling, he shook his head. "You need to stop thinking of me just as your boss, Beth. In fact, that role doesn't even matter anymore. And no, not that you would make a good sub—you *are* a sub. Need I remind you that you're not wearing any underwear? That you've already given me your obedience and made yourself sexually available for me in public?"

Thank God there was no one else near enough to hear *that* statement. Then Beth remembered similar scenes from books she'd read, where Doms made apparently outrageous demands, but actually did nothing that would jeopardise their subs' safety or reputation. As she processed the thought, she realised that Alex would do nothing to cause her shame or embarrassment in public.

Completely unabashed, Alex continued. "Shall I tell you what I see in you? A warm, witty, intelligent, caring woman who is almost in denial of the submissive side to her nature—she knows it exists, but lacks the courage to take that step. If you acknowledge your inner submissive and let her into your life, I can teach you all that's great about what she is.

"She's an essential part of you, Beth. You'll be no less of a woman if you never let her in, but you'll always wonder how good it might have been."

She was already wondering—had been for a long time. She'd devoured books on the subject of Domination and submission and trying to deal with her secret desires was part of her motivation for writing about them in a fictional context. Writing was safe; her heroine's Dom was Beth's fantasy man, and while he only existed on her computer screen, he could do nothing to hurt her.

But the man seated opposite her was real. He was her fantasy come to life, he desired her, and he wanted to be her guide on the road to submission. He was the model for the man of her dreams, and she'd quietly lusted after him for years.

She was doomed.

"Beth, I brought you here to spend a pleasant evening with you. Whatever's going through your mind, put it to one side—leave it for tomorrow. Tonight, we are going to have a delicious meal and get to know one other a little better."

He was right; the food was delicious, and so was the wine chosen by the sommelier—it complemented the meal perfectly, and when the time came to return to Alex's apartment, Beth was distinctly light-headed. Seated in the back of the Rolls again, she fired a somewhat exaggerated, narrow-eyed, Medusa-like glare at Alex, who gave every annoying sign of being stone-cold sober.

"So," he said, thoroughly at ease, "what do you think of the restaurant?"

"I can understand why it's your favourite, Alex. I've never been anywhere like that before."

"But you enjoyed the food?"

She chuckled softly. "How could I not? I've never tasted anything like it—sheer heaven."

"And the wine?"

At that question, she looked a little sheepish. "I know absolutely nothing about wine, but what we had really suited the food."

"Mark knows his subject inside out," Alex agreed. "I know what I like, but it doesn't always go with what I'm eating. That's why he's the sommelier and I'm not. And now for the killer question—what about the company?"

The company of the Dom with whom she was now having a relationship. The evening might have got off to a slightly prickly start, but thinking about it, Beth realised that she'd just had a wonderful time with a devastatingly attractive man, and right now, she felt like the luckiest woman in the world.

Earlier, she'd wondered how long it would take her to get used to the idea of being Alex's... Alex's what? Or just... Alex's? The answer was *next to no time at all.*

"Alex," she said, linking her arm through his, "I have had a wonderful evening, and I have enjoyed your company, very, very much."

"Then you'll have no objection to repeating the experience. And next time I'm taking you dancing."

It was a statement, not a question. She was mentally alert enough to work that one out, so she didn't reply. Instead, she leaned her head against his shoulder and closed her eyes, imagining what it would be like to be held in his arms as they swayed to a slow, romantic ballad. He'd hold her close... her head would rest close to his. If she had that, she would need nothing more in life.

Her sigh was one of pure contentment.

Alex glanced at the woman nestled against him and felt a tightening of his body that had been absent for six long months. What the hell was it about her that had turned him into the arrogant boor who told her what she was wearing and what she was going to have for dinner?

He was a sexual Dominant, not a lifestyle Dom—he took control when it came to sex and physical intimacy, and that was it. Except that Beth unwittingly made his common sense fly out of the window and magnified his usual feelings towards a sub beyond all reason. He didn't just want to protect her—his feelings were borderline possessive.

Putting that thought to one side—in the knowledge that once Beth sobered up, he'd likely have some fences to mend—he smiled to himself. All things considered, it had been a good evening, one he'd truly enjoyed, and his decision to share his favourite restaurant with this woman had been totally justified. The perfect end to the evening would have been knowing that he was taking Beth back home to make love to her, but as much as he wanted her, he knew that it would have to wait. Anticipation would make it all the sweeter when the time came.

It was important, he realised, that he find out the true extent of her interest in Domination and submission. He'd pushed her far enough to begin with, by instructing her to go without underwear for their visit to the restaurant. Had she shown any real sign of aversion to the idea, he would have produced the bag of silky lingerie he'd also purchased at the boutique and added "wearing underwear" to her list of hard limits.

In spite of his instruction on that matter, Alex wasn't comfortable with the thought of being a lifestyle Dom. Outside the bedroom, he wanted a woman who could think for herself, a woman who would stimulate him mentally—not a slave who looked to him for direction in every aspect of her life. He'd met enough subs like that to know that it wasn't for him. He enjoyed the contrast of having a confident, independent woman on his arm out-

side the bedroom, and having that same woman kneel before him inside the bedroom and lose all control in his
arms.

As Alex slid a careful arm around Beth's shoulders, he
knew to the very depths of his soul and beyond that not
only was Beth that woman, she would be until the day he
died.

CHAPTER SIX

When they arrived back at the apartment, Beth let Alex take her coat. The light-headed feeling had now given way to a desire for sleep—it was what usually happened on those rare occasions when she consumed a little too much alcohol. Part of her wanted to head straight for bed, but good manners dictated otherwise.

Not only that—she wanted to see what happened next. She slipped off her shoes and limped towards one of the large, comfortable sofas, wondering if Alex would join her. No, not if—*when*. She sat down with her good leg curled under her. Within moments, in spite of her best intentions, her eyelids seemed to acquire lead weights.

"Hey, sleepyhead, time for a nightcap. How's your ankle?"

Dear Lord, if he'd been attractive before, he was a thousand times more potent now. Her brain could only produce a garbled response to his enquiry about her injury, while her eyes were fully occupied in gorging themselves on the man himself. Devilishly handsome with his dark hair still ruffled from the breeze as they'd exited the limousine, he'd shed his jacket and tie and unfastened the top buttons of his shirt.

In the dimmed lighting, he scored a direct hit on her pussy. Remembering that she was still without underwear, Beth winced, hoping that any evidence of her barely controlled lust for this man would not soak her dress—the glossy fabric would make it impossible to conceal. She took the offered brandy snifter in both hands, swirling the glass to warm the measure of cognac, while Alex took a seat directly opposite her.

With the first careful sip, the fine spirit burned its way down her throat and settled in a puddle of molten fire in her stomach. For a moment or two, she stared into the amber depths of the glass, aware of Alex's gaze upon her but not yet ready to respond to it. His posture was as relaxed as her own; she would only need to lift her head slightly for her eyes to lock with his. Under the influence of fine food and wine, not to mention her own raging feelings and desires, it wouldn't take much for her to agree to anything he might suggest.

And it was just as much a mistake to focus on his legs, the fabric of his trousers pulled taut over his muscular thighs—and what looked like a substantial erection.

"Are you blushing, Beth?" His amusement was evident in his voice. "That's the effect you have on me, but you needn't worry—tonight is not the night. You need to sleep, and when you have a somewhat clearer head you need to think about what we've discussed. We'll talk more tomorrow.

"Now, I want you to take your drink, and go and get yourself into bed. I'll be out here; you have nothing to worry about."

Nothing to worry about, he said. She peered at the clock again; it was 3 a.m., precisely seventeen minutes since she'd last checked the time.

Beth had managed to get some sleep since Alex had ushered her off to the bedroom, but once she'd woken up about an hour earlier—feeling sober even if legally she wasn't—she hadn't been able to settle down again, due to thinking about the things Alex had said to her and what it had been like to go out with him.

And most of all, about what it felt like to be his woman.

All of a sudden, Beth knew what was wrong—she needed to take a look at Alex just to reassure herself that this wasn't all a dream, one of her erotic fantasies come to life. She could sneak out there for a quick peek without waking him.

What she didn't expect was to see him standing by the floor-to-ceiling windows on the far side of the room, just standing there, looking out over the city. With no lights on, he was in silhouette against the backdrop of the city lights, but she could still just make out the scars on his back in the subdued light. He seemed so alone, so vulnerable. That didn't make sense, not in the context of Alex Lombard, but the urge to be with him, to wrap her arms around him in a gesture of protection, overwhelmed her. She'd only taken a step or two when he turned towards her. At that moment she realised that he was completely naked. Her mouth went dry.

"Beth."

His voice was little more than a hoarse whisper. As she drew closer, Beth caught a glimpse of the harrowed expression on his face, an expression she guessed she wasn't supposed to see, judging by how quickly he turned away from her. Questions tumbled through her mind.

"Alex, what's wrong?" She laid her hand on his arm. In spite of the ambient warmth, his skin was chilled in a way that made her want to hold him even more.

"It's nothing. Go back to bed, Beth." His tone told her that he expected her to do as he said immediately. "I mean it."

If he expected blind obedience every time he gave her an order, he was in for a big surprise—she wasn't having any of it, not this time. They weren't in the office, and they sure as hell weren't in the bedroom. Novice though she was, Beth was sure that any sub would rebel when it came to her Dom's health and wellbeing.

"No. You're going to talk to me, Alex. Tell me what's going on."

"Beth. Go. To. Bed. *Now.*"

She pulled herself up to her full height—no match for

him, of course, but it gave her the confidence to face him down, or at least, try to.

"Alex Lombard, you're getting far too fond of telling me to do things *now*. Something's not right, and I am not going to waltz off to bed and leave you like this."

"Then take me with you." The voice was husky—the challenge, direct.

Oh God. Her confidence wavered for a moment, and then she faced him head-on. "If that's what it takes."

Although still a little nervous, Beth offered him her hand, her eyes locked with his. Whatever would be, would be.

"Beth, no. It's the alcohol talking, and I am not taking advantage of that." He looked away from her again.

That was the honourable man she'd always seen at the office. "I may well fail a breath test, Alex, but I'm sober enough to know what I'm doing with you." Again, she offered her hand, determined that he wouldn't brush her off. "You're not sleeping alone tonight."

The haunted look became slightly less intense. "Beth Harrison, a sub isn't supposed to be bossy."

Growing bolder by the second, she raised an eyebrow at him. "So spank me. A Dom should have more sense. I've done a lot of reading, and as far as I can see, it's part of a sub's role to take care of her Dom. And even if it weren't, I'd still be making it part of my role in your life."

Fire flared in his eyes. "You do realise what you've just admitted?"

She had, hadn't she? The words had come out without

conscious thought—if ever there was a case of *fools rush in*, this was it. She'd accepted him as her Master.

Still he resisted. "And you want to share a bed with a naked Dom?"

"You don't have to be naked, although I don't have any objections." She made the statement with every bit of brazen intent she could muster, almost drooling at the thought of being close to that magnificent body. She pushed that thought to one side—right now, whatever was bothering Alex so much had to take priority. "It's a large bed—I'm sure we can avoid one another completely, if that's what you want?"

His bark of laughter was totally devoid of humour. "You really think I'd get you into my bed and then avoid you? You're mine now, Beth, now more than ever, and there's no way I wouldn't touch you. After all, what would be the point in taking me to bed with you, if we're not going to touch?"

Beth took a deep breath. The thought of being touched in all sorts of ways by Alex was playing havoc with her equilibrium. "The point is that you wouldn't be alone."

For the third time, she offered her hand. This time he took it, and together they went to the bedroom.

It was obvious that Beth had been sleeping to one side of the bed. She headed for that side, while Alex went to the other. At the movement of the mattress as he lay down beside her, she felt a little of her bravery evaporate—maybe this wasn't such a good idea after all.

No. She dismissed the thought almost as soon as it

formed. This wasn't about her, it was about Alex and what he needed—not her precious sensibilities.

Lying on her side with her back to him, she waited for Alex to close the distance between them, to touch her as he had declared he would—and why not? She was his girlfriend, his woman, his sub—it was only natural that they'd make love, or whatever a Dom did with his sub when she was totally inexperienced. He might even just want to talk.

"Would you like to tell me what's bothering you?" she offered.

"Not especially."

"Then is there anything else that would help?" Beth asked the question in spite of knowing what she could be letting herself in for. Or was that *because of*, rather than *in spite of*?

"I already told you."

He shifted position, and all of a sudden the heat of his body was at her back as he fitted himself to her, his arm coming over to anchor her to him. She should have been scared, or at the very least a little nervous. Instead, she felt as if she were where she belonged. And judging by the erection pressing against her bottom, where she was wanted.

"We're just going to sleep together, Beth," he told her softly, his voice a warm caress. "We've both had too much alcohol to play safely tonight, but make no mistake—in here, whether we play or not, I'm in control."

The warmth and the closeness of a very male human body combined to wake Beth a few hours later. That shared body heat was something she hadn't experienced for too long.

If it hadn't been for the very real arm draped across her waist, she'd almost have been tempted to think that last night had been a dream. She also remembered that the very real hand at the end of the very real arm had started off resting on her stomach, over the T-shirt. At some point during the night, it had found its way under the garment, and right now it was splayed possessively across her belly. It wouldn't have to travel far south to find its way between her legs and discover that she'd woken up in a state of arousal and need.

A sexual Dominant, he'd said. Now that she was faced with the fact—in what would soon be the cold light of day—all sorts of worries made themselves known. Yes, she'd admitted she wanted to be his submissive, but what if she discovered that that sort of relationship wasn't for her? What would happen then? Was it an irreconcilable difference? Was there any feasible compromise?

"I don't know what you're thinking, Beth, but stop it. It's making you frown, and I don't want you frowning."

He was behind her. How in the name of heaven could he possibly know what her expression was?

"I can feel it," Alex said in response to her question. "Why don't you turn around, and we'll see what we can do to make you smile again."

This was it—now or never. Beth inhaled slowly, and then turned within his embrace so that they were facing each other. The sight that met her scored a bull's-eye on her libido again. He looked every bit as roguishly attractive as he had when she'd woken up next to him yesterday. Those eyes, that chest… that chest *again*—the whole package was a lethal weapon doing crazy things to her common sense. The hand that had been resting on her stomach was now curved possessively over her hip, drawing her inexorably towards him.

"Now, Beth, you know we have to talk. Don't be afraid. There's nothing you can say that will shock me."

Beth laid a tentative hand on his chest, enjoying the crisp hair beneath her fingertips, as real as the rest of Alex, as real as his being a Dom. She focused on the sensation, trying not to want him so much because she was afraid that she might not be what he wanted.

"Shall I start?" Alex asked, his voice low and gentle. "You're wondering if this really is right for you. I know you've fantasised about submission, Beth. You know that I'm a Dom, but now that you have the opportunity, now that you've admitted it to yourself and to me, you're scared. There's no need to be scared, love—I'm right here, with you."

He was. She could see it in his eyes, the promise that she'd be safe with him, no matter what. And along with that promise of protection was a desire that took her breath away.

"You know I want you," he continued, "and it's fairly obvious, given our current situation and the fact that you're in no hurry to move away from me, that you are attracted to me. We all have our comfort zones—I don't want yours to become your prison. It's time to explore who you really are, and you can do that with me. We'll take it in baby steps, just one at a time. I'll keep you safe, I promise."

And that included providing an environment where she could be honest, without fear of recrimination or ridicule.

"Alex, I'm afraid," she admitted, her voice a moment away from disappearing into the pit of her stomach. "This has all happened so fast. I know I've said yes, but I'm still scared about what would happen if it all went wrong."

"Come here." He gathered her to him. "I won't let it go wrong. I know you're worried about that, but I will not let it go wrong."

"It's not just that, Alex. You're a Dom. Even though I think I want to be your sub now, what would happen if I eventually found I'd made a huge mistake and I'm not submissive after all? What would happen then?"

"Don't worry about something that isn't going to happen. Trust me, Beth," he said, stroking her hair from her face. The look in his eyes, one of calm confidence, would have inspired her to do just that if she hadn't already been prepared to trust him with her life. "If you could see what I see… Don't be afraid of what you want. Put yourself in my hands. I won't let you fall."

The heat of his palm on her cheek warmed her

through; it was so easy—too easy—to imagine giving herself up to this man, being his in a way that most people probably wouldn't understand, handing him the responsibility for her safety... for her life. She thought about the previous evening, and how it felt to be close to him right now, about the fantasies she'd written about, wanting the reality but being too scared to go looking for it.

Instead, that reality had found her—in the most perfect way she could ever have wanted.

Alex watched his gorgeous new sub close her eyes as a variety of emotions chased one another across her adorable face. He was going to have to work on teaching her not to conceal her eyes from him. They were a means of communication—and far too beautiful to be hidden away from him.

He pondered the idea of taking her to the club, as he'd thought of doing a little over a week ago—never imagining for one moment that it might actually become a possibility. When fully trained, Beth would be a sub any Dom would be proud of, and he wanted to show her off—but only when she was ready, and that was a long way off yet. There was still no way he'd share her, not in the way that some Doms chose to share their subs—although if Cam happened to be around... Alex allowed himself a small smile. Maybe together, he and Beth could persuade his old friend of the beauty to be found in commitment to one special person.

"There's something bothering you, sweetheart," he observed. "What is it?"

"I know I said yes, and I mean it, but… what will you expect from me?"

He lifted her chin so that he could kiss her, a kiss meant to convey care, reassurance, safety. "I will expect you to be Beth—outside this room." He gestured around the bedroom. "In here, in any bedroom we share, in addition to when we're scening, I will expect you to obey me at all times. I will expect you to give up control, so that I can show you all the pleasure your body can give you."

He kissed her again. "In here, your body is mine. You'll keep nothing from me, including your thoughts. You'll have your safe word, Beth, but I promise you'll never need to use it."

He brushed the back of his fingers over her cheek. "I've made that sound very one-sided, I know, but in return, you will have my protection at all times; the gift of your submission will be an honour, and it will be treasured and cherished, as you will be treasured and cherished. And pleasured."

Alex couldn't resist the lure of her mouth; he had to claim it for a third time. This time, her response was electric. She pressed herself against him, grinding her hips against him. If she'd been his sub for longer, he'd have spanked her for that—he'd have put her over his knee and paddled her bottom until it was glowing pink. Beth was passionate all right—it would be a delectable challenge to teach her, and an infinite reward to see her develop.

"My beautiful lady, you have a lot to get used to." He

looked at her face; his stubble had burned her cheek a little, branding her temporarily with his mark in a way that appealed to the primitive, uncivilised male that dwelt within him. "Go and have a shower, and see how you feel about it when you're not in my bed."

A few minutes later Beth was under the shower, letting the water flow over her like a tropical storm while she cleared her mind and her senses of everything, save Alex's kisses and how it had felt to lie beside him. Put simply, it had been the quintessence of almost every secret fantasy she'd had since she met the man.

All cleaned up, she wrapped herself in one of Alex's huge fluffy towels, leaving the robe for him. Now for the hard part—hard, because she had no first-hand experience of a relationship such as this. She'd read so much, but the fact of the matter was she had to learn everything from the bottom up.

Alex was sitting on the edge of the bed by the time she emerged from the bathroom, his back towards her. All she saw was the man, not the scars... and the man was everything. Beth took a deep breath. When she'd last gone to sleep in the loneliness of her own bed, she'd had no idea that she was in love with Alex Lombard.

Understanding didn't come with a bolt of lightning; it came with the warmth of an embrace, enfolding her slowly in a comforting blanket of promise for the future—however limited that future might be. There could be no fireworks for something that had been growing slowly but surely over time. He was what she wanted. For now. For ever. For however long he wanted her.

And whatever price he came with, he would be worth it, down to the last penny.

She dropped the towel, slightly anxious about her nudity, even though he'd seen everything just yesterday and seemed to like it. What if he changed his mind on a second viewing? *Too late now...*

Her stomach rose to her chest as she took up a position in front of him and his eyes met hers. Following her instincts she knelt in front of him, feeling self-conscious and clumsy, and all the while a part of her mind was almost screaming at her, asking her what she was playing at, telling her she was making an almighty fool of herself. Her heart was racing.

Please let me have the courage and the trust to do this. Please don't let him laugh at me.

"I don't know... exactly what I'm supposed to do," she admitted hesitantly, "but this feels right... Sir."

Alex looked down at Beth. She was a truly remarkable woman. What she'd just done showed courage and character. There was no way he was going to reject that bravery.

"First of all, call me by my name for now, no matter where we are. It's taken me three years to get you to use it and I kind of like the way you say it. For future reference, though, there will come a point where I'm 'Sir' in here—unless, of course," he added, his eyes full of teasing humour, "you give me a reason in here to have you call me 'Sir' out there."

He looked at the woman kneeling before him. Eyes downcast, she only needed a little guidance regarding her posture. Pride in her gave him a warm feeling around his heart. He tried to think of the last time he'd felt anything vaguely similar and the simple answer was... he hadn't. Not even with the woman he'd married.

"Widen your knees, Beth. More... that's better. Just lower your eyes, not your head—you're not a slave. That's right, it shows respect. Rest your hands on your thighs, palms up. Good. Now, how does that feel? Could you hold that position for a few minutes without pain?"

"Yes, Alex."

He sensed that she was a little confused by the question. "D/s isn't about inflicting pain to the point of agony, Beth," he explained patiently. "I'm not a sadist, and I don't expect you to be a masochist. Yes, you will be subject to discomfort, and there will be brief—I stress, *brief*—spells of pain which you will come to love because of what happens after the pain, but it's not in my interest or yours to force you to assume a pose that leaves you hurting."

She visibly relaxed a little at that. While she'd clearly researched D/s for her writing, there was still a lot she had to learn. How he relished the prospect of being the one to teach her.

"From now on, that is your first position. You will assume it when told, and you will also learn when to assume it without being told explicitly. And should this, or anything else, *ever* cause you real pain, you will tell me immediately. Understood?"

"Yes, Alex."

"I also want you to understand this: you will come to me, as your Dom, if you have any problems or issues of any kind. You will tell me about anything and everything that bothers you, or makes you happy, no matter how small or insignificant you think it might be. Inside the bedroom and out of it, I'm the one you lean on now. I'll always protect you and support you. No arguments."

"Yes, Alex."

He nodded, trying not to be distracted by how good those two words sounded when spoken by his Beth. He scrutinised her appearance in fine detail. For a beginner, she was doing very well. Not perfectly, but for a beginner she showed plenty of promise. "And before we go any further, your safe words will be red to stop immediately, yellow to slow things down and discuss them, and green if I need positive confirmation from you that you wish to continue. Got that?"

She nodded and gave him one of her beautiful smiles. Why was he only realising now just how beautiful those smiles were?

"Yes, Alex. Red to stop, yellow to slow down and green for go. Just like traffic lights."

"Just like traffic lights," he agreed. "I know I said that I didn't expect you to need to use a safe word, but don't ever let that stop you if you feel you need to."

He could sit here and watch her all day, except for three things: her hair was wet, her ankle hadn't yet healed fully, and he needed a shave and a shower.

"Okay then. I'd like you to stand up now. Take your time, love; remember, everything you do now is to please me, and it pleases me to watch you move with poise and grace." He offered her his hand.

All things considered, again, she managed fairly well. Her balance was a little off, but that was hardly surprising with the problem with her ankle—he noted that the bruising was showing visible signs of healing already, judging by the way the colour was changing. "Stand up straight, hands behind your head, eyes lowered, feet shoulder-width apart. That will be your second position. Does your ankle hurt?"

"A little, Alex."

Probably more than she was willing to admit. That was a habit he was going to have to break. "I'm going to get cleaned up now, Beth. While I'm attending to that, I want you to sit here and dry your hair. If your hair isn't dry by the time I'm done, I'll finish it off for you.

"And don't get dressed," he added, having decided that he quite liked to have Beth as nature intended. He wanted to enjoy her a little longer. "Not yet, anyway. I thought that later, we'd go for a stroll in the park—not far, just for some fresh air, and while we're out, we'll get some lunch."

CHAPTER SEVEN

The bathroom door closed behind him; at that point, Beth drew in great lungfuls of air to feed her oxygen-starved body. *So far, so good.*

Actually… more than good. Involuntary warmth flooded through her at the memory of the way he'd touched her before heading for the bathroom, his hands gentle, his touch tender as he'd caressed her arms, almost as if she were the most precious thing in his life. His eyes had roamed over her face and body before he'd lowered his head and claimed her mouth with a kiss that promised heaven.

She went to the drawer where Alex kept the hairdryer. He'd promised to finish off drying her hair for her if she hadn't completed the task by the time he'd showered, so she'd better get a move on. She remembered all too well the fireworks he'd set off when he'd done that for her yesterday.

Just concentrate on drying your hair. Don't go off into a daydream.

She didn't know why, but it seemed like nothing—not her hair, not the dryer itself—was going to cooperate. In next to no time the shower stopped, and moments later the bathroom door opened.

Alex sat behind her again, his legs framing hers. The brush and hairdryer were taken from her and that delicious feeling tore through her again as he began to dry her hair.

Oh God. Oh God, oh God, oh God! He was barely touching her and she was still turning into a wreck.

"Sit up straight, Beth. That's it. Perfect."

His voice was silk and cream and honey, all mixed together in a way that made Beth melt from the inside out. She couldn't get enough of it—she was addicted. Whatever Alex wanted from her, she'd gladly give. He was communicating directly with a place inside her that was so secret, she'd merely skimmed the surface of its existence—the part of her that craved the surrender of all control, and craved it with an intensity she'd never before experienced.

A few minutes later the hairdryer was switched off. Beth sensed Alex's movements as he put it to one side. She was expecting him to tell her to stand up, but no, he said nothing. All she could feel, when he swept her hair to one side, was the gentle caress of his breath at the nape of her neck.

"That's it, sweetheart," she heard him murmur eventually, and then his hands exerted a gentle pressure on her shoulders. "When we're alone together, you'll accept my touch whenever and wherever I choose. To arouse you, to discipline you… or to guide you. Now, keep your back straight and look straight ahead. I want you to remain absolutely silent."

The sensation of his hands stroking down her back was exquisite, as was the moment when his arms came around her and pulled her back against his chest. His right arm pinned her to him, while his left hand began a sensual exploration of her breasts and nipples. A fierce, pulsating ache started up between her legs almost immediately and a soft moan escaped her lips. All of a sudden, simply breathing required a huge effort.

"Hush, Beth," he remonstrated, his voice both stern and sensual. "Did I give you permission to make any sound?"

She was about to answer, but shook her head instead. His words, the control they implied, were making her melt with need.

"Excellent. You're learning. Now, I want you to lift your legs up and hook them over mine if you can—that's it."

The shift in position tilted her pelvis up, opening her wide for him, while her weight rested fully on his broad chest. The heat of him flooded her body. The arm that had been around her waist moved, and then she felt his hand between her legs. God, she so wanted to close her legs against the invasion—it was too, too much—but she could do nothing. In this room, she was his possession.

He was massaging her pussy with deep, slow, sensual strokes. Before he even came out of the bathroom she'd been wet from just thinking about what might happen, but now—and he hadn't even touched her clit yet—she was soaked with arousal. Her hips writhed as she hungered for more of what he was doing to her. The mere act of thinking was impossible as feeling consumed her entire being.

A stroke went deeper, separating her labia, allowing his middle finger to dip inside her, and on the upward stroke, he pressed that finger to her swollen clit. She couldn't help but cry out as her back arched in reaction. She tried to push his hand away, but he would have none of it.

"Beth, in here, you will deny me nothing, unless you use your safe words," he reminded her, his touch picking up pace and pressure. "You may speak now. What do you want? Do you want to call red?"

"Please, Alex!" She writhed in his embrace, desperate for a release from the mounting need in every atom of her being.

"What, Beth?" he asked, his voice calm and controlled. "Tell me exactly what you want."

If she could tell him she would... except the words were tumbling around in her mind and refused to organise themselves into an even vaguely coherent sentence. His name was all she could manage to articulate.

"Not good enough, Beth. Tell me."

She couldn't—but if she didn't, she wouldn't get what

she wanted and she wanted it so damn much. "Please… please let me come, Alex!" Overwhelmed by need and now desperately embarrassed, it was the best she could manage.

"Not yet, my love. I know you need to come, but you're not ready. You need to learn self-control, and I am going to teach you."

Beth could have screamed. She was ready… oh, she was *so* ready, but not for the hand between her thighs. The finger dipping into her pussy was like being in the path of a sensual tsunami—the tidal wave was rushing towards her and she could do nothing to save herself from it. She couldn't pull herself away from that hand, she couldn't push it away, she felt as if she were going to explode. "Please, Alex—please!" she whimpered.

"Self-control, Beth." His voice was intractable, compelling, almost totally devoid of emotion. "Remember: you're stronger than this. Tell me what you need."

She was crying now, the pleasure becoming unbearable as it boiled through her veins. She wanted it to stop, she needed it to stop, but it was just going on relentlessly, endlessly, that hand ceaselessly working her clit to drive her out of her mind, the fingers dipping inside her instead of his cock filling her, the torment going on and on…

"Please!" she sobbed. "Please, Alex, I need to come—may I come?"

Silently she begged for release, pleading with Alex in her mind, to let her give in to the sensations he was creating in her treacherous body. All that happened was that he increased the pressure and the rhythm yet again—she felt her body pulse and contract around his fingers, dazzling white light exploded in her mind and then finally he allowed her what she craved.

"You may. Come for me now, sweetheart."

Alex wrapped his arms around his sub as her body writhed under the force of her orgasm. His hand remained between her legs, drenched from the sexual ecstasy that was crashing through her body. Like this, Beth was pure, carnal woman, made for a man's pleasure—the cool exterior was gone, banished by the torrent of passion he'd always suspected might lie beneath. His frustrated erection was hard as granite and giving him hell, but she was worth it.

Dropping his voice to a low murmur, he began to calm her, stroked her soft skin and dropped light kisses on her shoulder and the nape of her neck. Finally her breathing settled as her senses returned—and so did her embarrassment. It was in every line of her suddenly tense body, the way her teeth clamped down on her lower lip—he was really starting to hate that habit now, it had to go—and when her head drooped to one side, it was in the scalding tear he felt drip onto his forearm.

"Beth, listen to me. What just happened… it was beautiful. Don't be ashamed. I wanted you to find out how holding off could let you lose yourself in pleasure, just like that. Do you understand?"

He looked across at the mirror through which he'd

watched her as he pleasured her; she was limp in his arms, her head still bowed, her glossy hair a cascade of shining waves. With an effort she sat up straight, and it was then that he saw her face—her mortified expression faded, became something softer and more feminine than he'd ever seen before.

He wanted nothing more than to bury himself forever in her glorious gentleness, but now wasn't the time. The second lesson he had for her was that her pleasure at his hand was a gift that came without expectation.

"Beth?"

"Yes, Alex?"

"Go and clean yourself up. Leave the bathroom door open. When you're done, come back here, and get dressed. I'll get some clothes ready for you. No arguments," he added, when she opened her mouth to protest. She hesitated for a moment, and then he watched her walk to the bathroom, unaware that he was holding his breath, waiting to see if she would look around at him. Just as he was resigned to losing the bet, Beth paused and turned. He nodded, acknowledging how well she'd done, and let his breath out on a long, silent sigh.

Alex continued to watch her for a few moments as she washed the copious moisture from her pussy. With each passing second his patience faded more and more, until he had no choice but to join her in the spacious shower.

"Give that to me." He took the handheld showerhead from her and began to play the warm water on her pussy. "Spread your legs. Hold on to me if you need help with your balance."

He crouched so that he could ensure that she was clean. His fingers flirted with the curls at the top of her thighs, and he made a mental note to do something about that. Beth would look even more gorgeous with a smooth mons—when she was ready, he would introduce her to the delights of waxing. The result would be delightful, at any rate, even if the procedure wasn't. He would have to ensure that he spoiled her rotten afterwards.

He felt her hand rest tentatively on his shoulder.

"Alex?"

"Yes, love?"

"Was it really… all right?"

She sounded so uncertain. Alex resolved to make her certain. "More than I could have hoped for, Beth," he confirmed, his tone warm and reassuring. It wasn't a lie; for someone so new to the scene, she'd done phenomenally well. "I'm proud of you. Very proud."

"But what about you?"

"What about me?"

He heard her take a deep breath.

"You didn't come."

Good one, Beth. Alex silently congratulated her on having the nerve to make the statement so plainly. "Not necessary." Now that *was* a lie, but a white one he could live with in the circumstances. He straightened up. "You gave me everything I needed. All done now. Dry off and then we'll get dressed."

He made her wait while he dressed; he enjoyed looking at her nude body. Her shoulders were set with the same quiet determination with which she'd taken on everything that he'd thrown at her in the office over the last three years. Her dedication had not gone unnoticed then; it did not go unnoticed now.

Once attired in faded jeans and a navy rugby shirt, he gave Beth the clothes he wanted her to wear: smart black trousers, and a violet-coloured roll-neck sweater. When she looked up at him, he saw the question in her eyes.

"No underwear, remember?" His tone wasn't unkind.

Her beautiful eyes widened, and then she smiled—in that smile there wasn't just acceptance of his instruction, but enjoyment of it as well. He wasn't fooled, not for one minute—he wasn't going to have an easy time of it with his Beth, not at all. *Thank God.*

The unseasonal sunshine had brought a lot of people to the park. As Alex strolled along with Beth at his side, it felt entirely natural to take her hand in his. So far, she appeared to be coping reasonably well with the changing dynamic of their relationship, although he could still detect a trace of tension in the way she gripped his hand.

At the first available park bench, he had her sit down and then made himself comfortable beside her. "How's your ankle holding up? I haven't dragged you too far, have I?"

She shook her head. "It just needs a rest for a few minutes."

Alex looked at her for a few moments. "Beth, tell me what you're thinking about right now."

She pressed her lips together for a second or two. "I feel like the way I fit into the world is different now, Alex—that I'm not the person I always thought I was."

"And how do you feel about that?"

A slight frown creased her brow. "I don't really know. It's not what I expected. Actually, I'm not sure what I expected."

Alex took a deep breath as he clasped her hand in his. Twining his fingers with hers gave him an extra few seconds to think. "Beth, don't be afraid. This is a huge change, but you're not alone anymore. And don't forget," he lifted her hand to kiss her fingers, "you have a Dom who adores you."

She blushed delightfully. The hint of colour went perfectly with the slightly hesitant, self-conscious smile.

Transferring her right hand to his right hand, he put his free arm around her, drawing her into his side, so that he could kiss her temple.

"Beth, you're not doing this by yourself. I'm here for you, don't ever forget that. I'm with you every step of the way, and I've been around the scene for years. And I trained in the US with the best—"

"You trained?" Her surprised expression spoke volumes.

He returned her look of astonishment with a quiet chuckle. "Of course. Didn't you realise that any Dom worth the title will have been trained to take his responsibility for his sub seriously? He needs to recognise all the implications, the possible consequences of what he's doing. Surely you came across that in your research?"

She shrugged. "I did, but I wasn't sure it was true." She gave a little self-conscious laugh.

"Oh, it's true all right. And as part of the training, we also have to be on the receiving end of the kind of treatment we dish out to the subs. That way, we know exactly how it feels when we apply any given amount of force to a flogging, for example."

"That's comforting. You don't exactly see the local college offering degrees or evening classes in Domination and submission."

Alex laughed along with her. "That's true." He became a little more serious. "You know the sort of activities that can take place—it would be the height of irresponsibility to go take part in those activities without knowing the possible consequences if you get it wrong. I wasn't born knowing all there is to know about D/s, nor was any other Dom. I had to learn, and I learned from some of the best in the business."

Alex broke off, brow furrowed as he scanned their surroundings. His skin was prickling in a way he hadn't experienced since he'd walked away from Spectrum Security. Back then, the sensation had been a precursor to trouble, but here? Now? If it was still the iron-clad guarantee of trouble it had once been, then maybe it meant that Cam's investigations were starting to stir things up. If they were and someone was following him... He needed to talk to Cam as a matter of urgency—he couldn't put Beth at risk from whatever was going on.

With an effort he turned his concentration back to the conversation and forced a levity into his tone that he was far from feeling. "This will be a learning experience for both of us, love."

"It will?"

She seemed surprised by that, but Alex wasn't going to tell her why—that, for the first time in his life, he was embarking on an intimate, physical relationship with a sub who would wear his collar. Or that he knew it would be the only time. That was the kind of disclosure that could overwhelm her and send her into hiding at this stage of their relationship.

He pressed a brief kiss to her lips. "Your nose is turning a delightful shade of pink, and it's getting to the time when we should be thinking of lunch. There's a pub I know not far from here, by the river, where they do a great Sunday roast. It's just a pity it's too cold to sit outside, overlooking the river, but I promise I'll take you there next summer."

Half an hour later, Beth was sitting opposite Alex, a glass of orange juice in front of her and a roast chicken lunch—*not* chosen for her by her companion—on order.

The hidden depths of the man amazed her. He'd given her so much to think about, not least of which was his comment about bringing her here in summer. A slip of the tongue, or a pointer to how he viewed the development of their relationship?

She rolled the concept around in her mind, testing it,

trying it on for size—she supposed she'd get used to it eventually. The man she worked for was right there in front of her, yet in the space of forty-eight hours he had become so much more—her lover and her Dom. She wondered, a little frivolously, if she could find the bag thief, so she could thank him for changing her life beyond all imagination.

She thought of what Alex had said to her, about telling him everything, and sharing her worries with him. Oddly, that was going to be one of the more difficult aspects of this relationship—she was so used to dealing with things for herself.

And then she remembered his arms around her in the night, his body next to hers, the strength and heat of him. Her eyes lifted, stealing a look at him as he gazed out of the window, across the deck and the river beyond, almost as if he were searching for something. She'd been struck by his outrageously good looks from the moment she walked into his office for the job interview, but now she saw more of the man beneath. How could a woman not love him? Half in love and totally in lust from the start, she'd stood no chance. Beth smiled to herself.

"Something amusing you, love?" the man in question asked, setting his glass of wine back in its place on the table.

She shook her head, hoping he wouldn't ask her to explain why she was smiling, because she wasn't quite sure that she could. Or should.

"That's okay." His manner was deceptively easy-going. "I suppose you won't mind a good spanking when I take you to bed when we get back home, then."

Heat rushed to her cheeks as her stomach turned gold-medal-standard somersaults. With Alex, she knew, down to the last cell in her body, that it was no idle threat. She closed her eyes against the vision of him stripping her of her clothes and putting her over his knee to spank her naked bottom, but when she opened them again, her face was lightly flushed and her eyes held a new sparkle.

"Hmm, maybe that wouldn't be such a good idea after all," he observed thoughtfully. "I think you might enjoy it just a little too much, and we can't have that."

"You said you'd only do things like that in the bedroom anyway," she reminded him. "We're not in the bedroom now."

"True—we will only do things like that in the bedroom and the playroom I mentioned, but I didn't say we wouldn't discuss these things elsewhere."

She risked a quick glance at his face, and saw that he was smiling—that smile that had scored a direct hit on her knees more times than she could count. It was reflected in his eyes, and if she had to put a label on that look, it would be mischievous. The damn man was enjoying himself!

Far from being outraged, Beth just about managed to contain her desire to join in with laughter of her own. Just a few short hours ago she'd been shaking with nerves, yet now she was relaxed and happy, and looking forward to feeling Alex's hand on her backside. The situation was verging on the surreal.

Lunch was over quickly and then it was back to the apartment. Ever thoughtful, Alex hailed a cab, offering Beth his hand as she climbed inside. Unaware of his earlier disquiet, she missed the way he cast one last look around before he followed her into the vehicle.

All the way back to the apartment, she wondered when he would take her to the bedroom, assuming he meant what he'd said. Once there, she shrugged off her jacket and hovered, waiting for some clue from Alex. He was heading for one of the sofas but stopped suddenly, looking back at her.

"Not yet," he told her with the tenderness she was starting to recognise would always make her feel special. "Take off your boots and come and sit with me for a while."

She kicked off her footwear as quickly as she could manage, took the offered hand and followed Alex to one of the sofas. He sat, pulling her down beside him. The next thing she knew, she was lying full-length on the sofa, half on top of the full-length sprawl of him, cradled between his body and the back of the sofa.

"Beth, my sweetheart, later on we are going to go to the bedroom to discuss your discipline for keeping secrets—remember, I told you I want to know about everything that makes you happy—but for now, I want to get to know you better."

With that, he began to kiss her.

"Sir…"

"Shh." He placed a gentle finger on her mouth to silence her. "Not here, not now. It's still Alex, remember? Until I change that, this is just Alex and Beth getting to know each other."

He resumed the kiss, cradling her close to his lean strength. Or he would have done, had Beth not placed her hand on his chest to slow things down.

"If this is just Alex and Beth getting to know other," she said, "does that mean I can go and put some underwear on?"

His grin was devilish, telling her without words what the answer would be. "You're forgetting—firstly, you don't have my permission to wear underwear, and secondly, there'd be no point—it'd be coming off soon anyway."

"It would?"

"It would," he confirmed absently, apparently far more interested in cupping her cheek in his hand and tracing the outline of her lower lip with his thumb. "I like having you naked around me."

Just as well she had no objection to that... no objection at all. At that precise moment, she found herself actually hungering for it. She could feel her mind moving into that space where she felt owned by this man whom she suddenly wanted beyond all reason.

"But I want to call you 'Sir'," she murmured, giving voice to one of her deepest desires.

"Do I have to remind you who's the boss when it comes to that part of our relationship? You will call me that when I tell you and not before, and you will do it whenever it's appropriate to do so." He was suddenly fascinated with the way her hair curled around his fingers.

"I suppose I'll have to wait, then." She couldn't keep the grin out of her voice. "So... How long?"

"Until I'm ready!" His hand insinuated itself under her sweater, exploring the silken flesh that covered her ribcage. "Aren't you hot and uncomfortable with this thing on?"

The trousers and socks made her hot and uncomfortable as well. Moments later, her clothing was in a heap on the floor, and she was naked in Alex's arms. He was still wearing his jeans and rugby shirt, and looked like sex on legs. The difference in their attire made a huge feeling of submissiveness unfurl and wrap itself around her like a soft fur blanket. She felt she belonged like this—belonged to him. When her gaze began to shift from his face to his chest, his finger under her chin halted the movement and reversed it.

"You didn't even realise you were doing that, did you? I think I'm just going to have to kiss you to stop you doing it again."

This time he didn't stop at just kissing her; his hand stroked down her side, curved over her hip and pulled her against him. His knee pushed ruthlessly between her legs, and the next thing she knew, she was straddling him, her mouth still on his while his hands roamed possessively over her back and bottom.

Instinct drove her to push herself up so that she could look at him, her hands on his chest supported her, and between her legs she felt the force of his erection under the fly of his jeans. She couldn't help herself—her hips began to rock back and forth, riding as instinct demanded. With perfect precision she lined her pussy up with the fly of his jeans and began to grind down in an attempt to stimulate her clit. God, it felt so good…

"That's it," he encouraged her. "Christ, you look beautiful like that." His eyes were half-closed as he found his own pleasure beneath her.

Beth didn't expect to feel his mouth on her breast, or the strong suckling at her nipple. Her body responded instantly, and she knew that if she hadn't already, she was going to leave a wet patch on his jeans, right over the hard cock that she was growing more and more desperate to have inside her. His hands bracketing her hips held her firmly in place.

"Alex."

"Tell me what you want, Beth."

Her response was a single word, barely breathed.

"You."

A little while later, with a thoughtful look on his face, Alex was standing at the door to his home office, just watching Beth while trying to work out the best way to convince her that she belonged under his roof.

He rubbed the back of his neck. He knew it was unreasonable to want her to move in so soon, but it wasn't like they'd only just met. Did they really need to go through the whole dating thing when they'd been around each other nearly every day for three damn years? They already knew each other, and as far as he could see, their attraction was both fierce and very mutual. So why delay?

Their make-out session on the sofa had been every bit as frustrating for him as it had been for her. By the time he'd called a halt to proceedings, she'd been teetering on the edge of what he was sure would have been an explosive orgasm and he'd had a hard-on that had felt as if it could have held up the tent for a three-ring circus. He was going to remember the look on her face when he'd told her he had to call Cam for a long time to come. She'd stomped over to the kitchen, giving him a stellar view of her beautiful arse in the process.

Oh, she was going to be a handful all right, and he relished the thought of witnessing every moment of her development as a sub—his sub. Thoughts of showing her the ropes turned his mind briefly to learning more about Kinbaku—she would look truly stunning, adorned in a complex, artistic arrangement of bindings and knots. A human work of art.

The thought planted an intriguing idea in his mind, and the more he considered it, the more attracted to it he became. Aegis often played host to Doms giving demonstrations of various D/s activities. Bondage was a favourite, and if he could acquire the knowledge—and Beth the confidence—she would be a truly awesome sight to witness. Oh yes, an intricate web passing above and below her breasts. He'd position the rope carefully between her pussy lips, so that it was riding her clit. She'd be constantly aroused as the demonstration progressed… and forbidden to come until he gave his permission. That would wait until they were in one of the private rooms.

Much though he wanted to drag Beth away from the kitchen and play, there were other priorities to which he needed to attend, not least of which was that call to Cam, to find out if there'd been any developments in the investigation in the last twenty-four hours. He had no intention of making that call in front of Beth. He didn't want to alarm her any more than necessary—he hoped it wouldn't be necessary at all.

Most people would probably label the disquiet he'd felt as some sort of paranoia, but not Alex. He'd experienced it too often in theatre to dismiss it out of hand now—not when there had been occasions where it had kept him and the men in his troop alive against all the odds.

The phone call was brief, and as he'd expected, Cam couldn't add anything to what he'd told Alex the previous day. When Alex informed his friend of the uneasiness he'd experienced, he immediately sensed an even greater keenness in Cam's focus on the matter. Having witnessed it in action on more than one occasion, his former staff sergeant had an unshakeable belief in Alex's sixth sense for danger.

Once the call was finished, Alex emerged from the office to find Beth still in the kitchen area, and from the aroma wafting over, she was making coffee. It felt good,

Alex realised, to have a gorgeous naked woman in his kitchen. Thank God the apartment was too high up to be overlooked—the idea of introducing a *no clothes* rule when they were there together was hugely appealing.

He slid down on the sofa, feet up on the coffee table as usual. He hadn't forgotten about the spanking she'd earned over lunch, and he had every intention of administering it soon.

As he continued to watch Beth in the kitchen, he found himself considering the matter of a collar. While some might consider it too early for a formal collaring, he wanted her to have the symbolism of a collar for the spanking he was shortly going to deliver. In his opinion, she'd benefit from the added sensation and the way it would help her to get into the mind-set of a sub.

So… What could he—

Of course… the ribbon. It had been tied around the box when he'd collected the diamond collar from the jeweller. At the time, Alex had tossed the piece of black velvet into the drawer and never given it another thought. His focus had been on the collar—he'd had it made just after Beth came to work for him. Given all his reasons for not getting involved with her, it was a rash extravagance, but he'd felt compelled to commission the piece for her. He'd never imagined how important the ribbon would be.

Beth brought the drinks over and sat beside him on the sofa, her legs curled under her. As he sipped the coffee, made just how he liked it, Alex slipped his arm around his woman, drawing her closer to him.

"Well," he said eventually, "now that you have your safe words, I seem to recall that I promised you a good spanking at lunch."

CHAPTER EIGHT

Alex led his submissive into the bedroom.

It was a powerful moment for him, taking a sub who would wear his collar and warm his bed. Not just any sub, though. This was Beth, the woman who had been an integral part of his professional life for so long, whom he'd wanted in his personal life for almost as long, and for Alex, it was a defining moment. Soon, when she was ready, he would take her to see Giorgio, a fellow Dom who specialised in crafting slave collars—not just collars suitable for play, but collars that could be worn as if they were jewellery, innocent-looking pieces in the vanilla world, but full of meaning in the community.

"On your knees."

He didn't intend to keep her there long. She obeyed immediately, assuming her designated first position. For a few moments Alex simply looked down at her, giving himself time to appreciate the impact of the picture she presented. For so long he'd believed that this could never become reality with any sub, let alone Beth.

The ribbon was in the drawer where he'd left it. He drew the narrow length of velvet through his fingers. *Perfect*.

"Beth, it's important to me that my sub knows her place when in a scene. I don't have a suitable collar for you yet, but in a scene like this I want you to be aware of your place in this relationship. As a symbol of my ownership, this will be your collar for the time being."

Beth gathered her hair together, lifting it out of the way so that he could tie the ribbon around her neck. With great care, he laid the band against her skin, ensuring that it wasn't twisted, tying it with a perfect double bow at the nape of her neck.

"Now you're mine."

In that moment, life was perfect. *Beth* was perfect. Even the power of his nightmares receded as he took in the sheer beauty before him.

Her eyes briefly met his and then lowered, in an automatic expression of submission that stoked all his dominant impulses into a blazing inferno. At her soft "Thank you, Sir", he needed every last bit of control he could muster to remove his shirt without firing buttons all around the bedroom. He flung the garment to one side and then offered Beth his hand to help her up. He wrapped his arms around her as she rose, and when he pulled her against his body, felt her skin next to his, it took all his resolve not to sweep her off her feet and onto the bed, cover her body with his and fuck both of them senseless.

Instead, he kissed her as if he would devour her body and soul.

At the end of the kiss, he looked into Beth's eyes—they were gentle and full of wonder and honesty... the eyes of an innocent he didn't deserve, but wanted anyway. And the collar—maybe he'd have to revise his plans, because the ribbon looked as sexy as hell. "Come and sit with me."

Once seated on the bed, he pulled her down onto his lap. "Open your legs, sweetheart."

At the first touch between her thighs, her eyes closed and a delightful little whimper passed her lips. The arm around his shoulders tightened too. She was already wet and growing more so with each determined stroke of his fingers. "Look at me, beautiful."

Her gaze meshed with his and he felt as if he were looking into her soul. No woman had ever looked at him quite like that—she was hiding nothing from him. Her arousal was a growing fire, consuming her from within. Alex altered the rhythm of his stroking, dipping a finger inside her. She cried out this time, bracing herself with a hand on his chest as her thighs started to close.

"Beth, keep your legs open." The reminder was a little sterner than he intended and her response to it was instant.

"I... can't." she gasped, "I have... have to—"

"You don't. You only have to please me. That's all you have to do. Lean on me, Beth. Put your arms around me and lean on me."

He gave an involuntary grunt; her breasts against his chest made his cock surge under his jeans again. Her curves were in all the right places, soft and feminine and voluptuous, the way a woman was supposed to be. If the sensation of holding her like this was a mere hint of what she would feel like when she was under him, then he was doomed.

Her clit was swelling beneath his touch. Not only that, he could feel her starting to fuck his hand. "Keep still, Beth," he ordered. "Have you ever tasted yourself?"

When she answered by shaking her head, he took his hand away from her and used the same hand under her chin to force her to look at him. "Open your mouth. Now suck my finger as if it were my cock. You didn't answer me properly, so this is your punishment."

Shit, he was going to have to take her soon. If she were sucking his cock rather than his finger, it would be a supreme test of his self-control not to come like some out-of-control teenager who'd just discovered what his dick was for. Her tongue swirled around his finger, filling his head with thoughts of how her mouth would feel on his cock.

"Tell me how you taste."

Colour rose to her cheeks, and again she shook her head—embarrassment, he guessed. He quickly swiped his fingers through her folds again, sweeping up her moisture, and then licked his own fingers. God, how the hell was he supposed to wait to go down on her? She was a perfect banquet and he was more than ready to gorge himself.

"Shall I tell you? Slightly salty, warm, delicious and all woman. Do you know how wet you are?" This time he scooped more of her juices and wiped his fingers over her cheek. "Does this tell you how sexy you are? How much you want to be fucked? I'm going to fuck you, Beth, but not before I put you over my knee and deliver on my promise. Stand up and lie face-down over my lap."

Once she was in position, with one of his hands on her back to keep her safely in place, his other hand explored the soft curves of her bottom, weighing up the best places to paddle her backside. Half a dozen to begin with—that should get the message across nicely, and give her a nice warm feeling where it counted.

At the first smack, she jerked and cried out, no doubt startled by the sharp sting on her flesh. Already he didn't think he'd ever get tired of seeing her skin acquire that radiance beneath his touch. As soon as he stroked the same area she quieted down, wriggling only slightly. "Keep still, Beth. Do not move, and above all, do not come."

"No, Alex, I won't." Her voice was little more than a whisper, poised between pleasure and pain. "Thank you."

Another smack landed. This time she flinched, her buttocks clenching beautifully before relaxing as he stroked her flesh again. "How many is that, Beth?"

"Two, Alex."

"Good. You will now count out the remainder."

He repeated the process four more times, the smack followed by the caress. She counted each stroke as he had ordered her to do, and at the end her bottom was glowing nicely.

"You've done well, Beth," he approved, his voice a little more gentle as he lifted her to her feet. "Did you enjoy that? If you did, don't be afraid to admit it—tell me properly."

Her eyes were fixed on the floor. The admission, when it came, was quiet and honest. "Yes, Alex, I enjoyed it."

An eyebrow rose in perfect accompaniment to the wry grin. "Which just proves that I can't use spanking to discipline you, Miss Harrison. You've been a good girl." He examined her face—there was something in her eyes that suggested something remained unsaid. "What else, Beth? Tell me."

"Alex." She knelt before him, hands clasped and resting on her thighs, eyes still lowered. "Please... I need... I don't know how to ask."

"Just ask, Beth. It's only words, and words can't hurt you. Tell me what you need. If you don't tell me, how can I give it to you?"

She took his hands and pressed a kiss to each palm. "Please may I ask if you would consider..." She took a deep breath. "If you would consider further correction?"

"In what way?"

Alex knew he was pushing her, but she had to learn to finish what she started and become entirely comfortable with communicating her needs, as well as speaking plainly.

Her voice was barely above a whisper when she responded with a single word. "More. Or harder. I'm not sure which."

"Good—not perfect, but we're getting there. All you have to do is put the two ideas together, and find your confidence. You have nothing to be afraid of."

He waited.

"Please, would you consider extending my discipline by using a paddle, Alex?"

"And how many strokes do you feel that you deserve for your transgression?"

"Would ten be appropriate?"

Alex frowned; she had no idea what she was asking for. "No, ten would not be appropriate, Beth—not with a paddle. In conjunction with the spanking you've already received, I consider that four would be sufficient for you, as a novice. If you feel you should have ten strokes, then it's ten strokes with the flogger." There was more flexibility with a flogger—it could be manipulated in a pleasing variety of ways. Not only that—he happened to possess one that was ideal for a beginner. "So what's it to be? Tell me what your disobedience deserves."

Her stunned expression told him that she wasn't expecting that response.

"The flogger, Alex." Her voice was quiet but decisive.

"Face-down, on the bed."

While she obeyed his instructions, Alex found what he sought in the toy chest. He stood beside the bed, swinging the implement in a figure of eight to get the feel of it again, while he weighed up where he would place the ten strokes.

With a gentle touch, he traced a path down Beth's spine. The colour in her backside was fading now. In spite of his claim that this was a punishment, he had no intention of making it painful for her—it would be just enough to stimulate her and return that enticing glow to her skin.

Her body trembled in response to the first stroke, a common-enough reaction, but before he had the opportunity to deliver the next, Alex heard a soft moan of what could only be described as beatific contentment.

He followed the stroke with a tender caress, to take the sting away. This time he didn't have her count out the strokes—he was more concerned with watching her reaction.

And all he saw was a blissed-out sub. She took the flogger well, and when it was done he stretched out beside her and kissed her cheek. "Well done, sweetheart," he whispered, stroking her hair away from her damp face.

"Thank you, Alex."

Her somewhat whimsical smile reminded him of the previous evening, when she'd had a little too much to drink. A slightly tipsy Beth and one surfing the endorphin waves were both far removed from the woman who ran his office so efficiently. He let her rest for a few minutes, and then helped her to turn over.

From his box of toys, Alex produced brand-new ankle and wrist cuffs on chains, which he proceeded to attach to discreet eyebolts set into the wooden bed frame, before fastening the well-padded cuffs to Beth's limbs, paying great attention to her injured ankle. "Does this one feel all right, love? If it starts to feel uncomfortable, tell me—use your safe words, if necessary."

"It's fine at the moment, thank you."

Alex looked at her closely. There was something different in her voice, in her eyes too, and after a moment he recognised exactly what it was—trust. Until that moment he hadn't realised just how much that would mean to him.

He sat on the edge of the bed. While he had every intention of burying his dick in her pussy before long, he wanted to start familiarising her with his touch.

"Your body belongs to me now, Beth," he began, his voice low and sensuous. "Each of your toes, your feet," he laid his palm on her instep, "you have beautiful feet, and I especially like your ankles, since one of them brought us to this wonderful place."

He reached for that tantalising delta at the top of her thighs again, drawing the sweetest of moans from her soft lips. "You'll get used to my touching you here, Beth, because I intend to touch you a lot. I'll teach you to control your orgasms so that they serve my pleasure alone.

"And so there are no surprises in the future, I also intend to teach you to take my cock here." With his fingertip he carefully stroked over her anus. From her reaction Alex guessed that he might be venturing into unexplored territory. "Don't be afraid, Beth; I promise— I'll only ever give you pleasure."

His hand massaged her belly, savouring its soft curves. Any man who preferred skinny women with no breasts had to be out of his ever-loving mind, not when there were women like Beth around.

"Do you know how arousing it is to have a woman with a figure like yours? You have beautiful breasts." He flicked his finger across her nipple, felt his body quicken at the way hers jerked in response, and then he pinched the bud between his thumb and forefinger, rolling the little nub of flesh, and watching the areola pucker in response. Jewelled clamps, he thought. She would look exquisite. He spread his hand, cupping her breast and squeezing it so that she arched off the bed. With her head thrown back, the temporary collar grabbed his attention.

His mark of ownership—just the sight of it was enough to stir feelings that he'd long since thought dead and gone. Primitive needs boiled in his blood. In one smooth movement, he stood and shed his jeans. From the nightstand drawer, he withdrew a foil packet and tossed it onto the bed where it would be within easy reach, and when he freed her wrists from the cuffs he used his own hands to pin hers to the pillows over her head.

He looked into Beth's eyes, searching their emerald beauty for the secrets and shadows in her soul—he saw only honesty, gentleness and a little apprehension before she averted her gaze before her Dom.

He loved her. Dear God above, he loved her. Alex closed his eyes, letting the emotion wrap itself around him, flood every last part of his being. The fire of it consumed him. He'd wanted her forever, but loving her? When had *that* happened? When had she stopped simply being his assistant and become the woman he loved? It felt as if it had always been that way.

Alex went very still. It felt as if it had always been that way simply because it *had* always been that way, hidden away under the layers of fear and self-deception that had been his way of life for so long. He'd started to love Beth the day she started working for him. For an allegedly intelligent man, he'd been spectacularly dim-witted. And afraid.

He released his hold on her wrists.

"Keep your hands where they are, Beth." His voice was steadier than he could have hoped for, in the circumstances. "I'm going to touch you, every part of you. While I touch you, I want you to lie perfectly still. You will make no sound, unless you need to use a safe word. Nod if you understand. Good—now close your eyes."

He began with the touch of two fingers, laying the back of the index and middle fingers of his left hand on her chest, over her breastbone—she quivered for a heartbeat and then quietened again.

His fingers resumed their journey, moving through the scented valley between her breasts, rising and falling with each measured breath she took. He paused there, close to her heart, taking in her calmness and serenity—attributes that reached out to soothe the darkest, most tormented parts of his soul, the way they always had, right from the start, when she first became special to him.

I wish I'd realised how special.

She gasped when he captured her nipple in his mouth,

holding it lightly between his teeth while his tongue teased the sensitive flesh. That gasp set his achingly hard shaft twitching to bury itself in her sweetness. *Not yet*. He wanted to savour her body as he would a fine wine, before he took her, slowly and deliberately... before his cock slid deeply into her slick, tight pussy and made her fully his.

His hands curved possessively around her breasts, gently measuring and squeezing their softness. In spite of his command for her to lie still, she arched into his touch. To have her respond so willingly to his touch... it was more than he could have hoped for. Way more than he deserved.

"Beth." He growled her name. "What did I tell you? If you disobey me again, you won't be sharing this bed with me tonight." It was an empty threat he had absolutely no intention of carrying out.

Tremors rippled through her body as she strove to regain control, teeth biting down hard on her lower lip.

"Don't do that, sweetheart, you'll hurt yourself." He pressed his thumb to her mouth, framing her cheek with his palm and fingers.

A man less observant than Alex would have missed the way she pursed her lips to place a tiny whisper of a kiss to the pad of his thumb. If he hadn't already been in love with her, he would have fallen for her in that moment. The emotion sang through his veins.

His tactile investigation of her body continued—her ribcage, her navel, her belly and hips, all soft skin and alluring curves. She was a delight to explore; each movement of his fingers elicited the tiniest shiver of reaction, over which she had no control. When he dipped his fingertip in her navel, her belly trembled.

"My sweet, sweet Beth," he began, his finger tracing a pattern over her abdomen. "What am I going to do with you? Let me think…"

His touch was sending her to heaven.

Beth's sense of self-consciousness had gone off the scale when Alex shackled her to the bed. She'd felt silly and vulnerable, and after the spanking, she could add confused to the list. Part of her mind had told her that she shouldn't like or want this, yet something stronger and more primal, something that dwelled deep inside her, had soared towards freedom the first time his hand dealt out the discipline she craved. It was that primitive hunger that had compelled her to ask for more. What she had received was more than she could have imagined.

It was easier with her eyes closed, and with Alex talking to her. She was able to give herself up to the sheer joy of knowing that she was pleasing him. His voice was hypnotic, leading her to a place she'd never been before, where all that existed was the sound of his words, the touch of his hand, and the way her body was responding to both.

When her Dom's attention returned to her pussy, Beth felt her legs go weak again. His hand was less gentle this time, more demanding; it was so hard not to writhe with the bliss he was bestowing upon her, but she couldn't move, she couldn't cry out, and she wasn't even aware of the tears that began to run down her cheeks.

And then his hand was gone, leaving her with emptiness and a raging hunger radiating from her core like a supernova.

"Open your eyes, Beth. Look at me."

The command was compelling. Even so, she was hesitant to look at Alex for fear of what she might see. What she did see was a man gazing down at her with desire of such intensity that it stopped her ability to breathe. His touch on her cheek was gentle as he wiped away her tears. "If you're ready to stop, use your safe word."

She shook her head. "No, Alex." Her eyes connected with his. "Green."

Was that relief she saw on his face? "Then it's time. I'm going to take you, Beth. You have you permission to speak—use it wisely—but you are not yet allowed to come. You may move your arms, but your legs remain bound. I want you open and available."

She watched him position himself between her legs, a dark, primitive force kneeling over her. This wasn't the civilised man who worked all the hours God sent—this was a raw male animal who wanted her as badly as she wanted him. She ached for him.

If he'd been handsome in formal attire at the restaurant last night, he was devastatingly masculine wearing nothing but a formidable erection. She devoured the sight of his broad shoulders; the sculpted, muscular chest above rock-hard abs; the carved obliques that begged to be caressed; the strong arms, powerful thighs—and the long, thick cock she desperately wanted inside her. She longed for him to fill her hard and fast.

Alex reached for the condom, ripped the pack open and rolled the sheath onto his rigid shaft. Then his hands were on her hips, sliding under her back to support her while he lifted her to straddle his hips. She held onto him as if he were the only fixed point in the universe. His arms tightened around her, and between them lay the solid length of his rock-hard cock. Beth wanted to rub herself against him like a cat in heat. Her hips pushed urgently against him and –

"Oh God!"

He pushed deep inside her, but it was the rhythmic, controlled strokes, the feel of his well-muscled body moving against her that was overwhelming her. *Fast* would have been good—*this* was a thousand times better, the slow perfection of him filling her in a way that made her completely his. Her clit, already supersensitive, was being brutally aroused by the closeness and the unrelenting stimulation, and as if that weren't enough, her breasts were pressed against his chest, her nipples stimulated to stiff points by the direct contact with his muscular flesh.

She tried to clasp her legs around him more tightly, but with the ankle restraints it was impossible—instead, she got an intense reminder of her status as this man's sub, a reminder that targeted the space inside her only he could fill.

A large masculine hand anchored itself in her hair,

pulling her head back and exposing her throat. His mouth was hot on her skin, she could feel his teeth grazing her flesh, then she was falling backwards, secure in his arms...

With her hands pinned to the pillow, Beth couldn't resist as he moved over her body. His hips continued to drive against her, hard and unrelenting. He was sheer animal power in human form, carefully controlled but with a hint of danger, as if any moment that control might disappear. *What if...*

She could take that wild ride with him, she knew she could. He was her Dom. He owned her. Everything she had to give was his.

If only this could last forever. He was the man she'd wanted all her life.

"Please, Alex," she gasped, "please let me come!"

"No!"

He released one of her hands so he could squeeze her breast as he picked up the pace, his rhythm faster now. Her pleading became sobs of tormented pleasure; she couldn't hold it in much longer.

"Come, Beth, come for me, now!"

She needed no more encouragement. A supernova burst in her mind and her body, her orgasm exploded on a panting cry of sexual ecstasy, the like of which she had never known until this day. Her climax felt like it would never end, wave after unrelenting wave crashing over her, robbing her of speech, thought, even her sense of self. And while she was in the throes of that ecstasy, Alex went deeper, harder, driving into her until he came too.

She whimpered when he rolled off her, only distantly aware of him moving to release her bonds before he gathered her to him, holding her while she came down from the heights. His low voice comforted her, muttered words she couldn't comprehend, such was the tumult inside her, until she reached the point where she could whisper her thanks against his sweating chest.

Alex wrapped his arms around his sub, pulling her tightly into the protection of his body. He knew he had to be her anchor while she came down from the heights they'd just shared, but inside he was shaken to the core by the strength and depth of the emotion that had swept through him while making love to the woman he held so tenderly. It was so long since he'd felt anything like this… no, he'd *never* felt anything like this. This was unique.

She was unique. And he adored her.

If he hadn't known better, he'd have thought Beth was showing signs of having flown in to subspace—her eyes were glazed and unfocused, and he felt the first hint of a shiver. He wouldn't normally have expected that to happen in such a relatively mild scene; however, it was her first scene, and not only that, she'd not had sex for a while, so maybe it wasn't all that surprising that she'd been affected so deeply.

He took a moment to dispose of the condom, and then drew the sheets over Beth, leaving her with an instruction not to move—not that she looked capable of going far.

Without bothering to pull on any clothes, he went out to the kitchen to pour a glass of orange juice, to which he added a splash of cognac. He also grabbed a bar of chocolate—Beth's favourite, if the frequency of the appearance of it on her desk was anything to judge by.

When he returned to the bedroom, she'd moved onto her side and was curled up in an almost foetal position. He deposited the juice and chocolate on the nightstand by the bed. At the moment, Beth needed warmth and comfort more than anything else. He was more than happy to provide that. With a curious lightness in his heart, he slipped under the covers and moved closer to her.

"Come here, beautiful," he encouraged, his tone soothing and gentle. "You've been a very good girl, and now it's time for me to take care of you."

She turned back towards him and snuggled closer—a good sign, he thought, she was responding to his voice and his commands, though the look in her eyes was still distant. He wrapped his arms around her again—Christ, she was cold.

Although she was the main focus of his attention as he went about warming her up, there was a part of Alex's mind that was replaying the session and evaluating how successful it had been. He was also evaluating his feelings.

For a first session with a new sub, it had gone very well. Best to keep it fairly simple and not too demanding, and she'd responded well to a little discipline, light bondage and verbal instruction.

For a first session with the woman he loved, it granted him a glimmer of hope that maybe he *could* give her what she needed, because hell, she was everything he wanted and needed out of life.

She moved slightly in his arms. When he looked down at her in response, she was looking at him with questions in her eyes.

"Everything's okay, love," he said quietly. "How do you feel?"

She shivered again. "Cold. Should I feel cold? It's been so long…"

Since she'd had sex. Alex didn't want to think of all the times he might have had her with him, just like this, if he hadn't been so hung up on letting the past rule his life. Doubtless there would be fallout he'd have to deal with, but not now. Now he had a sweet sub to take care of.

"I'll keep you warm," he promised her. "You'll never be cold again. Are you ready to sit up? I have something that might help."

Still holding her close, he held the glass of juice to her lips, letting her take a couple of sips. He tried not to laugh at the face she made at the first one—her expression could have curdled milk. It conveyed precisely what she thought of the taste.

"Cognac." He turned the burgeoning laughter into a solicitous smile. "Hey, it's supposed to make you feel better."

From the doubtful look she gave him, Alex figured she was starting to regain her equilibrium. "Maybe the chocolate will go down better."

He broke off a couple of generously sized pieces, feeding them to her as he had fed her the cheese and biscuits a couple of nights earlier. Alex was a man who prided himself on not much being able to trip him up, but what Beth did next completely stunned him—when she finished the chocolate, she took hold of his hand and proceeded to lick the melted smears from his fingers.

Although the display of natural submissiveness stunned him, Alex was more concerned about how she'd react to what had happened once she recovered fully. It was quite possible that embarrassment, even shame would kick in, and he wanted to be on hand if and when that happened. Taking her out for dinner again, as he'd planned, no longer appealed—all of a sudden, pizza, beer and a bad movie, with Beth curled up on the sofa beside him, seemed like a far better idea.

"Alex... I need to go to the bathroom."

"No problem." He kissed the top of her head. "I'll help you."

"No!" Her face flamed. "I mean, thank you, but I need to—"

"You need me to make sure you're all right, Beth," he overruled her. "It's my job, as your Dom, to take care of you, and I take it very seriously."

He carried her into the bathroom, letting her attend to her needs while he ran the shower to the right temperature. When she was ready, he removed the velvet ribbon, with a promise that it would be replaced when they were done, and then followed her into the spacious enclosure.

"Alex?"

He picked up a bottle of shampoo and poured some into his palm, then made a circular motion with his index finger to indicate that she should turn away from him. He lathered up the shampoo, and then began to massage it into her hair, finding great pleasure in carrying out the simple task for the woman who meant so much to him.

And now would seem an opportune moment to go back to basics. "Beth, as my sub, what is your only purpose?"

"To please you," she replied.

"Good girl. And it pleases me to bathe you and wash your hair just as much as it pleases me to fuck you and spank you."

The juxtaposition of his matter-of-fact tone and the raw language he used clearly amused Beth, judging by her reaction. Her quiet chuckle brought a smile to his face as he rinsed away the shampoo. Using his fingers to comb conditioner through her hair, Alex decided that he liked making her smile and laugh. Her mere presence lifted his soul from the darkness that still threatened to overwhelm it more frequently than he cared to contemplate.

And he liked washing her body with the fragrant, creamy shower gel too. He could easily spend a lifetime getting to know every part of her intimately—every curve and hollow, and every reaction to his touch. Was she ticklish? Maybe now wasn't quite the best time to find out.

He was about to start showering himself when her

hands stilled the movement of his. "May I?"

The sensation of her touch on his body was sheer torture. She washed his back first, her soapy hands never faltering as she gently cleansed the scarred skin, left to right, shoulders to waist. He sensed her drop to one knee, and she was carrying on down, over his buttocks and then down each leg. When she came around to the front of him, her gaze dropped to the erection jutting from his groin.

"Don't look so surprised, Beth. That's the effect you have on me."

She looked up at him. For a heart-stopping moment, he thought she might shrink away, but then a slow smile lit her flushed face. "I think I can do something to help you with this, Alex. If I may?"

Oh shit. If he gave in to whatever was going on in her devious mind…

What he did or didn't want went by the board. He could only watch as she moved closer, close enough to take his nipple between her soft lips and begin to suckle, sending a bolt of sensual lightning straight to his cock.

"Beth."

Her name was a growled warning. If she carried on like that, he'd have to take her again—and he hadn't intended to do that quite so soon, no matter what opinion his dick might have on the subject.

"Please, Alex." She looked up at his face, her eyes full of what he could only describe as adoration. For him? "Let me give you this."

Alex hesitated for a moment, and then nodded. He didn't deserve this, but that didn't stop him wanting it… wanting her.

His sub had a wicked mouth. He felt her teeth grazing across his nipple before her tongue started working its magic again. He leaned back, the coolness of the tiles nowhere near enough to calm his growing arousal—especially when Beth's mouth transferred to his other nipple, while her fingers began to play with the first.

And when her mouth began to travel down his torso, it only grew worse. He watched her move lower and lower, until she was kneeling before him. It didn't take a genius to work out what she had in mind. He braced himself for the onslaught.

Her tongue stroked his heated flesh, his inner thighs, his groin, until she reached his balls, where she promptly drove him out of his mind with arousal and a raging need. When she licked up the underside of his cock, he could do nothing to prevent the low, guttural groan that rumbled past his lips. When her tongue traced the prominent veins along its pulsating length, he moaned again. When he felt the gentle suction she applied to the head, he thought his skull was going to explode. With his balls cradled tenderly in her palm, Beth used her mouth and free hand to send him to sweet oblivion.

His hands clenched into fists for a few seconds, until he could force his fingers to uncurl enough for him to lay his palms flat against the tiles. He needed the chill to turn down his desire to fuck her wonderful mouth. The alternating kisses and licks were like nothing he'd felt before, and the most distant part of his brain, the microscopic part that was still able to put together a coherent thought, wondered how Beth, who behaved with such decorum in the office, could be so skilled in such a carnal art. Was it natural talent, or had some lucky bastard had the pleasure of teaching her how to suck a cock?

Alex pressed his back harder to the cold wall, using it to bring himself back from the brink of orgasm—he wasn't ready to come yet, he had to know...

"Who taught you, Beth?" he managed to get out, looking down at her, dreading the answer but needing it more. The thought of her in this position in front of another man was killing him.

She looked down, a slight flush rising to her cheeks. "I'm sorry, Alex. I wanted it to be good for you."

Without her mouth wrapped around his cock, he was a little more capable of articulating what was on his mind. "Did I say it wasn't? Answer my question."

"No one. I've never... I never wanted to do it for anyone before. I'm sorry."

She was sorry. *Sorry?* "For what? For having a beautiful mouth and knowing how to use it to please me? Never be sorry about that, sweetheart."

She looked up at him, her eyes glowing with emerald fire. "Please... may I continue?"

He nodded. "But I'll tell you when I'm about to come—then it's your choice."

He could give her that, at least. And her choice, when

the time came, was to give him a gift that almost brought him to his knees in front of her. He gave her the warning he'd promised, expecting her to back away, but no, she remained in position, taking him deep into her mouth as he climaxed and licking him clean when he was spent.

Afterwards he allowed her to finish the task of washing him, so that they could get on with the serious business of relaxing for the rest of the evening.

Relaxing—now that was a laugh, Alex thought some time later as he lay in bed. For the last few minutes the ceiling had held a curious fascination for him. The half-finished pizza was abandoned on the coffee table, along with his beer and Beth's wine. Neither of them knew how the film ended, and he suspected that Beth cared as little as he did.

She was already asleep at his side, naked apart from the ribbon. His stomach clenched at the memories she'd given him, of her kneeling in front of him while her mouth gave him pleasures that had blown him apart, and then kneeling again, holding out the makeshift collar for him to replace after the shower. He had done so with warmth, gentleness and care, and a silent prayer of gratitude.

And above all, so much love that he thought his heart might break from it.

But now it was time for sleep. Alex began his usual ritual of controlling his respiration, counting each breath as he tried to get into the right frame of mind, hoping, as he did each night, that the terrors would stay away. Tonight of all nights, he needed them to stay away. He couldn't bear to think of the consequences if Beth were to discover the terrible secrets from his past and the power they still held over him...

CHAPTER NINE

On Monday morning Beth sat at her desk, feeling like a totally different woman from the one who'd left the office on Friday night. And her concentration was shot to pieces. The last time she'd occupied this space, she'd been nursing a turned ankle and reporting the theft of her bag. Now she was here with Alex's temporary collar around her neck and a whole new perspective on their relationship.

A week might be a long time in politics, but a weekend in the world of Domination and submission could beat it hands down. As yet, Beth wasn't sure whether the beating would be done with a flogger, a crop or a paddle…

She'd arrived at the office fifteen minutes earlier, accompanied by the man who was no longer just her employer. It was only quarter past eight now, but it had been a very strange morning, right from the moment she had dared to wake her sleeping companion with a kiss. For a brief instant an odd expression had passed over his face; then it was gone and he was leaping out of bed and dragging her off to the bathroom with him. Beth could swear she'd spent more of the weekend in that bathroom than out of it.

Of course, on the flip side of all that prune-like skin was the sinful deliciousness that was communal bathing.

A finger ran across the velvet ribbon—yep, it was still there. Not that she needed it to remind her of her new circumstances—there was a certain lack of underwear that performed that function quite nicely, thank you very much. Especially when she got up to finish making Alex's coffee and take it into his office.

He was on the phone to Japan again; while Beth was fluent in French and could get by in a couple of other European languages, her employer's command of a wide variety of foreign tongues—some of them quite exotic— was seriously impressive. She was about to leave when he signalled her to stay.

"Thank God that's all sorted out now," he said with a long sigh when he put the phone down. "Come here." She went around the desk, only to be pulled unceremoniously onto his lap for a deep, lingering kiss. She remained silent while he simply looked at her and looped a stray strand of hair around her ear. Under his gaze, she felt a warm contentment flow through her soul.

"Beth, you have no idea how often I've wanted to do that since you started working for me. I think I'll start every working day just like this."

She wasn't about to argue with that.

"I should have mentioned this over breakfast—Cam's coming in just before nine to give me the latest on the security problem we've been having. I just want you to be prepared for when he notices this." His touch was gentle on her throat. "You know you don't have to wear it in the office?"

"I know—I want to."

The words left her lips before she realised they were spoken, and in the space of a heartbeat, she knew they were true. She felt protected by Alex... as well as more informed. Over the weekend, he hadn't been reticent in sharing information she'd need to know—she could now see the Dom in his friend too, and she had no doubt that Cam would respect that protection.

"Good morning, Beth," the man in question greeted her when he breezed into her office a short time later. To his credit, Cam's initial reaction was barely perceptible— an uninformed observer certainly wouldn't have noticed it, but as he approached her she could see that his gaze was drawn, like a compass needle pointing north, to the ribbon.

When he reached for her hand and kissed the back of it, her eyes automatically dropped. And when he spoke again, his tone was completely different—warmer and more intimate, with the hint of a shared secret. "So he finally did it. Welcome to the community."

"If you say anything that starts with 'I', ends with 'so' and has 'told you' in the middle, Fraser, I'm dragging you down to the car park and turning you into chopped bloody liver." Alex glared at his old friend to reinforce the threat, and was rewarded with a who-gives-a-shit grin.

"Leaving aside the minor point that it will be a cold day in hell before you get the better of me in a hand-to-hand combat situation, all I can say is it's about bloody time, Alex. But what's with the ribbon? Don't you think she deserves something better?"

"Of course she bloody does, and we're taking the afternoon off to do something about it."

"Where are you taking her?"

"Giorgio's. I want to get her fitted for something special for daywear, and a suitable play collar. I wasn't planning on doing it so soon, but, hell, I just want her collared so I can start to build her confidence."

Cam nodded. "Have you thought about taking her to the club, or is it too early for that?"

"Too early—way too early. She needs time to come to terms with everything before I even tell her about the place, never mind take her there. She needs to trust me fully to take care of her."

"Of course." The other man's tone was sober. "So what's eating you?"

Alex watched him sit down before speaking. "She woke me up with a kiss this morning."

Cam let out a low whistle. "Sweet. And your problem is?" Then the light dawned. "You didn't have the usual problem?"

"No. I can't remember falling asleep, nor can I remember waking up, not until this morning."

Cam had known about Alex's nocturnal demons for a long time—they were a major factor in his decision to walk away from the private security firm they'd founded together after leaving the military. Apart from the medics, Cam was the only one who knew about the problems Alex had—and the only one who knew the cause of them. Consequently, he was the only one with whom Alex could or would discuss the matter.

As much as alpha males could ever be said to discuss anything remotely personal.

"Then perhaps Beth's the answer, Alex."

A troubled look passed over Alex's features. "She's the answer to a lot of things, Cam. There was a time when I didn't want to do anything to scare away the best assistant I've ever had. Now, I don't want to scare away the woman I—"

He broke off abruptly. The first person to hear what he was about to say shouldn't be the man opposite him. Besides, he wasn't sure he was ready to hear himself say the words aloud—not yet, anyway.

"Cam, what's the latest with the investigation? Are we talking industrial espionage?"

"Nice segue," the blond man observed with a knowing nod and a raised eyebrow. Then he became serious. *Very* serious. "I can't prove anything yet, Alex, but my gut's telling me that this isn't just common or garden industrial espionage—there's a lot more to it than that. I may be wrong, but I have a hunch it's personal. Maybe connected to the old days. Especially after what you felt yesterday."

"You've no evidence yet?"

"Nothing we can use. We're working on it, though. Got a couple of leads to chase up—they got sloppy with some of the equipment they installed. If it had been me, I'd have removed the manufacturer's labels and the serial numbers. Unless…" He paused, his mouth pressed into a thin line.

"Unless what?"

"Unless they were left there as bait to lure us into some sort of trap." Cam shook his head. "Shit, I've been watching too many spy movies. The investigation is still ongoing, but we're contacting the manufacturer, which should lead us to the supplier and eventually to the bastards responsible for installing it."

"What if the supplier won't give up the information? Client confidentiality and all that?"

"You remember those two guys I worked with a couple of years ago? The cyber experts, used to work for MI5 until they decided their talents could be better utilised in the private sector?"

"Lee Carmichael and Tristan Rhodes?" Alex remembered them well. Although he'd never had occasion to work alongside the two men—partners in more than just the business sense—he knew them from Aegis and had seen a couple of the smoking-hot demonstrations they'd given. Anyone looking at Rhodes would without question tag him as a Dom… until they saw him on his knees for Carmichael.

"Yeah. I bumped into them at the club a couple of days ago. I happened to mention our current problem, and they offered their expertise. They can get into almost any computer system in the world, so when I say we're contacting the manufacturer, it might be… indirectly?" Cam at least had the grace to look a little shame-faced. "Same with the supplier."

"I did not need to hear that, Fraser." For a moment Alex lapsed into officer mode. He knew all about the slightly and not-so-slightly questionable methods that could be employed when it came to investigating a situation such as this.

"Yeah, well, I have a gut feeling that whoever it is, the end customer may be just a third party working on behalf of the real enemy."

"If that's the case, then until we find out who that is, we have no way of knowing what this is about."

"My best guess is still revenge," Cam offered. "And if I'm right, both you and Beth could be in real danger."

"Revenge for what, though? If that *is* what this is about…"

"If it is, then it's someone who's been bearing a grudge for a long time. You've been out of the security game for years, and frankly, I don't think anyone we came across in the beginning is a likely candidate—we weren't involved in anything that could possibly warrant it."

Cam paused, apparently deep in thought. "No, I think this relates to something that happened while we were in the Regiment. I'll look into it from that angle, but whoever it is, if they've justified it to themselves, that's all they need. We've got their equipment, so they'll know we're onto them—"

"So it's possible they'll make their move sooner rather than later." Alex's tone was grim. "I can't let anything happen to Beth. I'll take her to Winterleigh—I can protect her better there."

Cam sighed heavily. "Alex, I know you don't want to hear this, and God knows I don't want to say it, but you know as well as I do that she'd be safer if you put some distance between the two of you, just until this is resolved."

Alex's refusal was immediate. "I can't. I have to see her, see that she's there and she's all right."

"It's okay. I'd feel the same. Just watch your back, all right? As soon as I get something we can act on, I'll be in touch."

The two men talked a while longer. Alex watched his friend leave, and then a cold, brooding darkness descended over him. It looked like his initial instincts probably weren't wrong. A threat from the old days? Even though Cam's opinion was that it had nothing to do with their work in the private sector, thinking about the past transported Alex back to that time and the darkest period of his life, to the heat, the dust, the danger, the adrenaline rush… and the pain. He looked at his hands, flexing his fingers to banish the image of broken bones and bloody flesh, starvation and raging thirst, the gut-wrenching degradation…

Damn it, he could even feel that prickling sensation moving down his spine, the one that had always warned him of an impending threat. His hand flexed again, as if getting comfortable around the grip of the semi-automatic pistol that had been his constant companion. It had always been enough, until he'd been thrown into that living hell…

Alex forced his mind back to the present. If it was personal, he had to protect Beth. He didn't care about himself, but some of the enemies he'd gone up against back then would think nothing of going through her to get to him, and he would not allow her safety to be compromised.

Cam was right, of course; the sensible thing would be to distance himself from her, but the chances of that were slim to none, and the last he heard, Slim left town. He'd just accelerate his plan to have her move in with him. She'd balk at the suggestion, but hell, she was his woman and his sub, and she'd damn well do as she was told. Even if she did bust his butt for it afterwards.

"Alex?"

Beth's sweet voice broke into his thoughts. His eyes swept over her as she stood in the doorway. So concerned… for him. He glanced at his watch—not quite ten-thirty. Way too early to call it a day, but shit, he was the boss, and truth be told, he'd made enough money out of this business over the years not just to take an extended leave of absence now but to walk away from it completely and not look back.

"Beth, I want you to cancel every appointment for the rest of the week. We've finished for the day, we have things to do, and then we need to talk, well away from here."

Just when she thought things were about to settle down.

As soon as she'd seen the expression on Alex's face, Beth had known that something major was going on, and clearly it was connected with the meeting. That look had made her feel very uncomfortable.

She put the phone down after cancelling the last of the week's appointments. Life was getting crazy all of a sudden and the craziness was showing no signs of going away. She switched off her computer, gathered her belongings together, and was putting her coat on when Alex emerged from his office.

"Ready? Good. Make sure you've got everything, because you won't be coming back here for a few days."

"I won't? Alex—"

"No questions, Beth." He cut across her, every inch the Dom and former officer. "The office can run fine without our being here for the next few days. You and I are going on a little shopping expedition, and then we're going to pick up what we need from your place and mine. When we've done that, we're moving to Winterleigh for a while."

"Whoa! Stop right there!" Beth dug her heels in— literally. Alex had hold of her hand and was almost dragging her out of the office. "I'm not—what are you talking about? I'm not moving anywhere with you! Are you crazy? It's too soon! We need to talk about this!" She tried to disengage her hand from his, but he wasn't having any of it. The look he turned on her froze her blood.

"Not now, Beth! You are coming with me and that's final—you *will* obey me!"

He'd said he was a sexual Dominant, not lifestyle. He could order her around all he wanted in the bedroom—heck, he could even dish out his sexy commands *outside* the bedroom and she'd take it, but this outrageous boorishness was taking things way too far. The safe word that would end it all hovered on her lips, and from the sudden look of—was that fear?—in his eyes, Alex knew it.

"Please, Beth." His voice was less harsh now. "Trust me. I know it's a lot to ask, but please… trust me. I'll explain later, I promise, but for now we have to move quickly. I have to keep you safe."

Something told Beth that whatever he was talking about, it had nothing to do with muggers and sprained ankles. Something much bigger was going on here. Questions tumbled through her mind as she accompanied Alex to the basement car park. Once they were in the Aston Martin and were heading out onto the street, she asked him about their destination.

"We're going to see a friend of mine—Giorgio. He's the best in the business."

"What business?" Beth could have sworn she hadn't heard Alex mention the name before.

They'd stopped at a set of traffic lights. Taking advantage of the standstill, Alex turned to face her. "Beth, from here on in, I really need you to trust me. Can you do that? Trust me implicitly?"

She wanted to argue but the intensity in his expression killed her impulse to ask the questions before she could give voice to them. Whatever was going on, he was seriously worried. "Alex—"

"I promise I'll tell you as much as I can—as much as I know—when we get home, to Winterleigh."

Beth reined in her desire to demand a full explanation there and then. Alex had always been a man of his word, and he wasn't about to change that now. She still needed to have some idea of what was going on, though. "Is it really that bad?"

"It could be."

She could see the war going on in his mind. Something was really bothering him. "And?" she prompted gently.

"And the safest thing for you would be to take a break and go as far away from here—from me—as you can."

"*No!*"

She would never leave him, especially if they were in the kind of danger that led him to believe she would be safer away from him. And at that single word, a little of the tension that had ridden him since they'd left the office ebbed away.

He was the man she loved—that was all that mattered. The somersaulting gymnast in her stomach disappeared, replaced by a sense of calm that was strangely at odds with… whatever this situation was.

A hand lifted to touch her cheek. He looked like he was about to say something but then the lights changed and the car moved off. With Alex's attention back on the road, Beth was left to her own thoughts and imagination. This all had to be related to the ongoing security issue, yet that hardly seemed possible. Alex was acting as if their lives were in danger, but how that connected with industrial espionage, Beth had no idea. As for revenge—the very idea was ludicrous. All she could do was be there for him—no matter what he thought the wisest course of action might be.

She glanced over at Alex, noting the firm set of his jaw and the hand resting on his thigh, now curled into a fist. She felt compelled to reassure him. The fist slowly uncurled beneath her touch and his thumb reached out to trap her fingers against his. He lifted her hand to his lips.

Ten minutes later the car pulled up outside a small, fairly nondescript office building—evidently, this was their destination, as Alex came around to open the car door and offer her his hand.

"We're here—this is Giorgio's place. He's well-known and highly respected in the community."

Beth swallowed hard. "Is he a Dom?"

"He is, but all you need to do is wait until he speaks to you, and address him as 'Sir' when he does speak to you. You'll be fine."

Alex took her hand and led her through the intercom-controlled security door, with its surveillance camera.

It was an adult store. Beth had been a reluctant visitor to such establishments once or twice in the past, accompanying one of her boyfriends who had been marginally more adventurous than the rest—ever since then, she'd had an aversion to pink fluffy handcuffs. Why it had been necessary to actually go to a place like that when there was the internet, she'd never known, but somehow now, with Alex, she didn't mind at all.

This place, however, was in a different league—the preponderance of black leather and chrome chain was overpowering. The scent of the former should have reminded her of safe things, like the first quality bag she'd ever bought, and the saddler's shop she'd walked past on her way to school. Instead she was thinking of the kind of place where these items, the harnesses, the gags, the cuffs, all the other D/s paraphernalia, would be worn and used. She'd read and written about establishments like that, but never experienced them first-hand. Was Alex a member of such a club? She caught her breath at the thought of him among the symbols of Domination and submission, dressed like the Doms in those books. Beth shoved the mental image aside, before it made her even wetter than she already was.

She was still trying to take it all in when a man appeared at the doorway to the back of the shop. He was a few inches shorter than Alex, but almost as physically imposing as him. Dressed entirely in black and with his long, silver-streaked, black hair drawn back in a sleek ponytail, he could have been any age from forty to fifty-five.

"Alex, good to see you again. I haven't seen you at the club in a while. How are you doing?"

The two men shook hands—they were obviously friends.

"I'm good, thanks, Giorgio. Work's been keeping me busy and away from the club more often than I'd like. How are you?" Alex waited for the other man to reply, then put his arm around Beth. "This is my new sub, and I want something special for her."

"Day and play? No problem. I have a couple of new day collars that I think you'll like the look of."

Alex glanced at the velvet ribbon. It looked good on her, but circumstances dictated that it was time to do things properly.

"Thanks, Giorgio. And for play, I want the best you've got."

The other man nodded, looking Beth up and down. "The private room's ready for you. May I use her name? I'll need to touch her as well—is that all right with you?"

It was a matter of courtesy, one Dom to another—after all, in the eyes of the community, subs were property, and one Dom would no more come between another and his sub than he would touch anything else the other owned.

"Giorgio, I'd like you to meet Beth. She's new to the scene, but she's a fast learner—and she's very special to me."

"I'm very pleased to meet you, Beth."

Beth kept her eyes lowered, and her hands clasped in front of her. "Thank you, Sir—I'm pleased to meet you too."

"Come with me, Beth. I have something for you that I think your Master will like."

Alex watched the two of them leave. Beth was about to be fitted with one of Giorgio's special play collars—an easy-to-wear combination of leather and soft suede that subs could wear for hours without discomfort. It was all too easy to imagine her kneeling before him and wearing nothing but the collar and heels… cuffs too, at her wrists and ankles, ready to be restrained for his pleasure. Desire coursed like molten lava through his veins.

He made his way to the private room, supremely conscious of his arousal, growing in anticipation of what was to come. Once Beth was fitted with her collar, she would be brought to the private room by Giorgio, who would then leave them while Beth modelled the collar for him. Having her then strip for him was an indulgence they really didn't have time for, but he longed to see Beth in all her naked glory, wearing just the collar, and he wasn't prepared to wait.

Making a mental note to pick up those matching ankle and wrist cuffs that had also made it into his fantasy, Alex made himself comfortable on the sofa. After a few minutes Giorgio came in and behind him, Beth. In her left hand she was clutching the velvet ribbon, but around her beautiful neck there was the collar—and God, it looked even better than he'd imagined.

"Thank you, Giorgio. We won't be long, but then we do need to look at those day collars."

"No problem, everything's ready."

Once the other man had left, Alex turned his attention to Beth. She was standing quietly, waiting to take her cue from him.

"Take your clothes off, Beth. I want to see you."

He was waiting for a protest, but it never came. Instead, lips pressed together to calm her nerves, she began to remove her clothing, and what she did next proved that she was everything he thought she was. She didn't just strip for him; when she'd done that, she assumed her first position in front of him. Hell, if only they'd been at home...

He had to do it, Alex realised. Before he dragged her fully into this pile of shit, he had to give her one last chance to walk away, but not just from the security issue. He also had to be sure that she wanted to be in this relationship, before it killed him to let her go. "Beth, I have to ask you this one last time—are you sure you want to stay with me? You'll be safer if you go away somewhere."

"I'm staying with you, Alex. I'm safe with you."

"And this relationship... it's what you want? If not, just say the word and I swear I'll never lay a finger on you again. I'll take you back to your apartment, on one condition—that you go away until this is over. I need to know you're safe until this is resolved. If you have any doubts, love, follow your instincts."

Hesitantly, she looked up at him, moved into an upright kneeling position, and took one of his hands in both of hers. He felt the brush of her lips on his palm, and then her eyes met his. "I'm staying, Alex. I want this. And I want to be with you, no matter what happens. I can't leave you. Now please... may I kiss you?"

He nodded, and their lips met in a gentle coming together that promised so much, yet also filled Alex with so much fear for what he might still lose.

"I'll never leave you," she whispered against his mouth. "If you want me to go, you'll have to tell me to go. Tell me that you don't want me—then I'll leave."

He couldn't tell her that—he could never tell her that. She was his now, his to cherish and his to protect.

With his life.

"We'll talk more about it later. For now, I'm going to take this collar off, and we'll go and choose your day collar—something you can wear every day without advertising your status to all and sundry. Get dressed now. And by the way—you look incredible."

The buckle of the collar was at her nape. While carefully unfastening it, Alex inhaled the perfume of her hair and her body, this woman he'd hungered after for so long. He let his forehead rest against hers for a moment, just a moment, so that a little of the ache could leave his soul.

As well as working in leather and suede, Giorgio was a master jeweller, a skill that enabled him to create magic from precious metals and gemstones. The pieces looked completely innocent to the vanilla world but conveyed a special message to those in the lifestyle.

Alex knew what he wanted for Beth as soon as he saw it. The ornate, heavy, gold chain, secured with a small working padlock, was perfect. A touch that Alex particularly liked was the discreet charm in the form of a tag that would soon have his initials engraved upon it. The advantage of the piece was that for ordinary day wear, it could be worn with the padlock and tag at the nape of her neck. If he wanted to make his ownership of her known, then he would direct her to wear it with the padlock resting over her heart.

"It's stunning, Giorgio," Alex approved, handing over his credit card. "And before I forget, I need the ankle and wrist cuffs to match the play collar."

"Already in the box, my friend. May I congratulate you on your choice of daywear for your sub? It suits her perfectly."

Alex had left the collar around Beth's neck. He turned to look at her, his eyes devouring her face and body. "It's as flawless as she is, Giorgio."

After stopping at Beth's place to pick up her belongings, they returned to Alex's apartment for a few more essentials before setting off for their real destination, well away from the capital.

The further they drove away from London, the more Beth became aware of a change in the man beside her. The urbane, sophisticated businessman she knew was vanishing more with each mile, and in his stead she saw appear the cool, focused, professional soldier he had once been. The authority he projected so effortlessly became an air of command and control. Less the boss, more the Dom. So much more the Dom.

One thing was for sure, though—he was also a man with a lot on his mind, and as such, Beth didn't feel inclined to press him about the mystery that was enveloping them—he had, after all, said that they would discuss things later. Of course, she wasn't entirely sure that *discuss* was the right word—he'd talk and she'd listen... and probably agree, unless he started going on about her leaving again. No way was *that* happening.

Beth fingered her new collar, conscious of the weight of it around her neck, and her mind drifted back to what had happened back at Giorgio's. The whole experience of being fitted for the play collar had seemed surreal, right from the instant that the other man had asked Alex for his permission to touch her and to use her name.

She still wasn't quite sure how she felt about that. No—she *did* know how she felt about it, Beth realised. Mainstream society might not find it acceptable, but the way Giorgio had spoken about her, the way he'd treated her, had all been an expression of respect not just for her relationship with Alex, but for her as a sub as well, even though she was so new to the world he and Alex inhabited.

So, what exactly was she getting herself into by staying with Alex? Whatever it was—she loved him. Was it time to let go of her independence and dismantle the wall that had protected the most vulnerable part of her for so long? Could she be brave enough to do that with Alex? She tried to imagine another man in his place—she gave this mythical man the face of others she knew among her colleagues and friends and drew a complete blank. Alex was the only man for her.

"Beth, tell me what you're thinking."

It would be easy to say "nothing", but she had no intention of knowingly deceiving Alex. "I started off just thinking about what happened at Giorgio's. It was… strange."

"Did it make you feel uncomfortable?"

"Not exactly. There was a surreal quality to it. I know this will sound weird, but I felt as if I belonged to you, and Giorgio knew and respected that, but he also treated me as if… as if I were on some sort of pedestal. Does that make *any* kind of sense?" She had to ask him, because it made not one iota of sense to her.

He gave a short, soft laugh. "It makes perfect sense, sweetheart. Any true Dom knows how special a submissive, any submissive, is. What else? There's more to what's bugging you than that."

Was she really so transparent? Or was it just that he was more tuned in to her than she could ever have suspected? "I'm sorry I was such a pain over leaving the office."

"You're not a pain, love. I'll tell you everything. Give me your hand."

He pressed her palm down on his thigh. "Why are you

trembling, Beth? Is there something else you're not telling me?"

In that instant, Beth's mind cleared. Those few words took the last bricks out of the walls that had defended her heart for so long. She so wanted to say it, to admit to how she felt. The words were there, battling to pass over the threshold of her lips, but was this the right place, the right time, in a car on the motorway? *If not here, where? If not now, when?*

She looked out of the car window, aware of the inadequacy of the words when measured against the feelings. Her throat felt so dry—funny what nerves could do.

"Alex—I love you."

CHAPTER TEN

God, that sounds so pathetic.

As soon as she said the words, Beth wished she'd left them unsaid. Not that they weren't true—she'd just sounded so pitiful. Even worse, tears of embarrassment made her eyes smart. All she'd probably done was make a bad situation worse.

"Beth." His voice made a verbal caress of her name. "We'll be at Winterleigh in about twenty minutes. When we get there, I'll let you get settled in the family room while I bring everything in from the car, and then we'll talk. There are things you need to know, but this isn't the best place to tell you."

Twenty miserable minutes had never passed so slowly. Beth watched the motorway turn into major roads and major roads turn into winding country lanes clothed in the russet shades of autumn. Then, in what appeared to be the middle of nowhere, Alex slowed the car and they were turning off the lane and into a drive guarded by huge electronic gates that swung open as they approached.

They passed between the towering structures and then carried on around a bend to the left, and after another curve back to the right, there before her was the most beautiful house Beth had ever seen. This was Winterleigh?

The car crunched over the honey-coloured gravel, following the sweep of the drive to draw to a halt at the front door. Alex came around to help Beth out. For a moment she simply stood there, looking up at the cream-coloured walls and leaded windows. She'd had no idea what to expect, but it wasn't anything like this.

"You have a beautiful home, Alex."

He glanced over his shoulder. "Maybe, but it's always been missing something vital," he said, with a hint of longing in his voice, before turning back to her. "Until now, that is."

He led her inside. The interior was every bit as impressive as the exterior. It was also light and modern, with a definite minimalist theme to the neutral décor. The family room was dove grey and white, with a luxurious carpet in pale oatmeal, and it was to that room that Alex escorted her, with an order to make herself at home. He would be back in a few minutes, and then they'd talk.

Beth was looking at the contents of the bookcases when he came back, carrying two cups of coffee.

"I'd have made it something stronger, but even I draw the line at alcohol at this time of the afternoon," he stated, depositing the cups on the coffee table. "Come here, Beth." He held out his hand. "Sit with me."

Though she wanted to curl up at his side, Beth sat demurely a few inches away from him on the cream leather sofa, dreading what was going to happen next. This would be where he told her that he was very flattered, but unfortunately he didn't feel the same way about her. He liked her and wanted her, but he didn't love her. The story of her life, and it wasn't about to change now.

His arm went around her shoulders, pulling her against his body. "About what you said in the car, Beth—"

"It's all right." She pushed away from him, suddenly feeling stiff and awkward as she fought to find the words that wouldn't humiliate her any further. "It was a stupid thing to say—"

"It wasn't," he countered softly, pulling her back to him. "It was brave and wonderful." A finger under her chin tilted her head up for a kiss that consumed her from her head to her toes. "And I should have been the first to say it. I love you, sweetheart. I never realised it, but I have for a long time."

She looked at him in silence, searching for some sign that he was just humouring her, but there was none—he truly meant it. Beth let out the breath she didn't know she'd been holding and rested her head against his chest, one arm draped across his abdomen. Suddenly, everything else faded into the distance. Whatever the reason behind their flight from London, it would be all right now. They'd see it through together. Alex loved her. Everything would be all right, she knew it. It had to be.

"Now, about… this." He waved his hand around the room. "Being here. You were right, this is too soon. Not knowing how you feel, I figured we'd date a while, spend a few nights together, and one day you'd wake up and realise you'd moved in with me while you weren't looking. Then you'd smile, and I'd kiss you and tell you that I'm in love with you."

Her heart felt as if it were going to burst out of her chest. The words were beautiful, but it was the way they were reflected in his eyes. It damn near broke her heart. With great reluctance, she tore her gaze away from his eyes and looked at the mouth she was desperate to kiss.

"I am, you know," he continued. "And that's why I had to hurry this up. I have to protect you, Beth, and I can do it better here than I can in London. This doesn't have to be for the long term, just for now, until we get to the bottom of the current situation. You need to be in possession of all the facts before making a decision about the rest of your life."

The rest of your life. He meant it—he really meant it. And as she imagined what it might be like to live with Alex and bind her life to his, Beth knew she had all the facts she needed already. When the time was right, she'd tell him. She wanted him to be as sure about her answer as she was.

"Okay. So why do I need protecting? What's going on?"

"I promised you an explanation." He sipped his coffee.

"By the time I'm finished, we may both need something stronger than this."

Beth listened intently as the man she loved began to tell her of his past, the years he'd spent in the military, and the transfer to Special Forces, where he'd been the linguist on the team. Without going into too much detail, he told her about the missions he'd been sent on to some of the world's most hostile hot spots, where he'd acquired the scars that marked his body. She wept silent tears for what he'd gone through, for the friends and comrades he'd lost.

"Shh, Beth, don't cry, not for me. It's all in the past now," he comforted her. "Or at least it was. Cam thinks— and I have to agree with him—that the bugs and cameras were planted by, or on behalf of, someone we ran into back then, someone who may be looking for revenge."

Eyes wide with shock, she looked at Alex. Her mind was struggling to comprehend how anyone could possibly have cause to seek vengeance against the man she knew him to be. "Revenge? I don't understand. I know you mentioned it as a possibility, but you said it was more likely to be industrial espionage. Why? Why would any-one want to ruin Paduan Ventures?"

Alex shook his head. "Who knows? Beth, it wasn't a picnic out there, we had to do things—"

She reached up to kiss him. "You did what you had to do, Alex. You had to protect innocent lives—how many did you save?"

"If this is someone out for revenge, then perhaps not

the one or ones that mattered," he replied, his voice almost haunted. "I brought you here because Winterleigh has state-of-the-art security—Cam had it installed it last year—and out here, I have the means to protect you with reasonable force, if it becomes necessary. I can't do that in London."

Beth went very still. "Wait a minute—I think I'm missing something. Someone's using electronic surveillance equipment to spy on your business and ruin you financially, but you're acting as if... as if there's some sort of threat to our lives. Why would 'reasonable force' come into it? And what sort of 'reasonable force' are you talking about?"

Alex sighed. "Industrial espionage comes from the head—it's a purely business decision, prompted by material greed, and as such, the risks involved will be weighed up with cold logic. Revenge, on the other hand... that's emotional. It comes from the gut and the heart, and it has no built-in boundaries. The measures taken to satisfy a desire for revenge could ramp up to the point where lives can be at risk."

That made sense. "And what about 'reasonable force'?"

"The house has a gun room—all legal, don't worry. It's out in what used to be the stable block. I normally only use the shotguns on clay pigeons."

A chill descended over Beth as she realised the implication of what he was saying. The danger they were in wasn't some abstract concept—it was very real and Alex was talking about the possibility of using firearms in their defence. "Is there anything I can do to help?"

"I'm not teaching you to shoot, if that's what you're asking," Alex stated in a tone that brooked no argument. "If someone sees you with a weapon, it makes you a target—you can leave that to me. What I want you to do is get to know this house inside out, so you can get to a secure room I'm going to show you from anywhere in the house."

"A panic room, you mean?"

"Not in the sense you're thinking, Beth—not like the movies. It's just a secure room with an independent communications system, so that if we're attacked and they cut the obvious lines of communication, the system in that room will still function."

For a moment, Beth wondered when reality had morphed into the pages of a thriller, the only place where any of this would make sense. She had to ask. "Why do you even have a secure room? Do you have a crystal ball I don't know about?"

Alex gave a short bark of humourless laughter. "Cam's idea—God knows why he thought I might need the damn thing, but it turns out he was right."

Well, it was an answer—of sorts. "Suppose something does happen—do I just call the police? Should I be calling anyone else?"

"Good questions, Beth, and they deserve good answers. Until it's confirmed, there's still an outside chance that this could just be industrial espionage, in which case there'll be no danger to us here, but if this does prove to be connected with my past and something does happen, call the police and then call Cam—he'll know what to do."

"And when I've done that?"

"Stay put—Cam will come for you."

Why Cam? Why not you?

He took a deep breath and let it out slowly as he held her close. "My love, we have to face facts—if something does happen, it's entirely possible I may not be in a position to come for you. It's always wise to have a backup plan."

Beth closed her eyes; something awful was rushing in her ears. No, that wasn't going to happen, it was a nightmare that didn't bear thinking about. She wasn't going to lose him—not now, not ever.

"And in order for that plan to work, I need to show you the secure room and give you a tour of the house, but I think that can all wait till tomorrow. What you need most right now is something to take your mind off that crap."

Alex pulled out his keys, including the one for the padlock on Beth's day collar. "Turn around and lift your hair up for me."

That was her Dom speaking. With a small smile making a gentle curve of her mouth, she did as he asked. The chain dropped from around her neck; Beth missed its weight immediately. She watched Alex lay it carefully on the coffee table.

"I left everything in the hall—go and get the collar and cuffs. They're in the small grey box."

Alex watched his sub walk out of the room. He hadn't intended to upset her, but she had to know what they were facing and what to do if the worst-case scenario happened. *Prepare for the worst, hope for the best.* It had served him well during his years of military service, and it would serve both of them just as well now.

And if it did all turn out to be nothing more perilous than industrial espionage, then at least some good would have come of it—he would have Beth.

Alex's immediate plan was relatively simple: for the remainder of the day, he was going to concentrate on Beth and give her something other than their predicament to focus on—even though he knew damn straight she wouldn't forget about it. Tomorrow he was going to start training in earnest, to get back to something approaching the level of fitness he had while in the Regiment—or at least try to. A daily stint in the gym and the odd run didn't equate to the endless, punishing PT sessions they'd endured in all weathers in the old days.

Some target practice wouldn't go amiss either. One of the advantages of living in the middle of nowhere, with several acres of land at his disposal, was that he could set up a target range and use it, and no one would give a second thought to the sound of a shotgun.

Before any of that, he had to give Beth the guided tour of the house. Her safety was paramount and might very well be dependent on her knowing the layout inside out. He didn't want to dwell on what might happen to bring that situation about, but avoiding planning for the possibility wouldn't prevent it from arising.

Today, though, his priority was Beth, and giving her a distraction now would aid both of them. It would take her mind off what was going on, and help him to visualise a future beyond this unholy mess—a future he was going to spend with her.

"Put the box down and take your clothes off—slowly." He settled back on the sofa. "I want you to perform for me, Beth. Pretend you're a stripper putting on a private show for a client, and at the end of it, instead of tipping you, you want me to fuck you. Show me how much."

He expected a fiery blush and some fumbling with the buttons of her shirt. What he got blew him away.

Completely entranced, he watched as she began to sway in time to music only she could hear. Her hands stroked over her still fully clothed body, drawing his attention—as if that were necessary—to the curves of her breasts and hips. However, what attracted him far more was her expression... the soft, dreamlike expression of a woman who knew she was loved—completely, thoroughly and for all time.

She shimmied elegantly out of her grey skirt, revealing legs clad in sheer, black, lace-topped nylons, and the smooth pussy he had taken great delight in shaving just a few hours ago. With arms raised as she seductively lifted her mane of hair, her shirt rode up, revealing voluptuous hips and the neat indentation of her navel. Blood surged south as he anticipated spreading those incredible thighs and sliding into her hot, welcoming body. Hell, he'd take her right now, up against the wall, one leg hooked around his hip to open her up for his cock.

The gorgeous little tease then turned her back to him while she unfastened the shirt. With a coquettish peek over each shoulder, she slid the shirt from her body. When it dropped to the floor, she turned to face him again—hands clasped in front of her, gaze modestly lowered, an appealing contrast to the flirtatious looks she'd just sent his way. She clearly thought she'd obeyed his orders.

However, since she looked so sexy in the nylons and heels and this was, after all, her second performance of the day, he was prepared to let it slide. Besides, it would give him the enormous pleasure of removing them himself when he fitted the cuffs to her ankles.

"Very good, Beth," he murmured appreciatively, loosening his tie and unfastening the top buttons of his shirt. "On the basis of that routine, I'd be more than happy to fuck you. Now, tell me how you felt while you were doing that. And tell me the truth."

She chewed on her bottom lip for a moment—another habit he needed to ensure that she broke—and then admitted that she'd felt really silly to begin with, but all of a sudden it was almost as if she'd slipped into that character and it became easier.

"That's better. Trust me, Beth, from where I'm sitting,

there was nothing silly about what you just did. It was beautiful to watch, and it'll come even more easily with practice, love. And I intend to give you a lot of practice.

"Now, pass me the box, then sit down on at that end of the sofa, lean back and put your feet on my lap."

With very precise movements, she presented the box to him and then obeyed the rest of his instructions, giving him a wonderful view of her almost-totally-naked body. Maybe he would revise his rule about *no knickers* and make it *no clothes* after all.

Her slim feet were on his lap, pressed together and perfectly still. With a touch that spoke of ownership, he ran his hand up her legs to her pubic mound. So smooth and silky to the back of his fingers. The effect on her was obvious, evident in the delicate quiver she gave as she closed her eyes.

After removing the shoes, Alex took his time with the nylons, savouring each moment as he rolled first one, then the other, down her endless legs. Completely naked, she was a real, live wet dream. A picture popped into his mind—when Beth was confident enough in their relationship, he'd take her to a very special spa for some very special treatment.

As well as being stunningly beautiful and an astute businesswoman, Alessandra was a Mistress—a Domme. One of her enterprises was a luxurious spa, where, for her friends in the community, she had set aside a secluded suite of treatment rooms.

The two members of staff who worked exclusively in

that suite were her subs, one male, one female. Both were trained in all the therapies available. Their services were reserved exclusively for members of the D/s community. A Dominant could take his or her sub there for a top-to-toe pampering session, and while it was taking place, he or she could watch, either in privacy from behind a two-way mirror or relaxing on a decadent chaise longue in the same room.

The thought of Beth being the subject of such a session put a seriously hot image in his mind, especially if the attending subs were to be given permission to touch her breasts and her pussy and he were to order her not to become aroused. Would her limits ever embrace a semi-public, semi-bi, fully ménage experience like that? At one time he'd have said no, but now he could only wonder.

With the cuffs buckled around her ankles, Alex instructed her to assume her first position in front of him and offer her wrists to him for the other set of cuffs.

Now for the collar. He took up a position behind his sub, held the leather strap to her throat, and when she'd gathered her hair together, he locked it in position with a small padlock.

"Beth, you need to know that the necklace you wore for me on Saturday night really was a collar. I had it made just for you. I've been waiting almost three years to put it on you."

Sitting on the sofa again, Alex regarded her startled expression, watched the questions race across her face. He gave a slight nod, granting her permission to ask him those questions.

"I don't understand—three years?"

He understood her confusion. His response to it was simple. "That's how long I've wanted you and loved you, beautiful. You and I know it's a collar, but it doesn't mean I expect you to behave like a sub when you're wearing it—its significance is a private thing, between us, and only someone else in the community might recognise it for what it is."

He'd loved her and wanted her almost from the time they first met. It hardly seemed possible, but Beth knew he was telling her the truth. He was a good man, an honourable man, and one she could trust without question.

A tumult of emotions was doing crazy things to her insides: excitement, nerves, apprehension—even shyness, although that, she realised with a mental jolt, was rapidly dissipating. She really was getting used to being naked around Alex.

In fact, now she thought about it, she *loved* being naked around Alex.

A small smile teased the corners of her mouth. He loved her, he thought her beautiful—she knew she wasn't, but around him, she could *feel* beautiful. And she was wanted—it would never cease to amaze her that a man such as Alex, who could have any woman who caught his eye, actually wanted *her*.

And had felt that way for so long. But what about all those women he'd dated, the ones she'd ordered flowers for, and booked restaurants for… why had he been seeing them when he said he'd been in love with *her*?

"What is it, Beth? What just happened?"

He must have seen her expression change with the memories. She took a deep breath. Communication was supposed to be key in this kind of relationship, but how could she ask the question without sounding like a jealous harpy? She said the first thing that came into her head.

"Nothing."

"Wrong answer, sweetheart. I've worked with you every day for three years," he said softly. "I've seen your face run through the whole gamut of emotions and expressions—so I know that when you look like this," he tapped her nose with his fingertip, "your quicksilver mind is bubbling with questions and concerns. Tell me."

Well, he wanted to know. Not her fault if he didn't like the question. "If you felt like that about me, Alex, why did you date all those other women? Some of them… they sounded so young…"

"Ah. Beth, they didn't mean anything, not one of them. In your research, did you ever come across an arrangement called a training contract? The terminology might vary, but it does exactly what it says on the tin."

Yes, she had heard of such a thing, and the sources she'd found seemed to indicate that sexual intimacy was often off the menu. "No sex? You *weren't* dating?"

"That's it exactly, sweetheart," he confirmed. "Those women were mostly subs-in-training; they wanted to learn how to serve a Master—or in a couple of cases, a Mistress—but they had no Master or Mistress of their own. They undertook a training contract with me, but I never had sex with any of them."

"You said 'mostly'." Beth had latched onto that word immediately. "What about the others?"

His smile was almost regretful. "I'm a man, not a monk, sweetheart. I couldn't have you—I had to do something."

For a moment Beth wasn't sure how to react to that confession. Then she realised that she had no right to react at all. It wasn't as if they'd been in anything other than a working relationship at the time. "Why couldn't you have me?"

"Because I don't date my employees and you weren't a sub. That was enough to protect you from me."

"You thought I needed protecting from you? What changed? Not just the thing with my ankle." Something else had to have happened for him to make his move.

"Your ankle provided the opportunity. Something else was the catalyst." He paused, as if weighing up his next words very carefully. "The other week, you left your notebook on your desk when you were out at lunch—I looked."

Oh, this was turning into one of those floor-open-up-and-swallow-me-now moments. Still, he'd read some of the other stuff she'd written, so no big deal, right?

"And then I took a chance."

That figured. And with *his* past...? "Who dares wins?"

The corner of his mouth turned up in that hitherto rare

wry smile she'd always found so attractive. "You live by that motto for long enough, you don't know any other way."

She could go ballistic, she supposed, but where would that get her? What would be the point? The situation was what it was. And it was a situation she rather liked anyway.

"I guess... you won?" She gave a little shrug and what she hoped was an encouraging smile of agreement. "Sir?"

"I guess I did."

And didn't he look pleased with himself.

"Stand up, put your shoes on and come with me."

He led her back into the hall and up the sweeping staircase, along the gallery to a locked door. She longed to look around and take in the details of Alex's house, but her concentration was on following him. There was plenty of time for the guided tour later.

She watched Alex unlock the door, and then followed him inside the room. With her eyes lowered, her range of vision was quite limited; the impression she had was of a light wood floor and a proliferation of beautifully crafted bondage equipment in more light wood and leather... and a magnificent four-poster bed that couldn't possibly be as innocuous as it appeared. This was Alex's playroom? Somehow she'd expected something a little darker and more Gothic, and while this was dark in places, it was light too. It was a room of many facets, just like its owner.

"Second position, Beth—wait there, I'll be back in a moment."

She sensed more than saw him disappear through another door at the other end of the room; it would be very easy to cheat and look around, even take her hands down, but that just seemed so wrong. Her Dom had commanded her to stand like this, so stand like this she would.

"Well done, Beth. You can put your arms at your sides now—and look up."

He was gorgeous. Movie-star-swashbuckling-hero gorgeous. Romantic-lead-in-a-costume-drama gorgeous. *Move over, Mr. Darcy*. Beth's mouth watered at the sight of him in the black leather trousers, black boots and flowing white shirt, left unbuttoned so that she could see his chest. Her knees turned to jelly in half a heartbeat—about the same length of time it would take to get herself off if she dared to touch her swelling clit.

"Aroused already, Miss Harrison? Your nipples are such a giveaway."

He wasn't wrong. They'd be only marginally more noticeable if she replaced them with bright-red LEDs that flashed out *come and get me* in Morse code.

Alex had moved and was standing in front of her now. In a gesture redolent of indisputable ownership, his right hand cradled her breast, the thumb flicking back and forth across the sensitive, puckered flesh. "Give me your thoughts, sub."

Oh, that Dom voice again. Beth half-expected to feel rivers of moisture flowing down her inner thighs at how the voice and the order it gave made her feel. She looked at him with openly adoring eyes, and gave him words that came straight from her heart. "You're the most beautiful man I've ever seen."

The flicking stopped short. One small movement of his head and he was looking straight into her soul; she held her nerve and never wavered, until his lips touched hers. Eyes closed, she gave herself up to the kiss.

"Oh, Beth." He breathed her name as he nuzzled her cheek. "Why didn't we do this years ago?"

She couldn't help the smile. "When you reach that part of the job interview where the interviewer asks you if you have any questions, 'Do you happen to be a Dom, because I need one badly?' isn't exactly on the list of suggested subjects for enquiry."

Alex raised an amused eyebrow. "And I suppose if I'd told you that your job description would include submitting to me, you'd have run a mile."

"Probably." Beth felt her confidence drain a little, and knew it showed in her expression.

"It's all right, love—you've been at war with yourself for a long time, so it's going to take time for you to fully embrace your submissive nature. And don't forget—when it comes to this game, we make our own rules up as we go along."

"Thank you, Alex." She took his hand and lifted it to kiss the palm.

"You're a natural, sweetheart." His voice held the warm honey of approval. "I think that maybe you deserve a little reward now—although with your stubbornness this morning…"

Beth lowered her eyes. "I apologise. I should have trusted you, Sir."

"Yes, you should. So... what should I do with my beautiful new sub now?"

"Whatever you see fit to do, Alex."

The St. Andrew's Cross. She'd seen pictures of them before, lots of them, read novel after novel where subs had been shackled to them and driven to the heights of ecstasy, but now she was the one being bound to the free-standing saltire that dominated one end of the playroom.

Alex took so much care with her bonds, far more than she anticipated. He didn't just clip the cuffs to eyebolts on the cross—he made a thorough examination of the contact with her tender skin, ensuring that there would be no chafing and that her circulation wouldn't be compromised, and all the while he murmured distracting, sexy nothings close to her ear. With her back to him, she was especially vulnerable. Secured in position, she could do nothing to stop the delicious sensation of his hands roaming freely over her body, stroking her flesh.

Or the crack of the open-handed slap on her bottom, followed by the soothing stroke of that same hand. The sharp contact made her flinch, but then warm waves of pleasure crashed through her. How many times over the last few years had she fantasised about this?

"Ah, Beth, we both know you like that, don't we?" He placed an open-mouthed kiss on the side of her neck while playing with her breast. For a fanciful moment she imagined herself being ravished by a vampire, the romantic anti-hero image enhanced by the outfit he was wearing. "In view of the fact that you've kept your submissive tendencies hidden from me all this time, I think I need to introduce you to something with a little more sting to it."

Moving around so that he could see her face, Alex produced a length of chain. "These are called tweezer clamps—ideal for someone new to the scene. I can vary how much pressure they apply to your nipples. Hold yourself away from the cross."

The pinch of the clamps on her nipples made her gasp.

"Because you're new to this, I'm going to ask you how this feels—in future, though, I will decide how much pressure is applied. Tell me."

"Thank you, Alex. Green. It feels good."

She started again at the touch of his hand between her legs.

"I can tell. Your pussy's dripping with need right now." He tapped her clit twice; her knees buckled when he followed that with a relentless pressure. "And now that we have your delicious nipples nicely adorned, it's time to reacquaint you with the flogger."

If such an implement could be said to be beautiful, then this one was a work of art. The sensation of the tails, fashioned from red suede, teasing her flesh as Alex draped them over her shoulder, was exquisite; when he used it in a sequence of figure of eight movements across her upper back, it felt divine. The rhythm matched the pulse of blood through her veins, while the impact made her skin feel alive.

"My darling Beth, I wish you could see what I see."

He dropped the flogger to one side and moved to stand close, his chest pressed against her back, arms lined up with hers. She let herself lean back against him, relying on his strength to hold both of them up. He was whispering close to her ear again, words she could barely hear but they thrilled her all the same, sensual promises of all the things he wanted to do to her.

His hands stroked down the sensitive skin of her sides. When he reached her hips, he pulled her back hard against him, leaving her in no doubt about his state of arousal when he ground his pelvis against her bottom. "You feel what you do to me, sub?" he growled into the side of her neck.

The impersonal mode of address still made her shiver. His hands wandered further, around to her breasts, where his fingers caught hold of the chain linking the nipple clamps. When he tugged gently, she whimpered with pleasure-pain, letting herself lean more heavily against his body, anchored now by the arm that had moved around her waist.

With her Dom's strength to rely on, Beth knew that she was where she was always supposed to be, with the man she was always supposed to be with. Every nerve ending she possessed buzzed with vitality at his closeness, she felt him in every cell in her body.

The heat of his body left hers, disturbing the haze that was enveloping her. Her breathing shallow, she awaited his return, and was rewarded a few moments later with the touch of something light and soft tracing the line of her spine.

"D/s isn't all about chains and whips and pain, my love." His velvet voice wrapped itself around her senses. "I can use pleasure to drive you out of your mind; I can torture you with feathers, and hold you captive in nothing more than silk and lace."

It wouldn't even take that, Beth recognised. That voice could hold her captive; a disapproving look in his eyes could torture her. He was holding her again, anchoring her against his heat and strength, so she had no chance of wriggling away from the feather that he was stroking across the delicate skin of her abdomen. She moaned softly, turning her head away from the exquisitely agonising sensation, only to feel the sharp spike of the clamps on her tender nipples.

How long the sheer torment of it all went on for, Beth had no idea. Each new implement drove her closer to a climax, only for Alex to draw back and choose something else with which to torment her all over again. Each time, a voice that wasn't hers but had to be hers begged him for release and each time he denied her. Neither would he give her time to recover before stimulating her anew. Sweat dewed her body and her heart was racing in preparation for the orgasm that never came.

"Please... Alex... Sir..." She moaned when his hand went between her legs again, to stroke her folds and lightly scratch his nail over her hypersensitive clit. The world beyond her body had ceased to exist—apart from the man who controlled every sensation inflicted upon her trembling flesh.

"You need to come, don't you, my love?" he murmured as he moved from one side to the other. His hand stroked her inner thigh, where the moisture that flooded her pussy now betrayed her raging arousal.

"Please..."

"You need my dick, don't you? Just here."

Two fingers scissored inside her. Beth moaned again, let her head fall back as her back arched in an attempt to force those fingers deeper inside her. She ached... oh, how she ached for him to fill her body as he filled her heart, to have Alex take her hard and fast and let her come while he was inside her.

Wet. Empty. Need. The words whirled around in her mind. She was barely aware of Alex bending to release her ankles, the rasp of his zip or the sound of him opening a foil packet, but then he was lifting her, and when she felt his cock drive deep inside her she cried out, unable to contain the detonation of sensation, an explosion that went on and on with each rhythmic thrust into her body. And when finally she came, so did he, with a guttural cry of fulfilment moments after she screamed her release and all but collapsed against him.

A few seconds later, she was freed from the cross. Alex had her in his arms and was carrying her to the huge bed, where he laid her down and attended to the nipple clamps. The sensation of blood rushing back to the tormented flesh had her arching against his mouth, and then his fingers replaced that sweet agony.

"Please, may I speak, Sir?" she whispered, loving him with her eyes.

He stroked the damp hair off her forehead. "You may, Beth. The scene's over now, it's just you and me."

"Thank you." She turned her face to rest her cheek against his palm. "That was… it just *was*…"

He was smiling down at her, a smile that spoke of a special intimacy that came along once in a lifetime. "I know. You're mine now, Beth. Let me be your guide and your protector—"

"Will you be my lover, too?"

He bent to kiss her forehead. "I already am, sweetheart." He frowned as she gave a little shiver. "Time to get you into bed, I think—you need to rest."

Beth giggled a little drunkenly, still high from the session. "I'm already in bed, Alex."

"Not this bed—our bed."

As if she were a fragile work of art, he carried her from the playroom to his bedroom. Once she was safely tucked in, he stripped off his own clothes—Beth watched him greedily, drinking in every perfect line of his body, the way his muscles flowed with his economical movements. He disappeared briefly, returning a few moments later with a bottle of water and a glass.

"You need to have a drink before we sleep," he said, filling the glass. "All of it." He remained by her side while she finished the water.

"Thank you, Alex."

"Beth, you don't need to keep thanking me."

"I do it because I want to do it, and because it feels right to do it." She sighed, the sigh turning into a yawn she tried to stifle. "I feel so tired."

"Then there's just one more thing I need to do."

Her neck felt too bare without the collar, and when she asked about the gold necklace, Alex shook his head. "Tomorrow, sweetheart. I want you to relax tonight, and I think you'll find it easier to rest without the chain."

Beth felt strangely bereft—it felt wrong to be without the mark of Alex's ownership. "Then, please, may I have the ribbon back?"

"No." His response was immediate. "You have your real collar now, Beth, and you are not going back to a bloody ribbon. It's not open for discussion."

He gave her a look that plainly said he knew best.

Beth knew she should be happier about that, but she wasn't going to argue the point now. She watched her Dom move around the bed, and when he joined her she turned into his embrace as if she'd always belonged there.

Her last thought, before sleep claimed her, was that at last she could be the woman she was always meant to be.

CHAPTER ELEVEN

Beth woke up alone.

It was early, not yet 6 a.m., and everywhere was in darkness. The other half of the bed was cold; wherever Alex had gone, it must have been a while ago. Given the lack of a note, it wasn't unreasonable to assume he'd be back soon.

A shower followed by breakfast seemed to be the best idea after such a good night's sleep. The session in the playroom hadn't been enough for Alex—when they'd finally headed for the bedroom late last night, he'd let her sleep for a while. When she woke again, after maybe a couple of hours, it was to find him watching her, his gaze intense enough to infect her with the same lust that rode him. He'd made her climax hard and often before finally letting her fall asleep again. He'd certainly excelled in his pursuit of ensuring she had multiple orgasms. A hot shower might help to ease some of the unfamiliar aches.

While the coffee machine was working its magic, Beth rummaged in the American-style fridge-freezer. It was well-stocked, so there had to be something in there suitable for a cooked breakfast. She was just reaching for the packet of bacon when all of a sudden the kitchen door behind her burst open, revealing Alex as she'd never seen him before. And boy, did the sight of him send her hormones into a frenzy. She blinked slowly, just to make sure she wasn't hallucinating... or fantasising. A quick lick of the lips ensured she wasn't drooling either, because... hellfire, he looked so droolworthy.

The camouflage gear and chunky boots harked back to his time in the military. Beth hadn't known him back then, but if he looked this hot in something close to battle dress, what must he have looked like in his dress uniform? That thought alone would have been enough to melt the knickers that, like a good sub, she wasn't wearing. Even the flex of his powerful shoulders as he shrugged off the heavy-looking pack was enough to get her thinking thoughts that didn't belong in a kitchen.

"Good morning, love. I hope I didn't disturb you."

In his arms, the last thing Beth cared about was the stubble that graced his jaw and the sweat that resulted from the run it was now obvious he'd taken. Strands of dark hair clung to his damp forehead. She resisted the urge to comb them into some sort of order with her fingers—a little boy in need of tidying up, he was not. There was nothing little about this man.

"Only by not being there when I woke up. I'd forgotten you'd said you were going for a run. Come to think of it," she added with a mischievous grin, "it was all I could do to remember my name when I woke up this morning."

He returned her grin, although there was something very male and very smug about it. Then he looked thoughtful. "If you could still remember your name, maybe I need to brush up on my technique."

Beth swatted his arm. "You brush up on your technique any more, and I'll have permanent amnesia! So... how did it go?"

His expression sobered. "Could have been better. God, it wasn't this difficult twenty years ago!"

Beth realised she was still holding onto the bacon. She deposited it on the kitchen counter so she could wrap her arms around the man she loved and focus her attention on him.

"Hey, what's this for?"

"Just because. So... I want details. How far did you get?" She looked up at Alex's face; even unshaven and glistening with sweat, he was still the man she craved beyond all others. She was addicted to him.

"Ten miles, and it took me too bloody long. Fifteen years ago, a performance like that would have had me drummed out of the Regiment."

A strange feeling rippled through Beth. Now that she knew the truth about Alex's past, as opposed to the gossip that periodically scuttled through the office, she could look at him with fresh eyes. She saw the man of action who'd put his life on the line countless times without a thought for his own safety. The things he must have done in the service of his country, things that would never make TV news reports and probably didn't even have an official record of their existence, made her blood run cold.

"Hey, come back to me, Beth. Where did you go just then?"

His genuine concern snapped her out of her dark thoughts and back to the present. "Nowhere." She smiled and gave him a peck on the cheek. "Why don't you get a shower and a shave, and I'll make breakfast?"

"Sounds good to me, sweetheart. Make it a good one—we have a lot to do today."

And with a playful slap to her behind, he disappeared.

Beth busied herself with putting together a gourmet cooked breakfast—eggs, bacon, sausages, tomatoes, the works. Once everything was cooking, she went to move the backpack from where Alex had dropped it, only to find that she could barely drag it, never mind lift it. He'd run ten miles with that on his back? What did he have in it? She opened it up, half-expecting to find a load of bricks.

She wasn't far wrong; it looked like half a quarry. What amazed her most was that he'd arrived back barely out of breath—that spoke volumes about his existing level of fitness. And he thought he was out of shape? No way!

He had perfect timing as well; she was just putting the finishing touches to his breakfast when he ambled back into the kitchen, his hair slick and damp from the shower. She looked up with a grin, only for her face to fall when she caught his disapproving look at the single plate.

"Beth, have you already eaten?"

"No, I thought I'd wait for you."

"Then where the hell's your breakfast?"

Beth looked from him to the plate, then back at him—and raised her eyebrows. Her glasses had slipped down her nose slightly, so she ended up looking at him over the top of the frames. She pointed to the grill. "If I have the same as you, it'll end up welded to my hips and I'll need a new wardrobe every three months! There are four rashers of bacon under there—I'm having a bacon sandwich. Now, go and sit down, and I'll be right with you."

Beth carried the groaning plate over to the informal dining table by the French windows, joining him in the seat opposite when her breakfast was ready. She shot him a look and pointed at the proof of what she'd told him.

Alex stopped with a laden fork halfway to his mouth, glanced at the sandwich... then put the fork down again, picked up the sandwich and helped himself to a bite—a big one. His eyebrows rose in appreciation as he chewed slowly, savouring the taste, and after he swallowed, he delivered his opinion. "That's good."

"Oh, I'm so glad you approve." Beth slowly folded her arms, with what she hoped was an appropriate degree of indignant menace. "I know it is. I make a mean bacon butty. How's your breakfast?"

"Excellent." The laden fork resumed its interrupted mission.

"So what was all the fuss about? You didn't think I

was going to wait for permission… did you?"

He shrugged. "It's been known. Some Doms—the minority, thank God—demand it. At the risk of stating what I hope is the obvious, I'm not one of them."

Beth put her sandwich down, so that she could give her full attention to the man in front of her. "I never thought for one instant that you were." Then she leaned across the table and gently kissed his cheek.

The moment passed; the look Alex gave her filled her with love for him all over again, but just for a moment, before he ruined it by speaking. "Anyway, you never told me you could cook. You make great coffee, but somehow I've always laboured under the impression you could burn water."

Beth's eyes narrowed; she knew he was just teasing her, but she could give as good as she got, up to and including kicking his ankle under the table if necessary. Maybe she'd keep that in her arsenal for another time. "You never specified cooking as an essential skill on the job advert, nor do I remember ever having to cook as part of my office duties."

"*Touché.*" Alex grinned. "My, we are grumpy this morning."

"I wasn't grumpy until someone helped himself to my breakfast. Just for that, I'm not cooking the steaks I found in the fridge for dinner tonight." She took a purposely dainty bite of her sandwich, relishing the taste of the crisp grilled bacon between the slices of wholegrain bread.

Alex didn't even look up from his plate when he

spoke. "That's okay; it'll save you turning them into a burnt offering to the gods of gastronomy."

Oh, that kick was so tempting. However, Beth responded with nothing more lethal than an irate glare, which was promptly defused by the roguish grin he gave her. His eyes were shining with humour.

She'd show him. Mustering all her dignity, she sat up straight and stuck her tongue out at him, before taking another bite of food.

"You know you just earned yourself a spanking."

"What?" Beth nearly choked. "But we're not... this is the *kitchen*!"

Alex made a point of looking around. "So it is. How about that?"

"Are you sure you're just a sexual Dominant?"

He shrugged again, loading his fork with hash brown, sausage and tomato. "I know I enjoy spanking you. Any chance of some coffee?"

After breakfast, the first item on the agenda for Alex was to lock his sub's day collar into place around her beautiful neck.

He really wasn't sure how she'd react to it. On one or two rare occasions, he'd collared subs for training, only for them to realise that submission wasn't for them after all. One in particular had looked like she was heading for full-blown hysteria in the seconds before she'd hightailed it out of Aegis. And then there'd been the blonde at the other end of the scale, who wanted nothing more than to be a 24/7 slave. She'd almost had an orgasm when the collar went on.

And now there was Beth, who gave him yet another reason to love her. Even standing behind her, while he locked the chain into place, he could sense the pride radiating from her. When he turned her to face him, her eyes positively sparkled and her smile made his heart hurt with wanting her. She looked utterly gorgeous.

It would be so easy to take her hand, go back to bed, and make love to her for the rest of the day. Unfortunately, that was a luxury they just didn't have.

"Just so there aren't any misunderstandings, Beth, this collar is here to protect you." He placed his palm over the padlock at the base of her throat, pressing it against her skin. "Anyone who's part of the scene will know what it means—that you belong to me. Understand?"

"Yes, Alex."

"And it doesn't mean that I expect you to submit to me in any way other than sexually. I want you to get used to the feel of it—it'll be there to tell any Dom that you're mine, but to anyone else, it's simply a beautiful piece of jewellery worn by a stunningly beautiful woman."

The flush that stained her cheeks was enchanting, and it had him fighting the urge to bed her all over again. If only they didn't have to... It was no use thinking like that. Beth had to know about the secure room, where it was and how to get to it from anywhere in the house, and for that he needed to show her around. Still, she'd found her way to the kitchen all right—and she'd looked right at home there.

An image exploded in his mind, generated by every primal male instinct he possessed responding to the warm female body he held so close—Beth, barefoot and pregnant. *Holy shit!* He really needed to stop thinking like that. What the hell kind of Neanderthal was he turning into?

Winterleigh was a far larger house than a man living alone needed, but it was the one thing he had fought to keep during the course of his divorce. The property had been a dilapidated wreck when he bought it on a whim at a knockdown price, and hadn't really improved much by the time his ex-wife walked out two years later. Fortunately, she'd been more interested in what she could spend, so she'd been more than happy to leave the money pit of a house in his hands. It had taken time and every spare penny he'd had, but eventually Winterleigh had been transformed into the closest thing he'd had to a home since he'd enrolled at Sandhurst.

So it was with no small sense of pride that he showed Beth around the sprawling mass that was his home, although he was more interested in her reactions to the property. He wanted her to feel that it could be her home, too. He wanted her to feel involved, and there was one room that might encourage that.

"When I bought this place, this was rather grandly referred to as 'the ballroom' in the brochure," Alex told her when they reached the large empty ground floor room at one end of the house. "At the viewing before the auction,

I thought the estate agent was rather more delusional than they usually are. The doors at the end open out onto the formal gardens. I was hoping you might have some ideas about what we could do with it."

He watched Beth as she wandered through the spacious room, looking up and down the walls and letting her fingers trail over the handles on the French windows at the far end. Then she came to a dead stop.

"You said *we*."

Of course he did—she'd be living there too, one day. He quirked an eyebrow to prompt her into elaborating.

"This is your home, Alex." She paused; Alex didn't like the look of the frown that creased her brow. "I'm not sure I have any business being included in the decision-making process—"

"Beth, don't you remember the conversation we had just yesterday? If you decide to stay with me, this will be your home too. Besides, who else am I going to trust with decorating and furnishing the largest room in the house? Cam?"

Alex refused to entertain the idea that she might not decide to stay—it just wasn't an option in his book. He was, however, pleased to see the idea of the former SAS staff sergeant venturing into the field of interior design amused her almost as much as it did him. Cam Fraser and fabric swatches were about as mutually exclusive as it was possible to be.

"Okay, point taken. What do you use it for now— besides storage?" She glanced over at the cluster of packing crates in one corner.

"What you see is what you get. Any ideas?"

Beth moved further into the room, turning in a full circle—he guessed to get a feel for the scale of it. "It's a large space—you could do a lot with this, it all depends how you see your life here unfolding." She flashed a grin at him. "Are you likely to hold many parties?"

Parties… the anniversary parties would have to wait for the wedding reception to happen first. A marquee in the garden, a huge wedding cake, Beth in a champagne-coloured dress that made the most of her curves…

Alex pushed the errant thought to one side—his subconscious was getting ideas well above its station. "Maybe. Come on, there's still a fair bit to see."

They ate lunch in the kitchen. After the meal, Alex quizzed Beth about the house. He was quietly impressed with how much she'd taken in so quickly, and then he turned his thoughts to the afternoon, as did Beth.

"Do you have anything in mind for this afternoon, Alex?"

He needed to get a range set up for some target practice, and was just about to tell her that when the machine-gun rattle of a sudden downpour hit the windows.

"I did," he admitted wryly. Hell, he still should have those same plans; he wouldn't dissolve in a bit of rain, but it had taken about three nanoseconds for him to talk himself into a pleasant afternoon of lounging around with Beth, talking her into keeping him occupied.

Ah, he was getting too easily distracted now. Anything to do with this woman distracted him. The thought of being Dom to the woman he loved gave him the kind of warm feeling in his chest that he'd thought he'd never be lucky enough to experience. So did the thought of this mess being over and settling down to living here at Winterleigh, with his whole life revolving around her.

Focus, Lombard. Stick with Plan A.

He wasn't the only one to lapse into a daydream, he realised. Beth was lost in thought, and though he couldn't be sure, it seemed that her eyes held a certain brightness that could only be attributable to tears.

"Earth to Beth—are you all right? You went away from me there for a moment."

"Sorry." She took a moment to gather herself together. "I'm sorry, I was miles away."

"What were you thinking?"

"It was just a silly thought triggered by the rain."

"Tell me."

Beth glanced down at her hands, clasped on her lap. "I just thought that if you went out to set up the shooting range, you'd get soaked to the skin, and then..." She closed her eyes briefly, as if she were fighting some sort of internal battle. "Then I thought that you'd probably seen, experienced far worse than a bit of bad weather when you were deployed. I told you it was silly."

Without speaking, Alex rose and came around to her, his arms enfolding her and lifting her off the stool she was sitting on. He sat down, so that they were almost on eye level with each other, and then pulled her between his muscular thighs, bringing her as close to him as humanly possible. She raised her hands to frame his face, the look in her eyes startlingly intense.

"Thank you," she whispered against his cheek.

"For what?"

"For loving me. For everything." She rested her head against his shoulder. "I love you."

Alex laid his cheek against the back of her head. His eyes closed automatically with the peace that this woman had unknowingly brought into his life. Now he understood fully what his comrades had fought for. It was never really about Queen and country, but the man beside you on the front line, he already knew that. What he'd never really understood, beyond the logic of it, was fighting for the family waiting back home.

He wasn't alone anymore. That empty place inside him, the one he'd clung to for so many years, the barrier that protected him from facing the reasons for his failings as a true Dom, was gone. The dark loneliness had been challenged and found wanting by the woman who held his heart and soul as surely as he now held her.

"I know, sweetheart. I know."

Regardless of what he really wanted to do, Alex kept his mind on his priorities and spent an hour outside on target practice, using the more contemporary weapons at his disposal. The antique shotguns, including a prized Purdey of which he was particularly fond, were excellent for taking out the local clay pigeon population. However, since clay pigeons didn't tend to shoot back, he'd elected to use one of his potentially lethal pump-action shotguns for the purposes of protection. When he'd satisfied himself that his eye was still good, Alex reloaded the weapon one more time and finished off with a satisfying crop of bull's-eyes.

As he was cleaning the shotgun back in the gun room, it occurred to him that it might be a good idea to take his old combat knives—also stored in the gun safe—back into the house as a backup plan. He had to consider all the options. Whoever it was, they'd waited a long time for revenge; if his past were coming back to haunt him, he was going to be prepared to meet it head-on.

Satisfied that he'd done all he could for now, Alex went in search of his woman. He'd held off thinking about her while he was cleaning the shotgun, but now he wanted to bury himself in her body and celebrate being alive with her.

"Beth!"

They almost collided in the hall. At the sound of her name, Beth had come running out of the family room. Alex caught hold of her and pressed her against the wall, his mouth crushing hers with the violence of his need for her. "Now I'm taking you to bed."

Alex headed for their bedroom rather than the playroom. He barely made it inside before he started to peel Beth's clothes from her body. When she was naked, he lifted her in his arms and laid her on the bed, stepping back to devour her with his eyes. She moved onto her side, facing him, her eyes never leaving his as she pillowed her head on one arm, one leg slightly bent for balance, almost as if she were posing for an artist. He was aware of her gaze never leaving him while he shed his clothes. If he didn't have her and soon, he'd go bat-shit crazy.

She'd been desperate to be with Alex for the last hour, and now the desperation was gone, replaced by pure animal desire.

Beth wanted him so badly—she'd never realised it was possible to ache with wanting someone until now. For the last hour, she'd been unable to concentrate on anything other than imagining being with this man, pure lust robbing her of the power to concentrate long enough to string words together into meaningful sentences. Right now, she'd be more than happy to spend the rest of her life in bed with him. What was it about this man that was turning her into a sex maniac?

Stupid question, Harrison. Stupid question.

"Has anyone ever told you you're perfect, Alex?" she wondered aloud, before lowering her head to lick his nipple, like a cat lapping a bowl of cream. A buzz of immense satisfaction came from the noise he made, somewhere between a purr and a growl.

And the taste of him—warm and sexy and male, and she wanted more of him, so much more.

"Beth." His voice was rough with desire. "Give me your mouth."

She obeyed, and in the same instant his hand parted her thighs so that his fingers could push into her pussy. She knew she was already wet with wanting him; his fingers moved slickly over her swelling clit, and her hips bucked in response, trying to fuck his hand.

"Easy, love," he murmured against her lips. His fingers dipped into her pussy again, and then his hand moved further—she felt the tip of his finger pushing against her anus. "Has anyone ever taken you here?"

Beth shook her head. "No one, Alex. Never..." She wanted him to be the one.

The fingertip pushed more insistently, opening her up a little. "Relax, Beth. You know I'll never do anything to hurt you. We'll take this at your pace."

She'd known he'd wanted this—he'd told her so. Even though she was more than willing, she braced herself for discomfort at best, pain at worst, but what Beth experienced was gentle care that robbed her of all sense of self, all sense of time. Alex's soft words serenaded her mind into acceptance, and his tender touch soothed her body into making the movements he required of her. His hand on her back calmed her when she whimpered at the easing open of the place only he would ever claim. He was the Master of her body, her mind and her senses, and when his cock finally filled her, she opened her eyes and saw their reflection in the huge mirror that almost covered one wall of the bedroom.

The eroticism of the image was stunning. The beautiful, muscular sculpture of Alex's body as he arched over her melted her insides all over again, and what Beth felt she was watching was not lovemaking or fucking, but a mating of two people who were meant to be together.

Forever.

Their eyes met in the mirror. Alex paused, balls-deep inside the woman he loved. Her hand was resting on the bed; he covered it with his, twining his fingers with her, the way he felt their lives were now entwined together. "Beth?"

The look in her eyes had a dreamlike quality—there was no sign of discomfort now, and it looked like she was enjoying the reward he'd promised her. Slowly, he began to move again, every stroke controlled to maximise her pleasure. It was all for her now.

Her fingers, still tangled with his, tightened their grasp. He knew how aroused she was without touching her pussy—he could smell the warm, feminine scent of her, a scent he could drown in, and one that told him she was close to orgasm.

He pushed her thighs further apart, took hold of her hips again, and began to increase the tempo of his fucking. He wanted Beth to be a wild woman under him, to hear her scream when her climax came.

Her back arched; she was getting closer, he knew it, as she pushed back against him, driving him deeper inside her. Instinct took over—one arm slipped under her waist, and as he lifted her upright, sitting back on his heels, his other arm went across her chest, pulling her hard against his body.

Her whimpers became impassioned cries. She was helpless in his embrace, vulnerable, totally dependent on him not to let her fall, impaled on his thrusting cock, arching back against his body as she surrendered to the pleasure he was giving her.

"Let it go, Beth," he encouraged her, his voice hoarse with restraint, from holding his own orgasm at bay. "Come for me."

He felt her clench around him; her head lolled back on his shoulder, and then it began, her body shaking as a wild howl signalled her climax.

Alex reached around to push the pillows out of the way, so he could lower his woman to the bed. His own need for release was increasing, to the point where he doubted he could control it for much longer. Taking his weight on his arms so as not to crush her, he increased his rhythm, feeling the ripples of her pleasure intensify once more. Those same ripples pulsated along his dick, his balls drew up, and an orgasm that cracked his spine forced every last drop of semen from his balls.

Almost drained of strength, he eased onto his side and took Beth with him. He held her while she calmed down, reluctant to let her go until he knew that she was settling. When his softening shaft slipped free, he was both surprised and gratified by the little grunt of complaint that she gave in response.

Beth, his beloved Beth, blew his mind. He thought of the woman he'd known a few days ago—his very proper, tightly controlled executive assistant—and looked at the sated, sensual female lying limply in his arms. The love he felt for her saturated every cell in his body—beyond any doubt, he'd go to hell and back to keep her in his life.

It was a sobering thought, but Alex knew, more surely than he knew that the sun would rise tomorrow, that his life would be worth nothing without her. He stroked her hair, lifting it away from her face and neck so that he could place a gentle kiss on that sensitive spot at the top of her shoulder.

Having taken a brief moment to remove the condom, he drew the sheets over her and slid in beside her. With gentle hands, he coaxed her to him, to warm her with his body and shelter her in his embrace. Although she was still in a post-orgasmic haze, she snuggled into him, her cheek pressed to his chest, her arm lying across his waist. He barely heard her sigh of contentment.

"Beth?" His voice was little more than a whisper. "Are you all right?"

He felt what he thought was a nod; it must have been a nod, because she nestled closer to him, a reaction so different from that of the last woman he'd made love to in this bed.

"Love, I know you want to go to sleep, but there's something I need to know. How do you feel?"

She looked up at him with a drowsy smile. Her hand lifted from his chest to touch his face. "Safe. Protected.

Loved. Like I could spend the rest of my life just like this. If I could bottle this moment, Alex, I'd keep it forever."

Her kiss was sweet and gentle. Her words brought warmth to his heart and reason to his life. What she said next made him feel cared for in a way that had been missing all his life, until the moment when Beth had walked into that life.

"May I keep you forever?"

Alex took a deep breath. "You mean the world to me, Beth. I love you. I want you in my bed and in my life for the rest of my life. Keep me for as long as you want."

He ran his finger under the gold chain around her neck, pausing when he reached the padlock. It was a work of art and she looked beautiful in it, but he had to know.

"Beth, are you really happy to wear this?"

He felt her lips against his chest, an inch or two above his nipple. "Alex, I love this collar. I love what it means. I want to be yours—this collar means that I am, and it lets everyone know who needs to know, that I am."

As they lay facing each other, Alex—overwhelmed by a feeling of possessiveness so primitive that it drove the last veneer of civilisation from him—tightened his arms around her and wrapped his leg over hers. She was the centre of his world, his holy grail, and he'd kill or die to protect her.

CHAPTER TWELVE

Beth and Alex had been sitting tight at Winterleigh for over a week. Their days had settled into some sort of routine, with Alex spending his mornings on the shooting range, out running or working out with weights, while Beth explored the house, familiarising herself with the layout of it.

She was also—grudgingly, it had to be said—joining Alex for some of his sessions in the gym. Somehow, he'd succeeded in persuading her that getting into better shape seemed like a sensible thing to do, although she had a hard job convincing herself of that when she was working up a sweat on the cross-trainer. What did he want to do? Bounce coins off her arse? Sometimes the only thing that kept her going was imagining all the things she could bounce off *his* arse in revenge. Still, she took his point— the sole aim of the exercise was to improve her fitness, should anything happen that required her to go somewhere in a hurry.

However, it was her novel that claimed the majority of Beth's attention when she wasn't with Alex. She still hadn't let him see it, and it was becoming more and more difficult to resist his cajoling. It was only a matter of time before he turned the Dom voice on her to get his own way. She was amazed he hadn't already.

One thing that was causing her some grief was Alex's flat-out refusal to let her stray beyond the bounds of the house and grounds. She would have loved to take a stroll to the nearest village, but her man insisted that she remain on his property for reasons of safety. Again, it was something eminently sensible, but that didn't mean she had to like it.

The one time she'd tried to defy him, he'd caught her before she reached the main gates, lifted her bodily into the Range Rover he kept to use while in the country, and driven her straight back to the house. He'd hauled her into the family room, put her over his knee, and proceeded to spank her bare bottom so hard, she hadn't been able to sit comfortably for hours. Looking daggers at him over dinner that evening hadn't helped her cause either—he'd taken great delight in denying her orgasms the next time they played. And the time after that.

At first she'd fumed about it—and not silently, either—but by the time she started thinking Alex's protective instincts were really quite sweet, she decided there was no hope for her.

Cam had called Alex regularly with the latest updates

on his investigation into who was intent on harming him, be it through industrial espionage or some sort of warped, personal vendetta. The last Beth had heard, both the men's instincts seemed to be leading them to conclude that the former was looking less and less likely. There hadn't been much to report up till now, but today Cam had insisted on a personal visit. The plan was for him to spend the day there and stay overnight in one of the guest suites.

"Beth, we're going to the shooting range," Alex informed her, dropping a sexy little kiss on her mouth. "Cam and I need to discuss a few things. While we're doing that, you go and do your homework."

She watched the two men leave, keenly aware of how grave their demeanour became once they left her and thought she wasn't looking. Over the last few days there'd been times when she'd almost forgotten how serious the situation was, to bring her to this house in the first place, but Cam's visit brought it all back. She could only hope that it would all be over soon.

And homework. *Really?* Beth frowned—there were days when she could happily kick Alex's legs from under him.

Think calm thoughts.

Oh, she knew he was taking care of her, which made her feel bad about being irritated by what he'd said. She also knew she should look at the positives: she was in love with and loved by a beautiful man who gave her the sexual domination she needed, who was giving her support and encouragement in her attempts to become a writer, and who was doing all he could to ensure her safety. In return she could give him the love and emotional support he needed, in spite of all his Dominant characteristics. They worked well together in so many different ways.

Back to homework. That meant two things: the first was more familiarisation with the layout of the house, and the second was working on her manuscript. She opted for the second.

Beth sat in front of her laptop. She hadn't wanted to impinge on Alex's work space in the office he kept at the house, but he'd insisted on it. He had occasionally spent time in there with her, keeping in touch with the office back in London; at the moment, though, she was alone—and couldn't concentrate worth a damn.

She stood and stretched; maybe some fresh air would help. It was dull outside, probably cold as well, but at least it wasn't raining. Wrapped up in a bright-red, knee-length duffle coat, feet shod in warm boots, she headed for the woods, away from the sound of shotguns—plural—being fired.

Boys and their toys.

Fallen leaves crackled and crunched satisfyingly beneath her feet as she walked through the trees, mostly denuded by autumn winds. Although she loved the colours of autumn, Beth's favourite season was spring, when all the trees would be sporting the light, fresh greens of new growth, birdsong would be making the woods come alive, and the days would be getting longer.

And by next spring, all of this would be nothing more than a bad memory.

Another barrage of shots sounded in the distance. Beth shivered—not through cold but through imagining what might happen to cause those weapons to be fired in anger. She really didn't want to dwell on it too much. It would all be over soon, it had to be. Perhaps that was the reason for Cam's visit—to tell them that it was all over and there was nothing to worry about.

She was only fooling herself. That was the sort of news the blond Dom could have imparted via a phone call; even if he'd felt a need to deliver it in person, he and Alex wouldn't have gone off to practice on the shooting range. Something must have happened that required the two of them to talk in person, and if that were the case, it couldn't be good.

She was washing dishes in the kitchen when the two men returned to the house. Masculine arms came around her waist, pulling her into a hard male body, while firm lips planted a sneaky kiss at the side of her neck.

"Did you lose the dishwasher again, love?"

Beth rolled her eyes. "It wasn't worth loading it with so few dishes, and you know I hate leaving the things lying around."

"Will you two quit already? You'll put me off my lunch."

Beth felt Alex chuckle at his friend's words, spoken with mock disapproval. If only things could have been like this without the threat that was hanging over them.

On the couple of evenings when Cam had ended up staying overnight, the three of them had been able to forget the spectre at the feast and have some fun, like the time they'd tried to teach her how to play poker. She was just so glad they hadn't insisted on playing *strip* poker...

"So, what have you two been talking about?"

She felt Alex tense up at her question. His tone, when he spoke, was as dismissive as his words. "Nothing much."

Cam cleared his throat in a way that did absolutely nothing to reassure Beth. "She should know, Alex."

"Yes, she should," Beth agreed. "Don't keep me in the dark, I need to know. This affects me just as much as it affects you."

Alex's arms tightened around her waist. "Come on. If we're going to talk, we might as well do it in comfort. Cam?"

All three of them went to the family room. Alex sat on the sofa with Beth, while Cam made himself comfortable in one of the armchairs.

"Beth, my love," Alex began, "we know what's going on now, and it's not industrial espionage. Cam's been able to confirm that someone from my past is responsible for the breaches in security at the office and is deliberately targeting me."

"So it is revenge." Without conscious thought, Beth moved closer to Alex. "Have you gone to the police?"

A look flashed between the two men. It was Alex who responded. "I don't want the police involved in this. Cam and I can handle it between us."

Beth couldn't believe what she was hearing. "Excuse me?"

"The evidence we have won't stand up in court, so there's no way they'll take action," Alex said soberly. "It's too flimsy. They'd need hard evidence, and that might mean waiting for the perpetrator to take this to the next level. I'm not prepared to put you at risk."

"That's why you wanted me to leave."

"And why you should still leave," Cam broke in. "I'm sorry, Beth, but that would be the safest—"

"Course of action—I know!" she bit back, more harshly than she intended. "Look, if something happens, I know what to do. I know where the safe room is and I know what to do when I get there. But I'm not leaving!"

Alex wrapped his arms around her and hugged her to his chest. "It's all right, sweetheart," he murmured. "You don't have to go anywhere—"

"Alex!"

"Cam, please... just don't. It'll be all right," he repeated.

Beth looked up at her man. "You really believe there's a threat then?"

"Yes," Cam responded tautly. "And Alex and I are working on a plan to deal with it."

She looked from one man to the other. "What can I do to help? There must be something I can do."

Alex gave her a brief, gentle kiss. "You already have by making sure you know where the secure room is and how to get there from anywhere in the house. If the worst happens, we can deal with it—so long as you're safe."

"You won't get in trouble with the police because of what you're doing, will you?"

The two men exchanged a swift look. Again it was Alex who answered the question, albeit in a roundabout way. "We know what we're doing, Beth. Like Cam said, we're putting a plan together to ensure that we keep you safe—"

"But what about you? Both of you. I don't want you to get hurt."

"We don't intend to get hurt," Cam said, his tone as serious as his manner. He was a million miles away from the light-hearted charmer she knew from her interactions with him in the office. "Trust us, Beth—we know what we're doing."

"Cam, I just had a thought. I don't suppose you've managed to convince Ros to come and work for you yet, have you?"

Cam grimaced. "Not for want of trying. She's still '*thinking about it.*'"

The heavy emphasis he placed on the last three words left Beth somewhat bemused. "Who's Ros?"

Alex gathered her to him in a reassuring hug. "Ros Edwards is someone I would trust with your life, love. I was thinking that if Cam had managed to charm her into quitting on her uncle and working for him instead, we'd get her down here to keep an eye on you."

"I've been trying to get her to ditch the life of a glorified civil servant and come and work for me for at least a year," Cam complained, "and every time I ask her, she says '*I'll think about it.*'"

Beth wanted to know more about this woman whom they both knew, and knew well, or so it seemed. "Not that I need babysitting, but what does she do?"

The two men glanced at each other; it was Alex who spoke first. "There's only so much we can tell you; what we do is covered by the OSA—"

"And what's that?" Beth felt like she was rapidly getting out of her depth and clutching at anything remotely resembling a lifeline.

"The Official Secrets Act," Cam supplied. "Ros used to be in the Army; she was a military police officer, but she left about eighteen months ago and went to work for her uncle. He commands a covert unit—"

"And that's as much as we can tell you about that," Alex finished off. "But, if Ros is still working for Guy, she's probably off somewhere we can't talk about, doing things you can't imagine, Beth. For which I am extremely grateful."

"You're absolutely certain that it's not just industrial espionage?" Beth knew she was clutching at straws.

"We're certain, sweetheart," Alex confirmed, his tone grave with resignation. "And we can't just sit here, waiting for something to happen so that the police will get involved. We have to be prepared to protect ourselves."

Beth turned her face into Alex's chest, her arm resting across his waist. Her mind was fighting the worst-case scenario—that she could lose the warm, vital man she loved. She breathed in the scent that was uniquely him, feeling her body respond in its usual way. "What's going to happen? What do you think they'll do?"

"Not they—he. Carmichael and Rhodes were able to uncover all the information we needed to identify the person responsible. It's one man, and now that we know who he is, we know why he's doing this." Alex paused; the look on his face was one of revisiting a past that wasn't a good place. "I killed his brother."

"That's bullshit and you know it, Alex!" Cam's disagreement was explosive. "Underwood was a damn fool and didn't obey your orders—"

"I as good as killed him. He was under my command when he died. There wasn't enough left to bring home for his family to bury," Alex said, his voice quiet, bleak under the assault of memories that clearly haunted him. Whatever it was that had happened, whatever the circumstances were, the tragedy had hit him hard. Beth nestled closer, offering her man the comfort of her body, in spite of Cam's presence just a few feet away. Any words could wait until they were alone.

"Jimmy Underwood was a loose cannon," Cam insisted. "You know that as well as I do. You gave the order to stay back but he charged into that building anyway. You didn't lay the IEDs, Alex, any more than any of us did, and if that idiot had followed orders—*your* orders—he'd still be alive now."

"When did this happen?" Beth asked.

"Fifteen years ago," Cam replied. "The building blew seconds after Underwood ran into it. Alex went in after him, and that was when a second wave of explosives were detonated. We were able to pull Alex out, but there was nothing left of Underwood."

Beth went very still, glancing from one man to the other as she took in what had been said. That was the incident that had given Alex the scars. It had to be. "You mean that that man deliberately disobeyed orders, Alex risked his life to try to save him, and now his brother's coming after Alex in some misguided desire for revenge? That's insane! And isn't fifteen years a long time to wait?"

She felt Alex's arms tighten around her. "I survived, Beth—Underwood didn't. I was in command of the mission. It's hardly surprising Ewan blames me for his brother's death. That family's been through enough—another reason why I'd like to keep the police out of this, if we can. If he does make a move on us, then maybe we can talk him out of it and get him some help—"

"And if we can't, then we have to be prepared for whatever he throws at us." Cam finished grimly.

"But why now? It all happened so long ago. That's what I really don't understand." Beth was genuinely puzzled.

"There could be any number of reasons," Cam said. "It was a covert op—it could have taken him years just to find out Alex was the officer commanding."

Beth's mind was racing. "If you know who it is, does

that mean you know where he is now?"

"He's gone to ground, so for the time being we've lost him," Alex told her. "Cam has contacts on the lookout, and as soon as they find out anything, they'll let us know.

"Beth, I don't want you to worry about this," he continued. "Ewan will make a mistake, and then we'll deal with him."

"You don't want me to worry? You'll deal with him?" She was incredulous. "First of all, you might as well tell me not to breathe as not to worry. And what does '*deal with him*' mean, exactly? He was either smart enough to get into the office and plant the surveillance equipment himself, or he knew who to pay to do it. And if he does track us down to Winterleigh, who's to say he'll come here alone? Do you know anything about him? Any training he might have had?"

All of a sudden, Beth stopped talking. It struck her that she'd just stepped into the realm of teaching her grandmother to suck eggs, judging by the look the two men levelled at her. And looking at Alex's face in particular, she had the strangest feeling that her backside was going to pay for her mouth's recklessness later.

"Everything will be all right, Beth," Alex reassured her. "We're putting a plan together, and we'll deal with Ewan Underwood." Even so, he still held her a little more tightly.

"I know what we can do," Cam said suddenly. "Get some of the boys down here for a training exercise out in the woods—if nothing else, it'll stop them getting too soft between jobs."

"Can't hurt," Alex agreed.

"They could do with some unarmed combat training and knife practice, and remembering how to live rough won't hurt them. I'll get them organised."

To Beth, it seemed like all of a sudden the conversation had headed off into parts unknown. "You've lost me."

"It's all right, sweetheart. It just means that a couple of Cam's operatives who aren't on assignment will be spending an indefinite, but hopefully short, period camping in the woods around the house." Alex's tone held an audible degree of satisfaction.

"Bodyguards. You're talking about bodyguards." Beth couldn't believe it—had they *really* implied that?

"Did I say that, Cam? I don't think I did."

Beth wasn't fooled by their apparently innocent expressions, but between them, the two men seemed determined to maintain the pretence.

Cam shook his head. "Nope, can't say I heard you say that. Don't think I said it either. Besides," he continued, struggling to keep the smirk off his face, "if we were going to say 'bodyguards', we wouldn't say 'bodyguards', we'd say 'close protection officers', wouldn't we?"

Beth sighed. They really were like two little kids at times.

No, she decided, they were *worse* than two little kids. Any woman could handle two little kids—it was the two big kids who were giving her a mammoth headache...

After lunch, Cam made his excuses and left—he had preparations to make for those of his employees who would be taking part in the training exercise, potentially half a dozen, all told. With no idea what sort of attack Ewan Underwood might mount, he'd insisted that it only made sense to bring as many men as were available. He would be returning later, though, having been invited for dinner and an overnight stay.

Alex saw his friend off and then went back into the house. To say that what Cam had told him that morning was disturbing would be a vast understatement. The threat had been a long time in the making, and the signs were that it would become a reality very soon. However, it wasn't so much the very real threat to his safety that bothered him so much—he could handle that, it was what he'd been trained to do even if it was a long time ago—as the very real possibility that Beth could get caught up in whatever act of violence Jimmy's brother was planning.

Alex had never met the elder Underwood; he'd still been in hospital at the time of the funeral. While on a visit to the ward, Alex's commanding officer had told him all about Ewan's angry outburst after the service, where he'd damned them all to hell for the perceived futility of his younger brother's demise. The last part of his tirade had taken the form of a violent, vehement promise to "get the bastard responsible."

Fast-forward to the current situation, and it appeared

that Ewan was a lot more resourceful than they might have given him credit for. It would have been no mean feat to discover the identity of the officer commanding on the mission, and then there was the bugging of the offices to consider and the sabotage of some of Alex's business deals. Alex's gut was telling him that it was only a matter of time before the man tracked him down to Winterleigh.

And now that the threat was so real, if Beth had still had any family left, he would have sent her to stay with them. Sadly, she didn't, and when he'd suggested it, she'd made it clear in no uncertain terms that she wasn't going to stay with friends either. She was determined to remain with him, and while his instincts were all in favour, his common sense, which was now in agreement with Cam's stance on the matter, was sounding the alarm.

He should make her leave. He knew he should. She would be safer away from him, but there was that stubborn part of him that wanted to keep her close, so that he knew exactly where she was and he could protect her—with his life, if necessary.

"Alex."

She was standing in the office doorway—so beautiful, but so vulnerable too, and compared to him, so fragile. Alex felt his body leap in response at the sight of her. "Beth, there's something I have to ask—"

"No. Don't you dare tell me to leave, Alex Lombard." He heard the tremble in her voice, even if he couldn't see it in her body. "I'm staying here with you, because if anything happens to you... he might as well do it to me, too."

A tight band wrapped itself around his heart. No, he would never—*never*—allow that to happen. "Beth, you're my life—I have to keep you safe."

She took a couple of steps towards him. "You think you're not the same to me? You think I'd want to be safe without you? Don't you know, Alex?"

He knew. Damn it, he knew with every last cell in his body just how much this woman loved him and that he had less than a snowball's chance in hell of convincing her to seek sanctuary elsewhere until the danger was over. Even if he tried, as her Dom, to order her to go, his instincts told him she'd defy him no matter what he threatened her with. He went to her.

"Please don't make me leave you, Alex. I'm begging you."

"Beth, let's go to bed."

He lifted her easily into his arms. Her arms went around his neck and he felt her lips, tender on his cheek, heard her quietly whispered words of love. Anxious to feel the soft satin of her delicate skin next to his body, he took the stairs two at a time, shouldering his way into the bedroom and slamming the door shut with his foot. He set Beth gently on her feet by the bed, exhorting her not to move while he closed the heavy chocolate velvet drapes and put the lights on a dimmed setting.

Beth stood where he'd left her, hands clasped in front of her, looking sexier than ever in black jeans that hugged her hips and a scarlet shirt with long sleeves. The fit was snug over her breasts and she'd left enough buttons undone to display her cleavage. The stupidity of the male sex dumbfounded him sometimes—he still hadn't worked out how she'd remained unattached so far, but he thanked heaven that she had.

He went to her slowly, savouring the anticipation. First, he released the silken sheen of her hair from the ponytail, threading his fingers through it to encourage the waves to find freedom. Her hair was only one of so many things he adored about her. No, he just adored her... completely... endlessly... hopelessly.

Then he watched her face as he let his palm almost touch her cheek, saw how she wanted to turn that cheek to seek his caress. The connection binding them together was a shining thread that ran between them and around them, one that Alex knew could never be cut. He'd love this woman till the day he died and beyond.

He stepped closer, framed Beth's face between his palms and tilted her head to receive his kiss. Her hands rested briefly at his waist, then went around him, in an embrace so tight that he could feel the hard peaks of her nipples through two layers of fabric.

Beth loved this man so much that she wanted her body to merge and become one with his. Perhaps that way, she could keep him safe.

She couldn't ignore the quiet desperation lurking within her heart, now that she knew there was someone out there, wanting to... what? Kill Alex? Kidnap him? She pushed the thoughts away; the trouble was, they pushed right back. Her mind ached from all the worry as much as her heart did.

"What are you thinking, Beth?" He lifted her chin to look into her eyes. "Tell me."

"I want it to be over," she said simply. "I want him to leave us alone—leave you alone. You don't deserve this."

"I don't deserve you." The intensity of the look in his dark eyes imprisoned her breath, froze it in her lungs.

"Tough. You're stuck with me, Lombard." She looked at his features, committing the tiniest details to memory, like the crinkles at the corners of his eyes that became more pronounced when he smiled, and the little furrow between his eyebrows that deepened when he frowned. "Alex, I belong here, with you... to you. I couldn't imagine being anywhere else with anyone else."

She glanced towards the bed. "In this room, you're my Dom, you own me, and I wouldn't have it any other way. Outside this room, you're the man I love and want to be with for the rest of my life. 'Deserving' doesn't come into it in either case." She moistened suddenly dry lips, wondering how he would react to what was going through her mind. She doubted he'd object.

"Sir," she chose the word carefully, "please may I undress you?"

The darkness in his eyes disappeared, replaced by the hot flame of need and complete understanding of her need for formality. "My sweet sub may do whatever she desires with me."

"Thank you, Sir."

She began with his shirt—slowly, taking her time, pressing a tender kiss to his skin for each button that she unfastened. When the garment was hanging open, she pushed it back, exposing the masculine contours of his impressive chest. Closing her eyes, she nuzzled into him, inhaling the clean, warm, male scent of him. She didn't have to see him to know he was perfect. Fierce emotion made her eyes sting with unshed tears—she'd protect this man with her life if she had to.

With the lightest touch she explored the textures of his body, the crisp hair adorning his pectorals, the smooth skin in the area of his collarbone, the brown nipples, small and already hard. When her tongue flicked over the sensitive flesh, his body jerked in reaction. He grunted but said nothing.

Beth suckled hungrily on each nipple, aware of two things—the growing wetness of her pussy and the extraordinary self-control of the man she loved. The only betraying sign of how the onslaught of her mouth was affecting him was the way his fists clenched and unclenched at his sides.

It was quite simple really, she thought with a secretive smile—she hungered for everything about this man. The way he smelled, so masculine, appealed to her most basic feminine desires, as did his intellect, his strength of mind and character, his powerful body and his dark, brooding good looks. And, above all, his courage... such a fundamental part of him.

She moved behind him, her left hand trailing across his

stomach with its clearly defined abs. The shirt was starting to annoy her—it had to go, so she grasped the collar with both hands and drew it down his back and arms, tossing it aside with impatience.

Her heart constricted for a moment at the sight of the scars on his back and what they represented—especially now that she knew the whole story, that he'd got them while trying to save the life of one of his men, without a thought for his own safety.

She put her arms around his waist, rested her head against his back for a few moments—not liking the way he flinched at the first contact, but feeling some relief when he visibly relaxed. He unwound some more when she began to litter his scars with light, loving kisses, his head dropping to assume an almost submissive posture.

"Master." Though she'd thought it many times, this was the first time she'd called him by that title. "I love you so much it hurts," she whispered, her voice aching with honesty. "You're beautiful. I want you every moment of every day, and every moment away from you is a moment I hate, because I'll never get it back. All I have to do is look at you, think about you, and I want you. No, don't move, please," she requested, when he would have turned around.

"This time is for you, Sir. Please let me please you."

CHAPTER THIRTEEN

"Yes, Mistress."

Beth froze. Her ears were playing tricks on her, surely? If those two words were what she thought she'd heard... she didn't even want to *think* of what it might mean. No, it had to be a mistake.

"Alex?" The question was in her voice.

He continued to look straight ahead, almost as if he were standing to attention. "I love you, Beth. You're the only woman I could ever trust enough for this. You're my future—I need you to help me banish the past."

The cryptic statement confused her even more. What was it about his past that had such a terrifying hold on him? Beth wished she understood. She couldn't even begin to guess how she could possibly help him. "How? How do I help you, Alex? Please, tell me."

"Something happened." His voice was as haunted as his face. "I can't... I can't tell you. I need you to do something for me."

"What? You know I'll do anything for you, Alex—just tell me what I need to do."

"Make me your slave."

A horrible coldness descended on her. Beth shook her head slowly, unable to take in the enormity of the request. He'd made it in such a matter-of-fact manner, which made it all the more unbelievable. He'd just turned her world upside down.

"Alex... I can't. *You* can't. I have no clue where to start. I don't have your training. I'd have no idea what I was doing. What if I hurt you?"

"You won't, Mistress."

How she wished he'd stop calling her that. "Alex, you don't mean this—you can't! It's not what you are!"

His shoulders lifted on a slow, deep breath. "It's what I need, Mistress." The normally even timbre of his voice was hoarse, as if he were facing some awful, terrible truth about himself, something he could no longer deny. "You won't hurt me—not in any way I don't need. Whatever you do to me, I can take it. But it has to be you."

"Then tell me why! Help me to understand! For God's sake, help me to understand... Give me that at least, Alex."

At that he turned and looked briefly into her eyes with an expression of such pain that her breath caught in her throat. She watched him kneel in front of her, head bowed, hands resting palms uppermost on his thighs. "I need to forget, Mistress," he said quietly. "Please. Help me to forget."

Forget what?

In that instant, her heart broke for him. Beth had seen the physical reminders of what he'd endured and thought she had an idea of what it had cost him mentally. She now realised that in the latter case, she had no idea at all. The saying went *"still waters run deep."* Alex, who was always so calm and in control, ran very deep. For a moment she faltered, unsure that she would be able to give him what he needed—in the next moment she knew that, no matter what it cost her, she could do nothing else.

Still slightly hesitant, she reached out, wondering if she should touch him, try to reassure him. When her hand rested lightly on his shoulder, she felt the way he shuddered, a quiver of movement that made everything shift into focus, even if she still didn't fully understand what was going on.

"Then you will remember that I am your Mistress." She tried to inject a confidence she didn't feel into her voice—her mouth was saying things her mind refused to take responsibility for. "You will refer to me as such until you are permitted to do otherwise. While you're my slave, you will keep your eyes lowered, unless I allow you to do otherwise. Do you understand?"

The change that overcame Alex was subtle but remarkable. The lost soul became the focused man once more, but there was a subtle difference. That difference was the shift of power... from him... to her.

"Yes, Mistress."

"And your safe word is garnet. It will bring a complete halt to whatever is going on. Do you understand?"

"Yes, Mistress."

"Tell me your safe word."

"Garnet, Mistress."

A strange feeling writhed in her belly, like nothing she'd ever felt before. Hearing Alex call her by that title was starting to turn her on in a completely different way, and she wasn't sure she should like it.

On the positive side, though, she was also gaining an awareness of the enormous weight of responsibility carried by every Dominant and a clearer understanding of the dynamic between them... and why Doms held such great respect for their subs. Alex obeyed instantly when she told him to remove his boots and socks; as he stood there wearing just the jeans, with his torso and feet bare, hers to do with as she wished, Beth thought she'd never seen him looking so fucking gorgeous. Alpha male through and through—and all hers.

"Hands at your sides, please, Alex."

A powerful, heady sense of control flared inside Beth. To have Alex, a magnificent male animal by anyone's standards, obey her without question was arousing her like she'd never imagined possible. The sense of power was like a drug, rolling through her bloodstream and infecting her with a compulsion to carry on having him do her bidding.

What she also recognised, though, and with a profound sense of humility, was the honour Alex had bestowed upon her by giving her such a special gift. It was a gift that she would never abuse, no matter how addictive she found being in control to be.

Finding a little peace with those thoughts, Beth turned her concentration back to the reality before her. Hunger roared—she hungered to possess this wonderful, beautiful man, who stood so calmly, his back straight, his eyes lowered in respect, and that chest that almost made her howl in needy arousal rising and falling with each deep, measured breath. Strength and energy radiated from him, all held in check, ready to be released at her command alone.

She placed her left forefinger on his breastbone, over his heart, with only the nail making contact with his skin. To his credit, he didn't move a muscle as she began to draw a line straight down the centre of his chest to his abs. That finger dipped briefly into his navel, a small gesture but one evocative of ownership, then it continued on its way, to the fastening of his jeans. His erection beneath the zip was unmistakable; when she laid her hand over the fabric, Beth swore she could feel its heat burning her skin.

"You want to come, don't you, Alex." It was a statement, not a question.

"Only when it pleases you to permit it, Mistress."

It pleased her to see and touch her property without the hindrance of his clothing. As she anticipated, he'd gone commando, and as she peeled away the faded denim, his erection sprang free, precum leaking from the slit. She could taste the glistening drop already, the memory of the subtly salty, undoubtedly masculine flavour of him drawing the tip of her tongue to lick her lips, even as her desire for him soaked her pussy.

Finding her focus again, she continued to push the worn jeans down his legs, her admiration for their muscular strength and stillness ever-present. When the fabric bunched at his ankles he lifted each foot in turn, so that she could remove the garment completely.

In this position, his cock was at eye level, standing to attention and presenting the temptation for her to lick the underside from root to tip. He was a work of art in mortal flesh, a living statue straight from the Renaissance. Beth leaned in and inhaled the clean, musky scent of him. *Oh, so tempting.* She could resist him no longer.

He tasted as divine as she knew he would, and when she heard the low, guttural growl of arousal, saw the hands form into fists again, Beth let her mouth curve into the satisfied smile of a successful apex predator. For that moment she was in familiar territory—the unfamiliar still awaited her.

She stood up and took a step back. What was she going to do with him? She'd never had reason to look at the Dominant side of the equation, not for real—it had only been for research and that wouldn't work here. To give Alex what he needed, to give him the full attention he deserved, the experience he needed, she had to get into the Dominant mind-set, behave how an experienced Top would behave.

"Lie down, Alex."

Again he obeyed immediately. In the absence of further clarification he lay on his back, his arms at his sides, hands palm-down on the bed, legs straight with feet about eighteen inches apart.

Think, Beth!

Her roving gaze fell on the toy box. Alex had moved some of the toys from the playroom into the bedroom—perhaps she'd find her inspiration in there. The flogger was out, as were the other impact toys—that was just plain wrong, and not only that, she hadn't been trained in the use of such implements. In spite of what Alex had said, she was still fearful of doing something wrong.

A quick rummage revealed wrist and ankle cuffs—they would do to start with. To go with the ankle restraints there was an adjustable spreader bar. That would put him in an open, vulnerable position, enabling her to make the most of the control she had over him. What to do with his arms, though?

Beth didn't want him spread-eagled, displayed as a living adaptation of da Vinci's Vitruvian Man. Legs yes, but she had a different vision for his arms. Another search of the box uncovered a shorter spreader bar—using that with the wrist cuffs, his arms would be stretched more vertically than horizontally. If she could just work out a way to anchor the bars in place...

A hot image flashed across her imagination. *Oh yes*. She found exactly what she needed, and a few moments later, Alex was in exactly the position she'd imagined, with pillows and cushions supporting his body where necessary.

"Are you all right?" she asked, checking his bonds as he'd checked hers so many times before. "Does anything hurt? Tell me if it does, now or at any time."

Until she asked those questions, her voice tender with concern, his control had been absolute. At that point, his eyes flicked over her face, briefly making contact with hers, and what she saw there could only be pure devotion. Then the contact ended and he averted his gaze.

"Forgive me, Mistress. I'm all right."

Still fully dressed, apart from having kicked off her boots, Beth sat on the bed by his legs. She felt his thigh muscle tense under her hand as she started a slow, deliberate, tactile exploration of his glorious nudity. His skin was hot beneath her touch, the texture of it so different from her own. The feel of it reminded her of all the ways they differed, man versus woman, and how those differences were like the opposite poles of a magnet, obeying laws of attraction that were as old as the universe itself.

He was exquisite, the most wonderful part of her life. That life could go on without him, but it would be a vast emptiness, a mere existence, not a real life at all. She hadn't even known that a part of her was missing until Alex had removed the boundary between them and slotted into that space as if it had been tailored to fit him.

"So, my love," she began, aware that she was trying to buy time to organise her thoughts and develop some sort of plan, "you said you need to submit to me. What can I give you that will satisfy that need?"

He swallowed hard; his Adam's apple bobbed visibly.

"I'm yours, Mistress. Now. Forever. Please… use me for your pleasure."

It gave her pleasure simply to look at him, to gorge her eyes on the magnificent male before her. For that he didn't need to be restrained—not for her benefit, at any rate, but this wasn't about her. It was about him and what he needed. The trust he'd placed in her was humbling.

She went to kiss his mouth, but stopped halfway to pause a moment or two. As gracefully as she could, she caged his body beneath hers, one hand on either side of his head, arms braced for support, while her knees were on either side of his hips.

From that position she could look down on him, her gaze burning with longing and desire as she slowly lowered her head to claim his mouth. When she caught his lower lip between her teeth and applied the same gentle suction as she had to his nipples, his suppressed moan of arousal thrilled her.

With her confidence bolstered a little, she invaded his mouth with her tongue, coaxing a response from every corner of his soul, light and dark. He began to make demands of his own, so she drew back, turning her attention to his jawline and throat, pressing a trail of hot, wet kisses towards his chest.

When she arrived at her destination, the ridges of muscle were too much of a temptation. With the tip of her tongue, she began to trace the lines. He tasted of salt and sweat, and delicious, virile male, and when she'd worked her way down to his navel, she licked a direct line straight up the centre of his body, to devour his mouth once more with a punishing kiss.

"Now… what of your pleasure, Alex?"

An innocuous-enough question, but when she watched the droplet of moisture trickle from the corner of his eye, she wished she hadn't asked it. Damn it, what was going on in his mind? The cause still baffled her, but its impact was unquestionable. "It's all right, my love—you're safe here, with me. Nothing can hurt you here."

With great calmness and sense of purpose, she leaned down and kissed his lips again. She heard the clink of chains as he moved, kissing her back.

"No, Mistress." His voice was a harsh whisper. "Hurt me. Please, I need you to hurt me. Take away the pain."

His hoarse plea sent her eyes back to his beloved face, even as she drew back, almost recoiling in horror at what he'd said.

She'd never seen such haunted bleakness before. Wherever he was, it wasn't here, it wasn't now—he was drowning in some past horror, something so terrible that it was overwhelming him and consuming him. Even as she watched, he sank deeper into its evil embrace, retreating further and further away from her.

Panic rose up and would have choked her, but Beth fought it down. Now was not the time for that—she need-ed to pull Alex back, get him out of the claws of whatever held him in a vise-like grip.

"Alex!"

There was a flicker of response at the sound of his

name; it gave Beth hope that he might not be lost to whatever was happening in his mind. Over and over, she said his name, shouted it, whispered it—she cajoled him, she remonstrated with him, she seduced him, and in between using his name as if it were a talisman, she told him she loved him.

And gradually, she watched him come back to her. Their eyes connected again, and a moment later his eyelids descended, as if he just couldn't face her.

His respiration, calming now, was still shallow. Beth stroked his hair back from his face. She wanted to run away from this with every atom of her being, but she couldn't let him down like that. What was she to do?

Beth knew she was avoiding the issue—he'd already told her.

He needed pain. And that meant she had to hurt him. *God help me.*

Unless somehow, she could distract him. Bracing her hands on his ribcage, she positioned herself precisely over his cock, and then lowered herself so that the rough material of her jeans came into contact with his sensitive, stimulated flesh. As his hips rose restlessly to meet her, a low moan escaped him.

"Remember your safe word, Alex, and use it if you want this to stop." She began to move, a gentle riding motion that would rub his dick and increase his arousal—an arousal she was determined should not culminate in orgasm just yet.

She felt him straining beneath her, hips rising in a

fruitless attempt to put his shaft inside her. Acting purely on instinct, she pinched and twisted his nipples to get his attention.

"Oh no, Alex, you're not getting away with that." Her voice was stern. "You're not putting *that* anywhere near me, nor are you allowed to come. Not yet."

She unfastened her shirt, opening it up to show him that she was naked beneath it, relishing the fire that fought the haunted look in his eyes. He wanted her as much as she wanted him.

Eager to feast on the man beneath her, she lay down on top of him, loving the heat of his skin next to hers. Wanting him was like a fever, burning her up—she could easily eat him alive. Her mouth branded him everywhere—everywhere except on his mouth, knowing as she did just how much he wanted that connection again. His erection was still pushing against her pussy, even though it remained shielded by her clothing.

Beth reached for his hands, twining her fingers with his, in full knowledge that the action would offer her breasts to his mouth. As her slave, he would not be allowed to draw her nipple into his mouth—she ordered him to resist the temptation.

"What do you want, Alex?" she breathed close to his cheek. "What do you need?"

The expressions that crossed his handsome face made her heart ache for him. "You, Mistress," he admitted. "I need you."

Beth needed him too. "In what way?"

Tears filled her eyes at the pain that had him turning away from her. No, not pain—torment. That was it—enough was enough. She couldn't let his anguish go on. She couldn't hurt him. She just couldn't. Enjoying the sense of control was one thing, but that wasn't her, not really. She just wanted to love him. There had to be another way for Alex to deal with this demon that rode him so hard.

"Garnet." She would say the word, even if he would not. "I can't—"

"No!" His eyes, the look in them almost wild, flashed back to her.

"I can't do this to you, Alex!" She was desperate to release him from his bonds.

"Beth, please—take it back! Take it back. You have to! *Take it back!*"

He was clearly as desperate to keep this going as she was to end it. She searched his face, and all she could see was distress and need. Knowing the level of self-control Alex habitually exhibited, something told her that what she saw was only the tip of the iceberg. She hated herself for what she was about to say, but he'd given her no choice—it was what he needed.

"I take it back."

Her head dropped beside his; plunged into misery, she was barely aware of him moving his head to rest his cheek against hers.

"Thank you, Mistress."

Beth took a deep breath, steeling herself for whatever

lay ahead. Whatever it was, however he wanted her to hurt him, it was something the man she loved needed so much that it drove him to go against everything that he was. She didn't want to think what could wield that kind of power over such a dominant man—it had to be truly terrible.

"Tell me exactly what you need, Alex." If he'd do that, she could do just enough to get him through this.

"Please, Mistress, I need you to fuck me."

Now she really did want to run away. Her eyes wet with tears, Beth turned her head away so that he couldn't see. This was a descent into hell itself. He'd managed to avoid inflicting any real pain, but this... Her luck had just run out.

She wanted to question his assertion, to make him stop and think, but her instincts were telling her that he'd thought about this more than once and now something had triggered a need to turn thought into reality.

Her fingers still entwined with his, she tightened her grip on his hands, teeth biting down on her lower lip to stop the tears from flowing. She had to be strong... for him.

"Please, Mistress... Beth. I need this. It has to be you."

He trusts you to do it for him. Don't let him down.

She let go of his hands and straightened up. Looking down at him, the entreaty in his eyes, the love she felt for him reminded her that it was a living thing inside her, a part of her that would never leave, no matter what. With great tenderness, she framed his face with her hands and kissed his mouth. "I'll need you to turn over."

Beth adjusted her Dom's bonds so that he could lie face-down, with pillows to make him both comfortable and more accessible. Regardless of the current situation, he was still in charge in the bedroom, and this was something he had asked her to do for him. She was aware of his eyes on her as she removed her clothing.

"Beth... my beautiful Mistress. You'll find what you need in the bottom drawer over there."

Her hands shook as she opened the drawer; there, brand new, still in its packaging, was a strap-on dildo. She was right. He had thought about this more than once, and had prepared for it. Beth's hand tightened around the toy—such an innocent word for something so hateful. She hated that Alex had prepared for this—she hated knowing that it was premeditated and now inevitable.

For Alex. The man I love.

Feeling sick, she buckled it in place, her vaginal muscles clenching around the shorter, thicker end that was supposed to be there for her pleasure. *A means to an end.* She silently recited the phrase over and over, brainwashing herself into accepting this for what it was.

A means to an end.

She slathered the longer, narrower protrusion with lube.

Alex was lying there so calmly, waiting for her to prepare him. She joined him on the bed—the first thing she was going to do was kiss him. For the sake of her own sanity, she had to believe that she was doing this for love.

"Alex, I want you to know how much I love you. You mean everything to me. Try to relax—I don't want to hurt you."

Alex could never tell Beth why he needed to step out of reality and into the fantasy where he was her slave. Not all of it, anyway. She helped him to sleep at night, but she could never know why he needed her to do this for him. Cam knew the full story behind it, as did the medics who'd treated his body after the kidnapping and the counsellor with whom he'd had no patience, but no one else. *No. One. Else.* With Beth in his bed, he'd been able to cope with the memories, but now he needed her to exorcise them completely.

If he was going to face death, he needed closure; he needed to replace that memory with another, one where the act was carried out with love, not hatred. He could only replace it with Beth beside him—there was no one else he could ever have trusted with this.

He hadn't intended this to happen when he'd brought her to their bedroom—he'd just wanted to be with her. But then, when she'd kissed his back, kissed scars left by the wounds that had nothing to do with the IED incident, a switch was flipped in his mind—he needed Beth to take the memories away for good. It seemed as if he'd always known that one day he'd ask this of her, and that day had finally arrived.

He watched her come closer. The pain and desolation in her eyes were like razor-sharp knives driving through his heart. The knowledge that she was doing this—doing it for him—was the broadsword among them. It told him—as if he needed telling—just how deep her feelings for him ran.

He was a bastard for doing this to her but the need that drove him to do it was too strong. As well as closure, he was convinced this could let him be the man he'd once been. The man he needed to be for her.

Her hand was gentle on his upper arm, stroking down to his wrist. "Will you at least let me remove these?" She rested her hand on the cuff.

He shook his head. Restraints were an integral part of the images that haunted his mind—they had to be there.

Her sense of resignation hit him like the shockwave from a nuclear blast.

Beth knelt beside him. She would have no way of knowing the reason for this, but in her eyes he saw the recognition that this wasn't some random impulse. He could only hope that it was enough for her to do what was needed.

Her hand was gentle on his hair, the back of his head, and at that simple contact, he felt himself calm down. Her hands moved to his shoulders and back, long caresses preceding the sweet, gentle kisses she dropped like blessings along his spine—blessings that touched the soul she'd given back to him and gave him hope for a future he'd never dared dream of.

If he survived…

Alex closed his eyes, recalling the destructive, harrowing memory of what was, without doubt, a visit to a version of hell so terrible no one could imagine it. He no longer felt Egyptian cotton under his cheek, but dirt and gravel; it wasn't Beth's subtle perfume he could smell, but the foul stench of stale sweat, urine and other human detritus. He was no longer lying on his bed at home, but shackled to stakes driven in the earth floor, stripped of his clothing, his dignity, his humanity, choking on the gag they'd stuffed into his mouth, listening to what his captors—who had no idea he could speak their language—were planning to do to him. He remembered his fight not to be sick, the struggle against the rising tide of nausea, the denial that screamed inside his head even as the rutting began.

The mental walls went up again, divorcing his mind, his heart and his soul from what was happening to his body. His breathing became shallow and rapid as the ruined walls of that godforsaken cellar in the abandoned house loomed up around him, creating that filthy, claustrophobic prison, where rough hands had tried and failed to shatter his will. It had taken every ounce of strength he possessed to hold on to his sanity—even now, it still terrified him to think of how close they'd come to breaking him, with the pain, the humiliation... and the act that, even now, even as only a memory, could still make him go cold with fear.

But no more. It was time—finally—to annihilate the nightmares. They had no place in his life with Beth. He was in his own home, lying on the big bed he shared with the woman he loved. It was her hands touching him, touching him so gently, with love and care; her warm, feminine perfume was wrapping itself around him; he lay on sheets that were clean and white... pure, just like her. Submitting to the act carried out with love was his choice—it wasn't being forced on him.

"Please, Alex, don't make me do this to you."

She was begging. In that moment, he hated himself for asking this of her, but she was the only one who could do it. He needed her love. "Mistress, I need you to do this. Please... help me."

He felt her lips on the back of his hand, then the gentle splash of her tears. She was going to run, his greatest fear, but then he felt her hands again, her touch tender as she stroked his back, working her way down from his shoulders. Heard her say over and over again how much she loved him.

He couldn't stop himself from tensing when she reached his hips, knew that Beth had felt that reaction when she paused and waited for a moment, her hands remaining in contact. Then she continued.

Bile burned his throat, a sickening wave of fire that brought with it the hellish visions of that prison in the desert, the torture that had been inflicted upon him and the unending pain and humiliation that followed. He felt it all again, but as his fist clenched he took hold of those memories and began to destroy them, one by stinking one.

No more.

No.

More.

CHAPTER FOURTEEN

Beth was crying. Her tears were silent, rolling freely down her pale cheeks. She could barely see to squeeze the lube onto her palm.

She wanted to stop, wanted it so much that it was tearing her up inside, but this wasn't about her, it was about him, the man lying so trustingly in front of her. She had to do it for him. She didn't understand what was going on, couldn't even begin to imagine what it was all about, but she knew one thing for certain—it was about *something*.

He has a reason. He has to have a reason.

"I'm sorry."

She barely whispered the words, knowing that even if he heard them, he wouldn't want them. Her soul, on the other hand, needed them. They were her salvation.

Her heart splintered when she heard his agonised moan at the first touch of her lube-coated finger to his anus, saw the way his body reacted. She felt sick to her stomach at the thought of what he must have been through, for him to react like that. His back arched for a moment, and then he was pushing against her. Beth applied more gel, and then knelt between his long, muscular legs.

Her resolution almost failed at the first hint of resistance. Although she'd applied lube to her fingers and his anus, the sphincter tightened defensively, protecting that most private part of his precious body. Not knowing what to do, she gently stroked the rosette, letting her fingertip linger over the centre, applying just a little more pressure there, to encourage the relaxation this would need.

His whole body was shaking. She reached towards his broad back, splayed her hand over as much of it as she could, hoping her touch would reassure and calm him.

He grabbed handfuls of the bed linen. From the way he was pulling at it, he wasn't putting them both through this for pleasure. So why, then? She looked at his face turned towards her, trying to get some idea of what was going through his mind, only for it to get a thousand times worse when she saw tears clinging to his eyelashes, the distant look in his captivating eyes once more.

He'd given her the power, but never in her life had Beth felt so powerless. Every cell in her body screamed to release him and hold him to her body, to give him the comfort that would take away whatever was causing his pain, but instead she concentrated on doing what he asked. The sooner it was done, the sooner this agony would end.

Her fingers began to work in earnest, her touch more insistent now. She murmured comforting words and felt him relax in response.

"Please, Mistress... may I ask you to carry on talking to me?"

For a moment, Beth's mind clutched at fresh air. She was struggling to find more meaningful words that would release him from whatever dreadful place was holding him when a curious calm descended over her. It really was simple. All she needed to do was enfold him in her love, wrap it around him until that was all he could think of.

"Alex, you're the only man I have ever taken into my heart and to the depths of my soul. What I do now is done out of the love I have for you." She stroked his back, crooning softly to calm him. "For this moment, you're my sub, Alex—much loved, much cherished, much adored."

Beth eased herself a little closer, working her fingers a little more, and knew a moment of alarm when she heard another low moan drift over the threshold of his lips. She realised then that it was a moan of acceptance as he relaxed into the sensation. Her teeth clamped down on her lower lip; the slight sting of pain served to remind her that the longing she felt had no place here. Even so, she allowed her hand to trail down his back to his behind, the muscles of a man in his prime thrillingly hard beneath her touch. In that instant, her inhibitions melted away.

"Do you know how beautiful you are, Alex? How desirable? I can't imagine having a day in my life when I don't want you. And I want you so very, very much. I didn't realise it, but it's been that way for all the time I've known you, right from the day I first met you. I think that's why I've never been involved, never wanted to be involved, with any other man since the day we met."

Beth didn't know if she was doing right or wrong, but her instincts were screaming at her to show Alex how close to him she wanted to be. She leaned forward and began to slide the lubricated dildo between the cheeks of his backside. The motion seemed to relax him even further, and then, in one smooth movement, she eased the tip into place and began to rock her hips against him.

"You're mine, Alex," she whispered against his back. "I own you, you belong to me. While there's breath in my body, no one else will have you."

"Yes, Mistress. I belong to you."

Something wonderful, something awe-inspiring, overwhelmed Beth in that instant—she felt Alex surrender to her, wholly and completely, giving everything that he was to her. In return, she could do nothing other than give him what he so craved. How she adored this gorgeous, wonderful man, for his strength, his integrity, all the qualities that made him the person he was.

She felt the agony of wanting that vibrated through him. Instinct took over, guiding her movements as she made love to Alex in a way she'd never made love to any other man. Somehow she managed to reach underneath him and found his cock, rock hard under his taut belly, steel sheathed in velvet, leaving her with no illusions about how aroused he was.

The heels of his hands pressed against the bed, forcing his upper body upright. Beth knew a moment's alarm, and then remembered that she was able to make him relax. She laid a gentle hand on his shoulder, the soothing touch enough to persuade him to resume his position.

Beth shifted slightly. With a little more room for manoeuvre, she was able to reach his balls, and as she thrust the dildo into him she squeezed, just enough to give him a bite of the pain he'd asked her for. Each small grunt of discomfort was like a poison dart through her heart—it was only the three words she kept reciting that enabled her to carry on.

He needs this.

And then she heard him, repeating one word over and over again, so quiet that at first she thought it was her imagination. She never would have guessed that the word "yes" could bring so much relief, but it lasted mere moments—with each repetition she sensed him going further away from her again. He was sinking into the world inside his mind, the world that had made him need this... this punishment. And with every passing second, Beth felt like she was losing his soul.

"Come back to me, Alex," she whispered, although she doubted he'd hear her. "Please come back."

His eyes snapped open. Beth gasped. He was back, and there was a fire in his eyes that scorched right through her.

"Please, Mistress—I need to come. May I come?"

His voice was strained with the effort of control. It was tempting to deny him his release, but she couldn't. She could deny this man nothing, especially if it meant that he could finally attain the peace he needed—the peace he deserved. If it meant that this would be over. "You may, Alex."

She held him through the most violent orgasm she had ever witnessed and when it was done, she flung the strap-on away from both of them and almost tore the bonds from his wrists and ankles, pushing the shackles, bars and chains away from him as if they were toxic. Her eyes stung with unshed tears when she moved beside him, wrapping her arms around him to pull him close.

He was saying something. Beth froze, struggling to hear what it was, and then she realised—he was thanking her.

When she felt his tears on her skin, she came crashing back down to earth. Dear God, what had she done?

"It's all right, Alex, I've got you," she comforted him, pushing aside the pain of her reaction. "It's over now. It's done. You're safe with me. I'll only be a moment."

She returned from the playroom with a bottle of water, wet wipes and soft, warm towels. With great care, she cleansed his body, her touch as gentle as she could make it. He didn't move at all, just let her do what she needed to do. At first, she thought he was mentally distancing himself again… until she saw that his attention was quietly focused on her. There was a calmness about him too, almost as if he'd come to the end of a long battle and finally won. When the job was done, she made him drink the water before lying down beside him, taking him in her arms again and pulling the blankets over both of them.

Beth waited until he fell asleep. Once she was sure that he wouldn't wake, she very carefully moved away from him and tucked the blankets around him again, all the while hating herself for what she'd done to him. She should have had more strength. She should have refused to do what he asked. She should have found a way to help him that didn't include… that.

How could she have done it to the man she professed to love? How on earth was she going to face him after that?

How could she face herself?

Alex knew, before he even opened his eyes, that Beth was gone. He knew because of the aching void in his heart. The emptiness of the bed echoed the emptiness in his soul.

He watched his hand move to the place where she should have been, watched the fingers clench the sheet. His selfishness had driven her away. He should never have given in to his weakness.

He'd lived with it for more than ten years, for Christ's sake. He could have lived with it for ten more—twenty more, for the rest of his life, if it meant keeping hold of Beth. Was trying to banish the hell that crouched like a malevolent demon at the back of his mind worth putting her through all of that?

She must have put the blankets over him before she left, but he had no way of knowing whether that was five minutes or an hour ago. It was dark outside, which told him precisely nothing. He needed to find Beth, but first he needed to make himself fit to find her.

Ten minutes later, cleaned up and dressed casually in jeans and a polo shirt, Alex went in search of his woman. The house was eerily quiet, and not knowing Beth's location was intensifying the anxiety gnawing at him.

He found her in the family room, curled up in an armchair, reading a book in the light cast by the freestanding lamp. The curtains were closed, adding to the air of cosy comfort. For a few moments, Alex just stood quietly in the hall, looking at her, letting his gaze absorb every inch of the lovely picture she made. He could never get enough of her. Every beat of his heart was just for her. How beautiful she'd be if she were sitting there nursing their child.

"Beth."

She looked up at the sound of her name, her expression portraying neither love nor hate. She had, however, been crying. He'd done that to her. Christ, he was a selfish bastard. He opened his mouth to speak—and realised there was nothing he could say to her. He turned on his heel and strode off, determined to distance himself from Beth as much as he could until he found the words.

After making sure that Alex was warm and safe, Beth had tidied herself up, gone down to one of her favourite rooms in the house, and made herself comfortable with a book. She'd been pretending to read for the last couple of hours, unable to concentrate for thinking about Alex. She hadn't dared to return to the bedroom, for fear of finding him awake and not knowing what to say to him.

She had no way of knowing how long he'd been standing there watching her. When she looked up at him, he looked as if he was about to say something, but instead had just stalked away. In those brief seconds, she'd felt her heart leap at the sight of him, looking so strong and vital and devastatingly handsome—as if the events of a couple of hours ago had never happened. Then he was gone, and all she'd got from him was a sense of a barrier going up between them. She was torn between wanting to go after him and leaving him to find his own way back to her.

Why did relationships have to be so damn difficult?

The sound of the doorbell was a welcome distraction—she'd forgotten that Cam was coming back, and that she'd promised him a steak dinner. If Alex had gone off to lick his wounds somewhere, then it was up to her to play the gracious hostess in his absence. She smiled; with Cam, that wouldn't exactly be a chore.

"Hi, angel," he greeted her when she let him in and he went to plant a friendly kiss on her cheek. "You okay?"

"Of course I am," she responded, aware that her voice was strained and Cam was astute enough to know her affirmation for the lie it was. "Come on in. I'd tell you to make yourself at home, but you already do anyway." She smiled, finding a little comfort in the presence of the big blond Dom. At least there wouldn't be any awkward silences while he was around.

Alex reappeared a few minutes after his friend's arrival. Beth left the two men talking while she went to prepare dinner, finding the kitchen a sanctuary after such a difficult afternoon. She needed that more than she needed to hear what news Cam had brought with him.

Still mystified, she put her best effort into trying not to work out what was going through Alex's mind for him to have made her do that to him, but the hardest thing to try to blank out of her mind was his tears. When the memory surfaced—and it did, many times—she found herself crying for him. And she didn't even have the excuse of chopping onions to explain the watery eyes. She was just thankful there was no one there to whom she had to explain.

Dinner was civil enough, and afterwards all three of them adjourned to the family room. Beth made sure that she chose an armchair, rather than one of the sofas. She needed to keep her distance from Alex; from their expressions and the quick look they exchanged, it didn't go unnoticed by either of the men, though they said nothing.

Her contribution to the conversation was minimal, to say the least. Beth was painfully aware of Cam's attempts to include her, but in the end she decided that it wasn't fair on him. And not only that—she couldn't stand the strain of trying, and clearly failing, to appear as if everything were normal. At least that was something she could do something about.

"If you'll excuse me, I think I'll go to bed. I could do with an early night."

The two men watched Beth leave the room, and then Cam turned to his friend and said, with a distinctly unfriendly edge to his voice, "Okay, what have you done to her now?"

Alex's face betrayed nothing. "She's had a long day. She's tired."

"She was fine before I left. As soon as I got back, I could see the difference in her. She looks lost. Have you dumped her?"

Alex remained silent for a few moments. "I haven't dumped her," he stated quietly.

"Then what the fucking bloody hell have you done?"

Cam's hands formed into fists. He and Alex were old friends, in some ways closer than brothers, but he was ready to beat the crap out of the other man for what he'd done to hurt Beth, no matter what it was. "You made her do something she didn't want to do, didn't you? What did you do to her, for God's sake?"

Alex's silence spoke volumes. "Not to her." His voice was as bleak as his eyes. "I asked her to do it to me."

Cam swore viciously. "*Asked* implies that you gave her the opportunity to refuse. I'd stake everything I own that one way or another, you gave her no choice in the matter. Hell, she'd do anything for you anyway. So what the hell—" He broke off what he was about to say, closing his eyes as an answer—*the* answer—occurred to him, and when he spoke again his voice was a lot calmer. "Christ, Alex, I'm sorry—"

"Not as sorry as I am," the other man admitted quietly. "She's hurting and it's all my fault."

"I'm not going to ask exactly what went on, that's between the two of you, but did you at least tell her why?"

Alex's defences went up. "No," he said curtly. "How could I tell her about that?"

Cam took a deep breath. He hated talking about what happened to his friend, even though it was more than a decade after the event. He'd seen the results of what they'd done to Alex, supported him on the long walk to the helicopter that had taken him to the hospital, and had sat with him every day while he was treated for his appalling injuries.

Cam had also been there when Alex, physically healed, had stormed out of his first therapy session, swearing blind he'd never go back—and never had. Since then, Alex had largely avoided discussing that horrendous time in his life, apart from one unforgettably distressing night.

After a few whiskies too many, he'd told Cam what he thought he needed to drive the memories away. Cam had done his best to convince Alex of the lunacy of his idea. He had his own thoughts on the matter, mostly involving a return to the therapist, but it looked like Alex had put his ill-conceived plan into action.

"I can't tell you what to do, my friend, how to put this

right, but she needs to know. At some point, you're going to have to tell her the whole story. Right now, she's hurting and she's confused, even I can see that, just as I can see her need to understand what's going on with you. And she will understand."

"How can you know that?"

"Easily." Cam knew he was on firm ground with what he was about to say. "She loves you. And you know what? Because she loves you, she'll help you to forgive yourself, and that's what you need more than anything else, Alex. For what happened today and what happened back then.

"Now, I suggest you go to her, talk to her, and I'll clear off to bed. I'm bloody knackered."

Alex had his doubts. He even doubted that he'd find her in their bedroom, so he was dumbstruck when he opened the door to find not an empty room in darkness but a room with romantic, dimmed lighting... and a beautiful woman naked in bed.

She was lying on her side with her back to him. He couldn't tell whether she was asleep or not, but at least she was there. Between them was the tempting expanse where he normally slept at her side.

A heavy sigh lifted his shoulders. He'd asked way too much of a novice sub... the woman he loved. How could he possibly explain his reasons for asking her to be his Domme? And even if he could find the words, once he told her what happened to him she'd run, as far and as fast as she could, and he couldn't blame her one iota. He'd let himself be raped, and he was still screwed up mentally because of it.

How the hell could he tell Beth that? Alex didn't know what to do—a feeling he wasn't used to. He'd always been in control—always had to be. Even during the assault, when he'd lost control of what happened to his body, he'd held on and kept control of his mind. Now, he had no control—if he did, he'd know what to do, what to say… whatever it took to stop the woman who was his life walking away from him, as she surely would once she'd recovered from what he'd inflicted on her.

He was on the point of talking himself into moving to one of the spare rooms when she turned over, and reached towards the place where he should have been lying beside her. She gave no sign of being aware of his presence.

He owed her an explanation, but when it came to Beth, he was vulnerable. It would probably be best if he left her alone tonight and they talked in the morning—if he took his place beside her in bed, he'd want to make love to her.

Not sexually dominate her, but make love to her, and after what happened that afternoon, she'd have every right to refuse him. He turned to go.

"Aren't you coming to bed?"

Alex felt like putting his fist through the wall. The pain would help him to decline and get out of there before he hurt her again. He sure as hell couldn't look at her or he'd be lost. "I thought you'd prefer to be alone tonight."

"And that's why you're here now?"

"I wanted to make sure you were all right—I thought you were asleep."

"I was. I'm not now."

She wasn't making it easy, and he couldn't blame her. Cam was right—he really needed to talk to her, but he couldn't burden her with the mess he'd carried with him for so long. In spite of his friend's confidence in the matter, Alex couldn't help but believe that if Beth knew the truth, he'd lose her.

"I know there was a reason for this afternoon, Alex. If you won't or can't tell me that reason, then at least tell me if it worked. Or was it all for nothing?"

The pain in her quiet, calm, honest voice sliced right through his soul. An answer was the least he owed her, and there was something in her tone that hinted at an expectation of hearing the worst.

The memory of the time he'd endured in that hell was one he'd never willingly called up, yet it had dominated his nights for a long, long time. He braced himself for the impact, waited for the trickle of sweat down his spine, but it didn't come.

And the reason it didn't come was that, although he still had that memory, it no longer had the power to carve him up into tiny little pieces. Its prominence and power had been usurped by a new memory, of an act carried out with love by the woman he'd cherish and protect for the rest of his life. She was in his bed, waiting for him. He should be on his knees in front of her, not a million miles away from her.

"It wasn't for nothing, Beth. Please believe me."

Silence, but he still couldn't turn around. She didn't believe him.

"Does that mean you don't need me anymore?"

He heard the stifled tears in her voice. "Need you? Beth, I need you more than I need air to breathe."

Go to her!

I can't!

"I know I'm not being a very good sub tonight, Sir," she said, her voice hesitant, "but surely we can work out whatever it is that's keeping you over there and out of this bed?"

Alex looked over his shoulder and lost the last shred of willpower that he had. She was sitting up, the covers bunched around her waist, oblivious to her nudity. He took a couple of steps towards her, into the light.

"You are my perfect sub, Beth, never doubt that, but tonight, I don't want you as my sub—I want you as my lover. Will you let me be your lover tonight?"

Her answer was eloquent in its simplicity. She said nothing, just drew the covers aside and offered him her hand.

CHAPTER FIFTEEN

"There'll be a couple of happy campers out there the day after tomorrow," Cam announced over breakfast. "I had to send a couple of the guys out on protection detail at short notice, but I still have a couple of very willing volunteers."

"Volunteers? Okay, Cam, who have we got?" Alex asked. He knew a lot of the men employed by Spectrum Security, having worked alongside them while in the Special Forces.

"Dylan Baxter and Conor Devlin will—"

"Oh, Christ. Not Baxter and Devlin. Please tell me you're joking, Cam. Those two clowns are the worst double act on the planet!"

"But they are good at what they do—you know that as well as I do." Cam was struggling to suppress a grin at Alex's deadpan reaction. The other man had been their officer commanding back in the day... and knew *exactly* how good they were at their jobs.

"As I was saying… Bax and Conor will be joining us. I've told them to keep out of the way… unless there's trouble," Cam qualified, his mood suddenly turning grim. "I've also got Rob doing the grunt work, trying to track down Underwood before he can get here."

Alex nodded—how Cam had assigned his men was Cam's decision to make, not his, but Alex would have allocated the assignments in much the same way. All ex-Special Forces, like himself and Cam, they had their own areas of expertise. He sighed heavily. "Thanks, Cam—I owe you."

Cam shook his head dismissively. He was clearly a man with something on his mind, though, and Alex didn't have to wait long to find out what it was. "Where's Beth this morning? Things all right between you two now?"

A memory filled Alex with warmth, of the moment when he'd joined Beth in bed and kissed her. "She's still sleeping. We're working on it, Cam."

"Have you told her?"

Tension formed a boulder in Alex's stomach. That was the elephant in the room—invisible as far as Beth was concerned, but for him, it was the one thing he truly feared, because of the threat that, for her, it could be a deal-breaker. *Would* be a deal-breaker.

"Alex, tell her." He heard the other man's sigh. "You were the victim, remember?"

"Yeah." The word was almost a snarl. *Victim*. The word stuck in Alex's throat. He was a man, a Dom, and no one's victim, for God's sake. He should have fought back harder. If he'd—

"And if you had, they would have turned on the boy. That's what you were afraid of, remember?"

Alex hadn't even realised he'd given voice to the bitter recrimination that had been his daily mantra for years. "Don't make me out to be some self-sacrificing hero, Cam."

"Not self-sacrificing, but yes, you are a hero. Don't hate yourself for being one man in the face of insurmountable odds."

He was going to be sick, would have been sick if he'd touched any of the food on the plate in front of him. The "insurmountable odds" had taken him and the son of his client captive because he, Alex, had been arrogant enough to think that he could do the job of two men. With two of them, he was sure they'd have been able to take care of the four men who'd attacked them, but odds of four against one had been too much.

What followed had shown him what the bowels of hell looked like.

He glanced at his friend—from the look of him, he wasn't ready to drop the subject. "Not now, Cam," he said quietly. "I promised Beth breakfast in bed this morning. Can you amuse yourself for a while?"

Thankfully, Cam knew a hint when he got one. "You're a lucky bastard. Look after her, Alex."

"I intend to—if she'll let me."

"Okay, then. Since breakfast will keep the two of you

amused for the next few hours, I'll see you at lunch."

Alex saw his friend off; the other man had already said that he intended to reconnoitre the nearest villages, to see if any strangers had been spotted in the area. Alex knew that he might or might not be back for the midday meal, depending on how much success he had with his enquiries.

And there was also the lure of a fine pub lunch at the *Dog and Partridge* to factor into the equation.

Alex busied himself in the kitchen, whipping up breakfast for the sleeping beauty he'd reluctantly left an hour or so ago. If he closed his eyes, he could still feel the heat of her body next to his.

He checked the contents of the tray—juice, coffee with milk and sugar, toast, egg and bacon, and a selection of fresh fruit. There was only one thing missing, and he could fix that by vandalising the vase of fresh flowers in the hall on the way back to the bedroom. His mouth curved into a smile for the first time that morning; he was definitely getting soft in his old age.

Beth was still asleep when he arrived at the bedroom. He wasn't surprised; the sex had been incredible—no, *making love* had been incredible. He'd given her his body with love and tenderness, and she had given him the same. Leaving the tray to one side, he got down on one knee by the bed, intending to wake her gently, but she beat him to it. Her smile warmed him through, banishing the coldness that had settled around him while he'd been talking to Cam.

"Why didn't you wake me?"

Alex grinned, feeling like a complete idiot. *Again.* "We had a busy night, if you remember—"

"If I remember? The torture you inflict on me every morning in the gym is less demanding!" Beth gave a somewhat theatrical yawn.

A wicked thought popped into Alex's mind. He leaned forward and kissed her. "In that case, tomorrow morning I'll just have to raise the ante and *really* give you something to complain about!"

He wasn't surprised when she hit him.

"Seriously," he continued, "you do know that the workouts are just intended to increase your level of fitness and give you a cardio workout?"

"Hmm, I'll let you have that one." Then the look in her eyes changed, to something less frivolous that told him he wasn't about to get away with anything. "There's something different about you today, Alex. Why... Last night, why didn't you... we... You made love to me without the things we've done before. Why?"

He couldn't give her the full explanation, not yet, but he did owe her some sort of reassurance. "Your breakfast's getting cold. You eat—I'll talk."

Alex made himself comfortable beside her, careful to stretch out on top of the covers fully dressed, rather than doing what he wanted to do, which was strip off, get into bed beside her and make love all over again... all day. At times, Beth really was too much temptation for him to withstand.

"I guess… I am different, sweet. Or starting to change, at any rate. Starting to feel free of something from the past that's had a hold on me for a long time. Thanks to you."

"Then yesterday…?"

"Began that process, yes. Do you want all that toast?"

Beth considered slapping his hand; instead, she buttered a slice and held it up to his mouth. He took a bite, and then plucked it from her fingers.

She glanced at the tray on her lap. "I didn't thank you for this."

"That's all right—we'll negotiate later."

She didn't have to be a genius to work out what that meant. The wicked grin told Beth all she needed to know, that while her Dom might have taken a temporary leave of absence the previous night, he would be back, and soon.

"You said there was something in the past that's had a hold on you—is that what you're not going to tell me about?"

He glanced away from her; she sensed his defences going up. He clearly wasn't ready to go into that yet—if ever. She sighed. "When… If you're ever ready, I'm a good listener, you know, Alex."

"I know."

All right, so they couldn't talk about the past—that left the present and the future, and while she assumed Alex would soon resume his role as her Dom, she needed to be sure. "There is something I need to know," she began.

"Am I still your sub, Sir?"

He turned back to her at that, his face fierce with a sensual hunger that thrilled her to her toes. His mouth crushed hers in a killer of a kiss. "Always," he growled, nuzzling into her neck. "Think of this as a brief holiday. I've no intention of letting my sub off the hook."

Well, that was one thing settled. "Since I'm still your sub, it makes the question more pertinent… Sir. Why was last night so different?"

"Beth, you've given me so much: not only your submission, but your love, your friendship, and your support. Last night, I wanted to give something back to you."

And he had. His caring and tenderness had rocked her to the depths of her soul. Beth had felt wrapped in love from head to foot when his magnificent, powerful body had stretched out beside her. He'd touched her face with his fingertips, as if he were a blind man imprinting her upon his memory, and then his lips had made sweet contact with hers—not taking love and passion from her, but giving her spirit what it needed to soar into the heavens.

She'd felt loved and worshipped and adored, and because it was Alex, it had blown her mind. Afterwards, he'd gathered her close and held her while, overwhelmed by all that had passed between them, she gave in to long-overdue tears. They'd slept, and then he'd made love to her again, still so loving and gentle.

No wonder she'd needed to sleep later, and now Alex was making it really difficult for her to concentrate on anything. His lips were making her crazy with need and his hand was cupping her breast, so that his fingers could roll and pinch her nipple.

"Alex," she got out on a breathless whisper. "Sir, if you don't stop doing that right now, this tray's going to go everywhere."

She had a moment's peace while the tray, along with her half-eaten breakfast, was whisked out of harm's way, and then Alex was back. This time it was his mouth that fastened on to her nipple, snagging it between his teeth and drawing it deeply into his mouth.

God, she could hardly speak. The man was a menace. The way he was damn well dressed, too, in those close-fitting black jeans and a skin-tight white T-shirt, was a reminder, as if she needed one, of just how formidably strong he was. The way the short sleeves clung to his impressive biceps was wicked—he could tempt a saint into sin. Beth threw her head back against the pillows stacked behind her, grabbing the sheets with both hands, trying to stop her sanity spinning off into the farthest reaches of the universe.

Her grip on the sheets disappeared when he dragged the covers away from her body, exposing her to his heated gaze. His hand pushed her thighs apart and then covered her sex, the palm resting on her smooth mound while his fingers thrust into the wetness of her pussy.

Aroused beyond reason, Beth moaned breathlessly, her hips pushing against his hand while all the time he suck-led on her breasts, alternating between them and sending her spiralling out of control. Her Dom had returned, sooner than anticipated, and he was making it abundantly clear that he was back in the driving seat.

"Please, may I come, Master?"

He raised his head from her breast. "Not yet." His voice was thick with desire.

No, he couldn't be doing this. Through half-closed eyes, she watched him move down her body, push her legs further apart, and then settle between her thighs. The next thing she felt was the swipe of his tongue over her labia, his thumbs pulling the folds apart, and then he was suckling on her clit the way he had her nipples, drawing it into his mouth, flicking his tongue over it, arousing her even more. What started off as a moan became a long, drawn-out wail.

There were no bonds holding her in place, no floggers or paddles there with the threat to redden her rear; her Dom held her where he wanted her by the force of his will alone. Her back arched away from the pillows, automatically forcing her hips into the bed and her pussy away from his devouring mouth.

Beth could do nothing to resist when he pulled her towards him, laying her flat on the bed. She heard a zip and then Alex was over her, his weight all on his muscular arms as his cock plunged into her.

God, he was so big, long and thick. Her pussy wanted to clench around him, to slow down the deep thrusts. His jeans were rough against her thighs, abrading the sensitive skin, making her spread her legs even wider, offering her pussy up to him.

Her orgasm was unbearably close. She begged again for permission to come, but the only response she received was to have her Master thrust more deeply into her. She didn't even realise that tears of pure, unadulterated, sensual ecstasy were rolling down her face.

"Now, Beth!"

Fulfilment came in an explosive rush, a volatile cascade that for a moment threatened to tear her apart. It was Alex's weight that kept her from going into orbit as he held her, keeping his own orgasm in check until hers was done.

She held him through the shockwaves of his climax, through the spasms that racked his body and the cries of fulfilment that told her his orgasm was every bit as intense as hers had been. He was deep inside her when he came, the hot wash of his seed filling her, mixing with her own wetness.

Breathing heavily, Alex rolled to one side, taking her with him so he could hold onto her as they both came back down from the heights. Waves of emotion crashed over Beth; over the last few hours she'd gone from hating what he'd asked her to do and hating herself for doing it, to daring to hope that she and Alex might have a chance for the long term after all.

She'd never felt his ownership of her more keenly than she did now, in her Dom's arms, naked save for his collar. Still caught in a post-orgasmic euphoria, she pressed closer to him, warmed by the ensuing deep male chuckle that vibrated through his chest.

"My sweet little sub," he murmured into her hair. "You see what you do to me, my love? I can't keep my hands off you."

That night, Beth found it difficult to fall asleep, even though Alex was by her side and Cam was just down the hall. What was keeping her awake was the news Cam had brought back with him.

A scruffy-looking stranger had been spotted in the area, his presence of note simply by the fact that strangers were a rarity in the villages around Winterleigh. People passed through, but this one was hanging around, to the extent that one or two of the locals Cam spoke to had wondered about calling the police to send him on his way. From their descriptions, the man sounded enough like Jimmy Underwood to be his brother, and therefore a cause for concern.

There had been a heated discussion about video surveillance. Cam wanted to put closed-circuit cameras around the estate, but not only did Alex not want them, regarding them as an invasion of his privacy, he maintained that it was too late, with the threat literally on the doorstep. In parts it was an almost word-for-word replay of the conversation they'd had twelve months earlier, when Cam had supervised the installation of the security system.

Beth slipped out of bed, pausing only to make sure that she hadn't disturbed Alex. She pulled on her dressing gown, a warm, fleecy and completely unalluring garment, and tiptoed out of the room, heading for the kitchen and that universal panacea, ice cream.

Okay, so it wasn't going to solve anything, but it would divert her attention for a little while, and she knew there was an unopened tub of her favourite flavour—chocolate—in the freezer. She was savouring her third spoonful when Alex appeared at the doorway. He was leaning against the frame, naked except for the black pyjama bottoms he wore slung low on his hips. He looked as sexy as hell. Beth felt an instant surge of lust set her pussy alight.

"I should spank you for sneaking off like that."

Beth's smile was half-hearted. "I couldn't sleep. Now that it looks like he's out there," she shivered, "I can't stop thinking about what he might be planning to do, and when. I'm sorry—I tried not to disturb you." Her tone was apologetic.

"I know. Beth, you should have woken me up—it's not your job to worry." He pushed himself away from the doorframe and padded over to her, his stride a hypnotic, sensual prowl that was more than enough to get her soaking wet with wanting him again. He sat down at the kitchen table opposite her and swiped a finger through the ice cream, scooping up a modest mouthful. He contemplated it for a moment; Beth expected him to polish off the dollop of luscious dessert himself, but instead, he offered it to her.

Her eyes never leaving his, Beth held his hand and

slowly, seductively, captured his finger in her mouth, relishing the melting treat almost as much as she relished the improvised spoon. Now *that* tasted especially delicious.

"Your job, Miss Harrison, begins and ends with pleasing your Master. You know I'll have to discipline you for this. You, it would appear, have a thing for chocolate," he observed, with a lazily raised eyebrow and half-suppressed smile.

"Of course I do," she admitted, licking up the last of the ice cream. "I'm a woman—chocolate's one of the five main food groups and essential for those of us with a second X chromosome. Isn't it?" Her eyes were full of wicked innocence, letting him know that she hadn't missed his comment about discipline.

"Looks like. Is this going to help you sleep?"

This time, his tone was serious—serious enough to make Beth wonder where this conversation was going to lead. "Probably not," she admitted on a sigh.

"Then why don't you put it back and come with me to the family room?"

A few moments later, Beth was cradled on Alex's lap on the sofa; he was busy untying the belt of her robe so that he could caress her breast. That was so Alex—a man who now had no problem with staking a claim and turning thought into deed. *Thank God*. She gave a contented sigh and rested her head next to his.

"It would seem we're all having trouble sleeping tonight."

The dry voice was Cam's; he was standing at the

doorway, in a similar state of dress to Alex. His pyjama bottoms were dark red, and like Alex, he too had a stunning physique—a perfect canvas for the bold lines and curves of the tribal ink that adorned his right arm from elbow to shoulder and strayed onto his chest.

There was something about subdued lighting and the intimacy of the small hours—the two combined to cast the kind of spell that could make a woman do things she wouldn't normally consider in the cold light of day. Beth started to cover up but then paused—she even stayed Alex's hand when he would have finished the task for her. She looked at him with complete trust, remembering what he'd once said about Cam possibly being involved in her discipline. "It's all right, Master. If you approve." Her gesture indicated a willingness to shrug out of the robe completely.

She held fast under Alex's searching gaze. He knew she wouldn't dream of doing this in front of anyone other than Cam. If she had any doubts about what she intended, he would detect them; if he wasn't happy about what she intended, he would stop her. The connection arced between them, and in that instant Beth saw pride and understanding flare in his dark eyes.

"I approve, Beth."

As she pulled her arms out of the robe, she was vaguely aware of her Dom's nod towards his friend. At that signal, Cam came over and hunkered down in front of her, one knee resting on the floor.

"May I touch her, Alex?"

For a brief moment, Beth knew a flare of panic, then it subsided as quickly as it came, replaced by a feeling of *déjà vu*. Giorgio had asked much the same thing, and she hadn't even known him—this was Cam. Even so, she still closed her eyes at the touch of a hand other than Alex's on her hair.

"She's beautiful. And brave. Beth, I would never hurt you. You belong to my best friend, and that makes it as much my duty as his to protect you."

Alex kissed her cheek. "He's right, sweetheart; you are brave. And you have my word of honour that no one will ever see you like this without your consent. Now, open your eyes and look at me."

Beth swallowed hard. She looked straight at Alex, but was keenly aware of Cam, still crouched beside her.

"Do you remember your safe words, Beth?"

"Yes, Sir."

"Good girl. Do you trust me to take care of you? Good. Now, remember your safe words and don't be afraid to use them. Cam?"

Some sort of unspoken communication flashed between the two men. Cam made himself comfortable at the other end of the long sofa, where he lounged at ease with his back resting against the arm. One foot was anchored on the floor while the other leg was bent at the knee and rested against the padded back of the sofa.

Beth was supremely conscious of her vulnerability, positioned as she was between two physically powerful, half-naked Doms. Ménage scenes from novels she'd read flashed through her mind. She knew this wouldn't go that far. Neither man would hurt her, she was absolutely certain of it—just as she knew that, whatever was going to happen, she could stop it in an instant.

"She's been a bad girl, Master Cameron. She was worried and didn't wake me, just came down here alone and raided the freezer for ice cream. I need your help to make her understand a sub's place and her responsibility."

Beth lifted her eyes in the direction of the other Dom; a gasp caught in her throat. She'd known about him for a while, but this was the first time she'd seen warm, friendly, protective Cam fully assume the mantle of a Dom. The same sensual power emanated from him as it did from Alex and in response, like some primal beast, an enticing apprehension unfurled inside her. Her pulse began to race.

"Take her, Master Cameron. I want to look at her."

Strong forearms came around her waist; Beth was lifted backwards, pulled abruptly but carefully against a hard, warm, male body. She breathed in sharply, for half a moment intending to use her safe word to call a halt, but she stopped herself when she saw the intensity of Alex's expression.

I'm safe.

She knew it without a shadow of doubt. Whatever happened, Alex would ensure that she wasn't hurt—he knew her limits.

Cam held her captive, her back against his chest, her bottom nestled between his thighs. If her proximity was affecting him, she felt no evidence of it. Her legs stretched out along the sofa, feet tucked against Alex's hip.

"Open your legs, Beth."

Dear God in heaven.

Alex sucked in his breath at the sight of Beth in his best friend's arms. He sensed her nervousness. She wasn't scared exactly—he knew she'd have used one of her safe words to slow things down or stop them altogether. It seemed more like she was just a touch anxious, but no more than that. And maybe a little—just a little—excited.

He'd never forgotten that her one fear had been that he would make her have sex with another man as a form of discipline, and while he, Alex, could enjoy the aesthetic image of his woman under the control of another Dom— Cam being the only one whom he would trust with her— Alex was the only one who would ever have her. She belonged to him and him alone.

She did look exquisite under Cam's control, though— pure sub, with the heavy gold chain he now allowed her to sleep in. Her eyes were chastely lowered, her pose elegant, revealing her pussy as he'd directed.

"Beth, I want you to bend your knees and let your legs fall apart. That's right."

Alex could feel his body tightening in response to the picture she made. She was the only woman who had ever reduced him to a mass of primitive male impulses, emotions and heated needs, and she was the only woman who could satisfy them.

He had to touch her. A couple of fingers slipped between her folds told him that she was getting aroused, as did the way she squirmed, causing the muscles in Cam's arms to flex as he held on to her. Alex was waiting for one of her safe words, but none came—she simply looked straight at him, absolute trust in her striking green eyes, along with a smouldering hint of arousal that he found intoxicating. He could be wrong, but she seemed barely aware of his friend—her focus was on her Dom, just as it should be.

And now he had a decision to make—to stimulate her to orgasm or not. He'd asked a lot of her, Alex knew. What stunned him was how well she was handling being naked and held by another Dom. Perhaps he would challenge her limits just a little; he would keep her orgasm for when he carried her back to their room, but right now, he found the prospect of seeing her in Cam's arms, restless with restrained arousal, quite appealing.

He leaned forward to kiss her mouth, uncaring that his closest friend would witness the love and intimacy of his relationship with his sub. "Isn't she beautiful, Master Cameron?" He twirled a lock of her hair in his fingers.

"I've always thought so, Master Alex," the other man agreed easily, his tone low and intimate. "You're lucky— I envy you."

Now, that was surprising. "How so?"

"You have love and a beautiful submissive, all wrapped up in one sinfully delightful package. I hope you've left a little of that luck for me."

Alex looked at his friend, took in the faintly sad quality of his wry, unguarded smile. In all the time he'd known Cam, he'd never imagined the time would come when he'd see the other man thinking about settling down.

Turning his attention back to his woman, Alex was stunned to see that her expression had taken on a slightly dreamlike quality. Then, as if she could feel his gaze upon her, she lifted her head to look at him. For a moment their eyes connected, and then she looked down again.

A muscle twitched in his cheek. She was aroused all right—he could see it in the way her nipples were beading. He didn't need to slide his fingers into her pussy to know how wet she'd be, but he did need the breathy moan in response and the way she leaned back against Cam for leverage to push her hips towards him. He slid his middle finger upwards, finishing the movement with a flick of his fingertip over her hypersensitive clit.

"I don't think I've ever seen such a responsive sub, Master Alex," Cam commented as his arms tightened around her quaking body. "How's her training going?"

"So far, I've barely scratched the surface with her." Alex intensified the torment with stronger, faster strokes. "I love her. And I'm enjoying her too much."

While talking to his friend, Alex continued to tease Beth's pussy and nipples. He was completely aware of the way he was arousing her, pushing her closer and closer to climax. Intimately acquainted with her tells, the little signs she gave as she neared orgasm, he knew exactly when to draw back... and how frustrated she was, even though she didn't show it.

He didn't know what made him offer her the fingers that had just been inside her, but the sensation of her kitten-like tongue cleaning him gave him a hard-on that damn near killed him. Just the sight of her with his finger in her mouth as she sucked it clean made him want to plunge his cock into her body. It was only the presence of his friend that prevented him pressing her back into the sofa and taking her.

"Thanks for indulging me, Cam."

The other man smiled. "My pleasure. I bet she looks something else."

"She surely does. Beth, you've done very well, but I think it's time we went back to bed. You don't need to worry about that bastard out there. We'll keep you safe."

Back in their bedroom, Alex gently laid his cherished sub on the bed, having carried her there from the family room in spite of her repeated protests about letting her walk—in his arms was where she belonged.

Now that she was safe in bed, he wanted to talk to her. For a long moment, though, he simply looked at her and the gentle smile that blossomed when he stroked her hair.

"How do you feel?" he asked, finally ready to hear the answer.

"Truthfully? I..." her voice faltered. "When you and Cam... when you were talking about me, I felt... owned. Protected. Even before, when Cam appeared..." She looked up at him, realisation like sunrise in her eyes. "I wasn't scared. I knew neither of you would hurt... harm me."

She'd known it in her head and felt it in her heart—he could see it in her eyes, hear it in her voice, feel it in the sense of calmness that radiated from her. She understood. "You surprised the hell out of me when you volunteered to be naked in front of Cam."

"I'm not sure I can explain fully, Sir. I'm not sure I know how to say this, but... I needed to..."

She frowned. Alex watched her struggle to find the right words. Though he burned to know what she was going to say, he found the patience to remain silent. The words had to be her own.

"I needed to show you what you mean to me and prove to myself that I can do whatever it takes to demonstrate that to anyone else. I trust you to protect me. I know it was only Cam—"

"Shh." Alex knew where she was going with that sentence and he wasn't having any of it. "Don't ever belittle what you just did, sweetheart. I'm not sure I can adequately convey how honoured I feel by what you did and the courage it took to do it." The kiss he placed on her lips was almost reverential.

"Thank you, Sir."

"There you go again," he said with a smile that was somehow both stern and indulgent, as he arranged the covers over her before sitting beside her. "Don't think I haven't noticed the Sirs and Masters you've been dropping into the conversation—against my express instructions. You know I'm going to have to do something about that, but for now would you like to tell me what else is on your mind?"

She hesitated only a moment. "I thought you might ask him to join us."

Another surprise he would never have imagined. "Would you have used your safe word if I had?"

"I don't know. Perhaps not initially," she continued, her apprehensive gaze searching his face. "It would depend on what you intended to happen next, Sir."

An old memory sprang to mind, back when he and Cam had been training in the US. Under supervision, they had shared a willing sub—but only for a bondage and discipline session, no more than that.

"I'd share our bed with him, but I wouldn't share you," he stated bluntly. "Sex is off the menu. But if you wanted to know how it would feel to have him touch you like this…" With his fingertips he traced the contour of her cheek, the line of her neck, continued until he cupped her breast in his palm. "How would you feel about that?"

"After tonight, I could do that, Sir. But would it be fair to Cam… Master Cameron?"

It didn't surprise Alex that she was so concerned about his friend; it was all part of the woman he loved. "You bring out the protective instinct in us. Cam and I… we've always known that if each of us ever found our special sub, the woman who meant everything to us, then the bond we have would grow stronger, not weaker. He'd consider it an honour and a privilege—as would I, if the positions were reversed."

He noted the small frown that creased her brow—he wondered if she found that to be more than she could accept, but her next question surprised him yet again.

"Does he have anyone special in his life, Sir? I've never heard either of you say anything about anyone. From what he said tonight, I got the impression that he doesn't."

At one time, Alex would have launched into the usual waffle about Cam being a confirmed bachelor, but given the things his friend had said about their relationship and the sincerity with which he'd said them, he now found himself ready to discard that assertion. There was no doubt in Alex's mind that the other man was well on the way to accepting that he'd been missing out on something unique.

"Not yet, love," he replied, "although it's going to take a very special woman—someone as special as you are to me—to pin him down and make him commit to her."

The next morning, Beth found herself on her own in the office, trying to concentrate on her writing. With the thought at the back of her mind that Alex and Cam were preparing to defend them in a life-or-death situation, Beth was finding it difficult to sort out the jumble of words. Even now, the two men were out there patrolling the grounds, armed with Alex's shotguns. Beth found it more than a little irksome that she'd been forbidden from taking a more active part in those defensive measures, for all that she could understand why the two men had taken that stance.

She could do with some fresh air and a long walk in the woods to take the edge off her frustration—the house, for all its luxury, was starting to feel like a prison, and she didn't want to risk incurring Alex's wrath by suggesting again that she'd like to take a walk to the village. Once was more than enough.

Clad in her winter coat and boots, she made her way to the kitchen and the door that led to the courtyard at the back of the house. When she opened it she found herself face-to-face with a stranger, a man whom she'd never seen before, but who appeared to boiling with a barely controlled anger directed straight at her. Fear paralysed her voice in her throat as she stared at the wild-eyed, unkempt stranger... and the lethal-looking automatic handgun he was pointing at her.

"Lombard's whore!" he spat at her. "Where's the bastard coward hiding?"

Terrified, Beth stepped backwards, her mind willing suddenly leaden feet to move faster. She had to get away, warn Alex and Cam that the threat was real and right here, right now. Irrational instinct overruled the common sense that would have told her not to risk being shot by trying to get away. She ran, only to be brought down not by a bullet but by a vicious tackle that sent her crashing headfirst into the wall.

With the last vestiges of consciousness slipping away and unable to defend herself, she felt rough hands ripping open her coat, removing her boots and tearing off her jeans.

CHAPTER SIXTEEN

It was all he could do not to charge in and tear the fucking sonofabitch limb from limb.

Alex came to an abrupt halt outside the family room, rage blazing through him like an all-consuming forest fire at what he saw in front of him as he took cover against the wall. His hand tightened on the thick haft of the lethal combat knife. In that split second, he was ready to slit Ewan Underwood's throat. Somehow the bastard had managed to get into the house and take Beth hostage. Alex's worst fear was now a terrifying reality.

His woman was on her knees in the centre of the room, clearly set there as bait in a trap for him. Duct tape covered her mouth, while more bound her hands together, only her right thumb left free to press down on the top of the slender cylindrical device enclosed by her clasped hands.

Alex identified it at once—it was a dead man's trigger,

the only thing keeping her alive, keeping her from being destroyed by the military-grade explosives packed into the suicide vest that held her torso in its deadly embrace. How the hell had Underwood got his hands on that? In Alex's estimation, there was enough to send them to kingdom come ten times over.

She didn't yet know he was there, Alex realised grimly. At first he thought her gaze, fixed unwaveringly on the switch, was like that of a petrified animal—almost as if by force of will she thought she could maintain her hold on the button. However, as he looked more closely, what he saw in her eyes wasn't just fear—there was steely resolve there as well. Pride flared through his nervous system. She was scared—who wouldn't be?—but she wasn't letting it get the better of her. If only she'd look up—then she'd see him and he could give her the reassurance she needed for both of them to survive this.

Alex didn't know what had made him suddenly decide to return to the house, leaving Cam to check the outbuildings and stables, but whatever it was, he wished to God it had happened earlier. Then he could have intercepted Underwood before the other man could make Beth an innocent victim of his grotesque desire for revenge.

As soon as he'd approached the house, Alex had felt the familiar prickling sensation, a portent that something was very wrong. Exercising extreme caution, he'd entered the kitchen. Signs of a struggle had sent cold fear through him. Hoping against hope, he'd checked the secure room first, desperate to believe that Beth might have made it there, that somehow she'd had sufficient warning to take refuge, but the emptiness of it had been a mockery of all his plans and promises to keep Beth out of harm's way. The ensuing silent search had led him to the family room, where he'd finally found the woman who was his life.

Hysteria won't help. Stay focused. Alex will find you. He'll come for you. He'll protect you. He promised. Alex always keeps his promises.

Beth repeated the words like a mantra, over and over again, but they couldn't control the tremors that had her visibly quaking or fight the cold terror that was washing through her body. Her head was still swimming from hitting it on the wall while trying to escape from her assailant, the man she now knew to be Ewan Underwood.

She must have lost consciousness with that initial assault, because the next thing she remembered was pain exploding in her jaw and a man's voice growling obscenity after obscenity at her. Another slap, and she'd registered the sensation of being dragged into a kneeling position while she struggled to tune back into reality.

While unconscious she'd been stripped of most of her clothes, though she was thankfully still decent enough; her ankles were bound together, probably with the same tape her assailant had used on her hands and mouth, and her feet were well on the way to losing all sensation and feeling. Her legs weren't feeling too good either.

She tasted the lingering metallic tang of blood. A covert examination of the inside of her mouth with the tip of her tongue revealed the spot where one of the blows she'd received had cut the inside of her lip. The stinging sensation reminded her again of what had happened after Underwood brought her round with another slap to the face.

"Shut up, bitch!" he'd snarled as he pressed the tape over her mouth with rough hands, her punishment for attempting to reason with him. Then he'd forced something into her hands, grabbed her thumb and pressed it to the end of the tubular object. He'd held it there while he wound more of the tape around her wrists and hands. "This is a dead man's switch; it's connected to your new designer outfit. Have a look." He'd pointed at her chest.

She'd known it was there, felt the bulk of it wrapped around her body but hadn't dared look until that moment. What she saw terrified her: a vest, with wires and blinking lights, and cylindrical blocks of what looked like clay. She didn't have to be an expert to reach the conclusion pretty quickly that PE4 was some sort of explosive.

"When I flip this switch," he'd held up a little black box, "your nice new jacket goes live, and so long as you don't let go of this," a shake of her wrists, "you won't go boom. Got it, bitch?"

Shaking with terror, Beth had barely been able to nod. Now, struggling to combat the threat of panic, all she could do was stare at the switch clasped in her hands, her thumb applying so much pressure that the knuckle was already white. The way her hands were restrained meant that she couldn't even find some relief by changing thumbs.

Alex was her anchor. She knew he'd come and get her, he *would*, and panicking wouldn't help either of them. She couldn't let fear get the better of her. If Alex knew what was happening, he'd be relying on her not to release the trigger. That was her job—he needed her to do her job until he could get there and take on the man who threatened all of them.

Beth was only distantly aware of Underwood's movements as he took cover behind the open door to the family room, gun in hand, leaving her kneeling in full view of whoever might be out in the hallway… and in no doubt whatsoever that she was intended to lure the man she loved to his death.

Alex knew he should wait for Cam to join him, it was the only sensible thing to do, but every primitive impulse in him was clamouring to charge in, rescue his woman and get her to safety. Before he could do that, however, he needed her to know he was there, so that he didn't scare her into letting go of the switch that was keeping her alive.

He needed a miracle.

Beth.

He couldn't have said whether he spoke her name or just thought it, but in that sweet moment she looked up and her eyes connected with his. While the fear twisted a knife through his heart yet again, he focused on the determination that, even as he watched, blossomed into a look that rewrote the book on love and complete trust.

Yet, even as he smiled and nodded to reassure her, the look in her eyes changed again, became intense and focused in a way that grabbed him by the balls and gave him hope that they might yet get out of this alive. In that instant they became a team. And she was talking to him—talking with her eyes, telling him that Underwood was hiding behind the family room door.

He nodded—she blinked.

He mouthed the words *I love you*, and she blinked again.

And still more blinking, except now there was a frantic urgency about it. She was trying to tell him something—but what? It was a wild stab in the dark, but he mimicked firing a gun... the single blink was slow and controlled, and told him what he needed to know.

Yes.

So he was facing a mad man armed with a gun, and he had nothing more than a combat knife. Christ, why had he thought it was a good idea to ask Cam to take the firearms back to the gun room?

Focus, Lombard. You've faced worse. Beth needs you to get her out of this.

Years of training and battlefield experience told him that the odds weren't good; on the plus side, combat and conflict had been his life, while Underwood was clearly deranged. That had to give him the upper hand, in spite of the disparity in their weapons.

In a fraction of a second, Alex called on all his military

expertise, the knowledge that had made him such a cool strategist under fire, to weigh up the best option for tackling the intruder. He couldn't wait for Cam to arrive; he had to do something now. If he'd had his friend's skill with the knife, he might have waited until Underwood came into view and taken the bastard down from a distance, but with Beth in such a precarious situation, Alex wasn't prepared to take the chance—there was no way she was going to be collateral damage.

Besides, he had no way of knowing how long she'd been forced to hold the trigger. If he waited for backup, Beth might well reach a point where she could no longer maintain the required pressure. No, he was going to get in there, neutralise Underwood, and then free her hands so that he could take over the switch until Cam arrived.

A shadow of movement in the tiny gap between the door and jamb caught his eye—it was enough.

"Underwood!"

On a surge of adrenaline that had him roaring the man's name, Alex charged through the doorway, forcing the door beyond the limit of the hinges and sending Underwood flying across the room. Alex lunged at his opponent, his eyes fixed on the other man's gun, knowing in that split second that if he and Beth were to survive this, there could only be one outcome.

Cam went through the house, looking for Alex and Beth. He'd found nothing around the outbuildings to indicate any trouble, but as soon as he'd entered through the kitchen he'd sensed the unnerving quiet—until the sound of all hell breaking loose, culminating in a single gunshot, had led him to bypass the secure room and go straight to the family room, his gut wrenching when he took in the scene that awaited him.

Ewan Underwood was dead, his neck broken. A cursory check was all Cam needed—he'd seen that method used too many times in war not to be certain that the unnatural angle of the neck indicated a fatal injury.

Holy shit.

Close by, Alex was unconscious and bleeding like a stuck pig—under normal circumstances, Cam would have examined him fully first, but jury-rigged explosives had a way of altering a man's priorities.

"Easy, Beth," he said softly as he knelt down in front of her, putting himself between her and Alex, and very carefully peeled the length of tape away from her mouth. "Everything's okay, it's all over.

"Alex... Help him... please..."

Her voice was a hoarse whisper, the pleading tone enough to send a bolt of pain through Cam. He thanked God that she didn't have a clear view of what had happened. "I will, angel, but I just need to check this first."

Acutely aware of how much blood Alex had already lost, Cam made a quick examination of the tape binding Beth's hands. With a heavy heart, he enclosed her hands in his. "I can't take the tape off just yet, I'm sorry. I need you to hold on a little while longer, just a few more minutes. If I take the tape off now, you might not have the strength to do what I need you to do. Can you hold on for me? For Alex?"

"Just help him. Please. I'm all right."

She had a death grip on the switch in front of her, and much though Cam hated leaving her like that, he needed to stop the flow of blood from Alex's wound. He tore off his jacket and sweater, wadded up the latter garment and wedged it against Alex's side, in an attempt to slow the flow of blood from his wound.

"Sorry, old friend," he muttered under his breath, hoping that the makeshift compress would buy Alex enough time while he dealt with Beth and the suicide vest.

"How bad is he?"

"Don't worry about him, Beth; he's tougher than you think. Now, I need to get us some help, but I can't use my mobile phone around this," he nodded at the explosives. "I have to use the phone in the office. I'll be as quick as I can, I promise."

She nodded stiffly. "Hurry, Cam. Please," she whispered. "He's lost so much blood. I can't lose him."

Jesus. Cam swore under his breath. She had to be in agony, yet all she could think about was Alex.

"Beth, don't worry." He shot a glance back at his friend, doing the very thing he'd just told her not to do; blood was soaking into the improvised dressing at an alarming rate. "Try to stay still—help will be here soon."

Cam could rewrite the book on frustration. After calling

the emergency services, he'd gone back into the family room to tend to Alex's wound and reassure Beth, although he still hadn't dared risk unwrapping her hands. He'd been banished when the paramedics arrived to take over care of his friend, while the RLC Explosive Ordnance Disposal operators dealt with the suicide vest, with the fire brigade on standby.

The police were hovering around too, wanting to ask him questions he really didn't want to have to deal with right now—not when a quick phone call to the right office in Whitehall, just as soon as he could make it, would get them off his back.

That sense of frustration mounted while he kicked his heels alongside the second team of paramedics who were waiting to take care of Beth once she was free of the hellish device that had been forced on her. The guys from the Royal Logistic Corps had already advised both him and the paramedics—quite forcefully—to get as far away from the house as possible, because if something went wrong it was highly likely that most of the house would go up. The paramedics had relocated, but not as far as the officer in charge of the bomb disposal squad would have preferred.

As for Cam, there was no way he was running like some craven coward. Not when Beth was in the middle of it all and had no choice. If they'd let him, he'd have been in there with her, reassuring her and encouraging her, the way her Master would have done, had he been able.

The paramedics tending Alex had stabilised his condition and taken him to hospital quite some time ago. Cam wanted to phone the hospital to find out what was going on, but he couldn't get in to use the landline in the house. Using his mobile phone was out of the question, in case an errant signal interfered with the circuits governing the detonation of the explosives packed into the vest. It was unlikely, but Cam wasn't taking any chances.

If ever there was a time he needed to be able to split himself in two, this was it. His only comfort came from knowing that, while he could do nothing practical for either Alex or Beth, Alex was being taken care of by the health professionals he needed, so he, Cam, could be here when Beth was free and no doubt would need a shoulder to lean on, no matter how strong she was. He could ensure that she was taken to hospital for the care she would need, and he would follow.

The all-clear, shouted by the EOD operator emerging from Alex's house, broke into Cam's reverie. That was the cue for the medics to enter. Cam followed them through the front door, unsure of what would greet him.

Beth was still in a kneeling position. Cam's heart broke at the sound of the gulping sobs that escaped her as she tried to stand with the assistance of one of the paramedics. Even after all she'd been through, she was still trying to be brave and not cry. Cam flexed his fingers, gritting his teeth and trying to prevent his hands forming into fists. If Underwood hadn't already been dispatched, he'd have been quite happy to finish off the job.

"Angel, let me help."

She looked up at him; he could see the question forming in her mind.

"Alex is on his way to hospital. They're taking good care of him, I promise, and I know he'd want me to take care of you until he can do it himself."

Ignoring the paramedics, Cam gently lifted Beth into his arms, letting her legs straighten out gradually, wincing as what must have been a ferocious attack of pins-and-needles savaged her circulation-starved limbs. She sniffled softly, burrowing her face into his neck, holding onto him for dear life. He looked at the senior paramedic, who nodded in answer to the unspoken question.

"I'm going to take you to the ambulance now, angel," he said softly. "They need to examine you and make sure you're all right." He started walking. "You've had a nasty bump to the head. There's a couple of other injuries we need to take a look at, and you're in danger of going into shock. Alex would kill me if I don't take good care of you. You'll be going to the same hospital where he is, and I'll be in the car, right behind the ambulance, okay?"

Hours later, Cam stood just inside the Intensive Care Unit, his purpose originally just to check on Alex. Beth was also an inpatient, under observation for a concussion. When he saw her sitting beside Alex's bed, clad in the god-awful hospital-issue clothing they'd given her when admitted and with the plastic identity bracelet encircling her wrist, Cam decided to come back later. He was unwilling to break the intimacy of the moment but then Beth softly called his name. He turned back. "How are you doing, angel? I'm glad they kept you in—you need someone to keep an eye on you for a while." He leaned down to kiss her cheek.

"I'm okay." Her smile was weary, though—she was still badly shaken up. "Thanks to you and Alex."

"Hey, no thanks ever necessary. Taking care of you is what we do. How's he doing?"

The sadness in her eyes tugged at his heart. He loved her dearly as his best friend's soul mate, and to see her like this, after all she'd been through, all her bravery through an ordeal that would test anyone to the extreme, left a solid lump in his throat.

It also made him wonder what it would be like to have someone care so very much about him.

Her lower lip trembled a little before she spoke. "They've been really good about letting me stay with him for a while. He hasn't regained consciousness yet. They said the surgery went as well as can be expected, so now it's just a matter of waiting."

Cam looked at the unconscious man, the wires, the tubes, the beeping monitors and the drips. They'd intimated that it could have been worse, and as a former medic, he knew that there could have been major organ damage. As it was… well, on balance Alex had been bloody lucky, even if it didn't look that way right now. "Beth—he needs you now more than ever. You have no idea how good you've been for him."

Holding Alex's hand in both of hers, Beth looked up at him, clearly puzzled by the gravity of his demeanour. "What do you mean? The nightmares?"

"The nightmares he hasn't had since you've been more than just his assistant. Until you, he hadn't had a full night's sleep in over ten years."

"Ten years?" She looked even more confused, if that were possible. "But the IED was fifteen years ago. What happened ten years ago?"

"You mean he hasn't told you yet? Shit." He frowned and then sighed. "Beth, I really don't think you should hear about it from me."

At that moment, the conversation was interrupted by the arrival of a nurse; the doctor was on his way, so would they mind leaving for a few minutes?

"Certainly. Mr. Fraser was just going to take me for a cup of coffee, weren't you?" Beth dropped the hint with all the subtlety of the Royal Tank Regiment on manoeuvres.

The best thing that could be said about the coffee was that it was hot and wet, she thought ruefully as she faced Cam over a table in a quiet corner of the hospital coffee shop. "Right. You'd better start talking."

"And to think I kept telling Alex about your submissive tendencies." He took his first sip of coffee and promptly glared at the mug. "Are you sure this stuff's fit for human consumption?"

"Stop trying to avoid the issue. What happened?

Please."

Cam's blue eyes became shadowed, as if he were re-calling events that were best left in the past. "You aren't going to take no for an answer, are you?"

"No, I'm not. And don't think," she continued, her voice low but no less determined, "that using your Dom voice will work, because I'll tell you now, it won't. I want answers."

"Bloody subs. You don't let a Dom get away with any-thing." He sighed. "We left the service a couple of years after Alex was injured in the IED incident, and like a lot of people in that position, we went into the private sec-tor."

"You started Spectrum Security together."

Cam nodded. "Some of the lads who left around the same time joined us, and then we went back."

"Back? To the Middle East? But why?"

"Initially, it was a means to an end. There was a lot of money to be made, we figured we'd do it for a couple of years, then come back to the UK and start our real lives on Civvy Street."

"What did you do there?" Beth wasn't sure whether she was more afraid of asking the question or hearing the answer.

"Security at high-profile installations, some personal protection, that sort of thing. There were—are—a lot of very wealthy, powerful people over there who like to feel secure as they go about their daily lives."

Cam's eyes became a little bleaker. "After the IED incident, Alex changed; it was as if his life didn't mean that much anymore. Oh, he never endangered anyone—in fact, he became more protective of everyone around him, but less protective of himself. I thought it would change once we left the Regiment and started the security business, but it didn't. He insisted on taking on the riskier jobs."

He contemplated his coffee, took another drink and grimaced. "This crap doesn't taste any better if you let it cool. This particular assignment was as escort to a foreign diplomat's son. Several threats had been made against the family before we even got there, so that's why Alex took that duty. Usually there'd be one of the other lads with him, but that particular day we were short-handed, so he was on his own. The job was usually pretty straightforward... he thought he could handle it."

Cam emerged from his plunge into the past. "Look, Beth, what happened to Alex isn't good to remember, and it's even less pleasant to hear. You should really let him tell you about it."

"So he can gloss over the details and make it sound like a walk in the park? You know he won't tell me everything. I need to know what's made him the man he is. I need to know why he asked me to..."

She broke off and looked straight at him. "Tell me everything, Cam."

Cam drained his coffee, made another face at the taste. "God knows how they can sell this and call it coffee— yours is a thousand times better, Beth."

"Cam."

He heard the warning in her voice. There was nothing to stop him getting up and leaving without telling her a word. Nothing except the fact that he could never and would never do that to Beth. He deliberated for a moment more.

"Alex and the boy were kidnapped by insurgents. For the first week, maybe ten days, we had no idea where they were being held. When they did make contact with their ransom demand, the boy's father insisted on paying it—it was just petty cash to him, but the kidnappers didn't leave the boy and Alex where they said we could find them.

"Eventually, close to two weeks and several demands for more and more money later, we managed to get our hands on some intel that led us to an abandoned house. When we got them out, the boy was pretty much fine physically, but Alex was more dead than alive."

Beth's face drained of colour. "What happened?"

"They hated the boy's father. They wanted to get at him through his son, but the boy was their bargaining chip—no sense in torturing him to the point where he couldn't plead with his father to comply with the ransom instructions, or risking going too far and losing their leverage. Instead, to make the boy's pleas more desperate, they tortured him psychologically by physically abusing Alex in front of him, with the implication that they'd do the same to him."

Cam looked at his hands and forced his fingers to straighten—he hadn't even been aware of clenching them into fists. "You see, during the time Alex had been the boy's personal protection, they'd built up a really good relationship—I think the boy almost saw Alex as a surrogate father-figure."

He paused. Though he hadn't thought about that dark period for a long time, he still hated remembering what had happened to Alex, hated even more that he was the one telling that story to the woman his friend loved. At that precise moment, knowing that Beth was smart enough to come to the correct conclusion from what he was about to say, he needed to gather his thoughts and get it over with as quickly as possible, for both their sakes.

"God knows what goes on in the minds of bastards like that. Alex already had the scars from the explosion; when we got him out, his back was like raw meat. He'd been severely beaten, there were burns all over his body, and they'd broken half of his fingers. He was severely dehydrated and starving—of the little food and water they'd been given, he let the boy have pretty much all the food and most of the water. There were other injuries, too."

"What do you mean? What... other injuries?" Beth's expression gradually changed to one of utter horror. "Oh, God, no. They didn't...?"

Cam bit back a curse. As he'd surmised, Beth put two and two together, but there was no way he could tell her that, had it gone on for much longer, Alex would most likely have been as good as emasculated.

It seemed that his silence, however, was enough. She was crying silently, great tears of sorrow and grief rolling down her face. Cam would have given anything to protect her from the knowledge of what Alex had been through in the past, why he'd had such disturbing nightmares for so long. He knew only too well how much she loved the man. And now she had to face up to him being seriously wounded while trying to rescue her.

"God, I'm sorry, Beth. I shouldn't have told you."

Her expression told him he was wrong, and when she spoke, her voice betrayed her grief. "Yes, you should, and I'm glad you did. I just wish I could have been there for him then."

And that was Beth. As strong as Alex had told him she was. Now Cam understood why his friend loved this woman so much, and why he himself was finding it more and more difficult to believe that he was perfectly happy with his status as a confirmed bachelor. Could there be another woman like Beth out there for him?

"You're here for him now, that's what counts. He'll be all right, angel—keep the faith. He's tough. He wouldn't let us carry him out of there. His body and mind had been subjected to the worst hell you can imagine and then some, but he was determined to walk to the helicopter with as little assistance as possible. He survived every-thing they threw at him back then." And the weeks in hospital while his damaged body recovered. As for his mind... Cam had learned long ago to let that sleeping dog well and truly lie. It was a reality that Alex flat-out re-fused to face.

He watched the bewildered shake of her head, knowing that the small gesture reflected only the tip of the emotional iceberg she was struggling with. He saw the way her expression changed in the fight to find something to say, but Cam knew there were no words—not for a woman who felt about a man the way Beth felt about Alex. The pain Cam had seen his friend suffer was reflected right there, in his woman's gentle gaze.

He reached across to cover Beth's hand with his, telling her silently that words were not necessary, because they both understood—they understood everything. She nodded in acknowledgement, but the revelation had left an older shadow in her eyes.

"After all that, I can understand him wanting to move into something completely different, but how did he end up in this business? It's light years away from security."

Cam took a deep breath. That was a tale and a half, and all this time later they'd still not got to the bottom of it. Again, it wasn't Cam's story to tell, but he didn't see any harm in sharing it with Beth. She needed to hear something positive, to take away some of the distress caused by what he'd just imparted.

"About a month after he left Spectrum, some money appeared in his bank account. It was a huge amount, Beth—seven figures, and neither of us could work out where it came from. He tried to get the bank to return it, but for reasons that to this day remain a mystery, it couldn't be done."

Cam toyed with his empty coffee cup. What he was about to tell her still sounded totally unbelievable, even after all this time. Nevertheless, in his opinion, she was entitled to know.

So he began the tale, with the arrival of the letter inviting Alex to a meeting at an exclusive hotel in London, with the wealthy foreign national who asked him to source a unique item of jewellery and provided him with the necessary contacts. Alex had been handsomely rewarded and more work of a similar nature had followed, from that source and other individuals of similar financial status.

"Now, we've never been able to prove it, but we suspect that initial sum was linked to the foreign diplomat whose son Alex was escorting—quite how and why, we don't know. Alex tried to send the money back time after time, but in the end he had to accept that he would never be able to return it, so he decided to donate it to ex-servicemen's charities instead."

"The money didn't come from that first client, then?"

Cam shook his head. "The client paid for the necklace, and for Alex's fees and expenses. The only thing that made the slightest sense was that there was some sort of connection between the deposit and the diplomat whose son Alex was escorting, and that diplomat was somehow connected to the first client. We even wondered if the money was intended as compensation for what Alex had suffered. If he hadn't been there, they may well have had different ideas about hurting the boy."

Beth's eyes narrowed. "Alex would never willingly take compensation for that."

"Agreed. That's why he tried to return it and when he couldn't, he donated it to a number of forces charities instead. Anyway, further commissions followed, and it turned out he has a knack for sourcing high-end collectibles—the rest, as the saying goes, is history."

He knew it was a lot for Beth to take in, but as he watched her, Cam became aware of a change in her demeanour. He could see she was mulling everything over, analysing it, extracting what mattered most from it.

"Cam, the nightmares. If he's been having them for years... surely he should have had some sort of therapy, counselling... something?"

"He was supposed to." Cam's tone was as cheerless as his memories of that time. "He did actually go to one session, but he didn't stay."

Beth snorted. "I wish I could say I was surprised. No wonder he had nightmares. Just because they seem to have stopped, though, it doesn't mean things are resolved."

Something that had concerned Cam for years, but even as he watched the shadows disappear from Beth's eyes, he saw her straighten up, as if she were developing a spine of carbon steel. The fight that had disappeared when he first told her about Alex's history was coming back with a vengeance. He could almost see her mind whirring with possibilities.

"Cam, I don't like loose ends. I like them even less when they affect Alex. I'll find a way to get him to accept the help he needs."

Cam believed her. For the first time in years, he was cautiously optimistic that in due course his friend might finally be fully healed of all that he'd suffered so long ago.

He checked his watch. "I hate to say this, but it's ridiculously late—you should get some rest. They're keeping you in here for a reason. I have to go now anyway, but remember—if there's anything you need, or there's anything I can do, call me, no matter what time, day or night."

"Where are you going?"

"Back to London. We've managed to keep a lid on this so far, but it's taking some heavy hitters to keep it that way. Alex and I have good friends in high places as well as low—friends who owe us a lot. I've called in the favours, but I have to go and see a couple of these people tonight, before I see the others in the morning. The local police won't bother you—I've already made the calls to take care of that—but once I've spoken to the right people, there'll be no comeback for all of this."

Beth reached across the table to squeeze Cam's hand. "Thank you—for everything."

"You're most welcome, Beth." He lifted her hand to press a brief kiss to the back of it. "Take good care of yourself—and him. He's a lucky man. Now, let me escort you back upstairs before I go."

Having said goodbye to Cam, Beth returned to the ICU. In spite of feeling a little light-headed, she was determined to see Alex before she went off to her own bed, and apart from anything else, she wanted to know what the doctor had said.

Having learned from the nurse on duty that his condition was officially classed as stable and that he was doing as well as could be expected in the circumstances, Beth resumed her place at his side, taking hold of the hand that lay so still on the sheets. She needed to talk to him—there was so much she needed to tell him.

"Please, Sir. Come back to me. I need you so much. I need to tell you how much I love you, how much you mean to me. Please, Alex."

She also needed to tell him that she knew about his past now, that she understood and it changed nothing, apart from one thing—his struggle was now hers too.

And then there was the simple fact that she couldn't forget the horror of watching Alex fight to save both of them, how powerless she'd been, at the same time terrified of letting go of the switch that stood between both of them and oblivion.

Most of all, though, what she couldn't get out of her mind was how Alex had repeatedly put himself between her and Underwood as the two men struggled for control of the gun. She couldn't even help by grabbing hold of the knife that Alex had dropped at the start of the fight, thanks to what Underwood had done to her hands—she could only watch until that dreadful moment when, with the gun between their two bodies, the trigger had been pulled, and with a final herculean effort Alex had dispatched their assailant by breaking his neck.

Almost in slow motion, she'd watched Alex collapse to his knees and look towards her before pitching forward, unconscious before he hit the floor. Too far away for her to get to him, to be with him, all she could do then was look on with growing horror as blood blossomed over his side.

There'd been so much blood, so red, so very red, spilling out of his body, taking his strength and his life with it, and she could do nothing to stop it. One false move and the suicide vest could have exploded, killing both of them. The only chance Alex had had was for her to stay put and wait for Cam to find them.

It was a nightmare that would live with her for the rest of her life.

At such close quarters, the gunshot wound could have been a hell of a lot worse—not the doctor's exact words, of course, but that was the message when they'd brought Alex back after surgery. He'd be unconscious for a while yet, to allow his body to start the healing process, and it was still impossible for them to say how long he'd have to remain in hospital.

She felt so tired—so very tired. Perhaps a little nap would help. She leaned forward, pillowing her head on her arm. Just a few moments, that was all she'd need. She'd be fine then.

CHAPTER SEVENTEEN

Alex groaned. A search through the fog that seemed to have replaced his memory had failed to uncover any recollection of his having been around any horses lately, but sure as hell, one had kicked him. Judging by the way everything was aching, it must have been a bloody carthorse.

And that was another thing—he couldn't remember painting his bedroom ceiling that insipid eggshell colour, either. As he continued to stare upwards, the smell started to intrude on his consciousness... it was the unmistakeable smell of a hospital, and for a second, he was transported to another time he'd woken up in a sickbay. He felt the razor-sharp shards of pain, nausea and shame all over again.

No, can't be. That was ten years ago...

"Beth!" Her name came out as an almost unintelligible croak, carried along on the tidal wave of harrowing images that suddenly crashed through his mind.

He tried to get up, but his head felt as if it weighed about two tons. When he tried again, he became aware of several things all at once—his side hurt like hell, even more than the rest of his body, and he was damn near strapped to the bed by a bunch of tubes and wires. A steady beeping provided a strangely comforting confirmation that he was still alive.

Movement drew his attention to the left; a middle-aged nurse with a cheerful smile was standing there. "Good afternoon, Mr. Lombard, good of you to join us at last." She checked the displays on the monitors around him. "How do you feel?"

"Like shit," he rasped unapologetically. His throat was like sandpaper and his mouth tasted like a particularly unhygienic monkey had died in it. "Where's Beth? Miss Harrison? How is she?"

"Your young lady? I believe they're getting ready to discharge her."

Discharge her? She'd been an inmate too? "Is she all right? I want to see her."

To his surprise, the nurse chuckled. "She'll be here soon, I'm sure. The only reason she isn't here now is because they have to go through the discharge paperwork. I don't know how, but she managed to persuade both her doctor and yours to let her spend most of the time here with you—she wouldn't leave your side unless one of the doctors ordered her out. I would imagine she'll be back here by the time the doctor's done with you. He's on his way now."

Alex felt his eyelids closing. *Bloody anaesthetic.* He had to stay awake... he had to see Beth, make sure she was all right. When the doctor arrived, he endured the prodding and poking, not to mention the man's endless questions, with mounting impatience. He knew he'd been relatively lucky that it was a low-velocity round that had hit him; he knew he'd been even luckier that it hadn't done any lasting damage to any major organs. He didn't need to hear the lecture from a medic; he'd seen enough battlefield injuries to know just how fortunate he was.

By the time the doctor was giving the nurse instructions for his further care, Alex had switched off mentally from what was going on around him and was looking beyond the hospital staff to the entrance to the ICU, waiting for the one person who could make this whole situation a lot more bearable.

Consequently, he was only vaguely aware of the doctor's departure—he'd spotted Beth peering into the unit, and as she came towards him, relief flooded his heart. *Thank God.* She was safe. Pale, tired and bruised, but safe—and that was all that mattered.

"You all right, sweetheart?" They'd given him something to drink, but it was still an effort to speak.

"I am now." She smiled, but he could see the unusual shine in her eyes. He watched her lift his hand to her cheek, brush her lips across the back of it. "They said I could have a few minutes with you, but they want you to rest."

"As if I have any choice." He touched the discolouration that marred her lower jaw. "I shouldn't have let this happen."

She held his hand to her face as she shook her head. "Don't, Alex. Don't blame yourself for something you couldn't control."

"I should have made you leave."

She tilted her head. "Didn't you hear what I just said? *Don't blame yourself for something you couldn't control.* You couldn't control Ewan Underwood, and do you really think you could have made me go anywhere without you?"

The guilt still made him feel sick, though. If it wasn't for him, she wouldn't have had to fight for her life—she wouldn't have known the kind of fear no civilian should ever know, nor would she ever have seen the kind of violence no civilian should ever have to witness.

"Cam's coming to pick me up soon," she continued quietly. "He had meetings in London this morning, something about ensuring that the right people were made aware of what happened, and that the appropriate steps are taken to deal with any consequences. What did he mean by that?"

Alex swallowed. His mind was still fuzzy, but he knew what Cam was up to. "It means there'll be no investigation into Underwood's untimely demise. I would guess that Cam has enough material to put together a valid case for self-defence."

She nodded, taking in what he'd told her. "He also said he'd stay at Winterleigh with me until you come home.

He was going to take me back to London, to his place, but I wanted to be here so I could come and see you.

"And," she added, suddenly unable to look him in the eyes, "we need... we need to talk, but not now."

He wondered exactly what she wanted to talk about. Statements like that seldom boded well. Had she decided that the experiences of the last couple of weeks were all too much?

All of a sudden, Alex felt an iron band tighten around his heart—was this her way of telling him that she was planning to say goodbye?

Previous painful experience told Alex that he wasn't going to get out of the hospital any time soon. Although the doctor treating him kept making encouraging noises about his progress, it was only Beth's daily visits that kept him from going insane with a combination of frustration and boredom. As for the dread, he pushed that back into the farthest recesses of his mind—he refused to waste his energy on trying to work out when she was going to tell him it was all over.

The cuts and bruises she'd sustained at the hands of Ewan Underwood were healing well; each day brought a marked improvement. However, what Alex was disturbed to note was the deepening of the shadows around her eyes. She clearly wasn't sleeping well, if at all, a fact that she confirmed when he questioned her about it.

"Don't worry about it, Alex," she told him, trying to

reassure him that it wasn't important. "It's just a phase. It'll pass."

"Tell me why you aren't sleeping," he insisted. By now, they'd taken away a lot of the equipment monitoring his condition, and were even making noises about moving him out of the ICU in a day or two. He was already having some light physiotherapy *in situ*.

"It's nothing."

"So help me, Beth, if it weren't for the fact that it would shock the hell out of the staff, I'd put you over my knee and spank some sense into you!" Alex kept his voice low and tightly controlled. "Just because I'm in here, it doesn't mean you can forget all about the rules!"

Her eyes widened in alarm, and then he saw the moment when her defences came down. She glanced down at her hands, clenched together on her lap. "Nightmares," she admitted, her voice barely more than a murmur. "I keep... I keep seeing you, that moment just before Cam came in, but in my nightmares, he's too late, and... I lose you. Over and over again. There's been a couple of nights when I've been afraid to go to sleep."

Christ. Alex knew all about that. He held out his hand and she came to his uninjured side, resting her head against him while he held her as best he could and murmured reassurance. "I'll be home soon," he promised. "Just as soon as I can, and you'll never have another nightmare, I swear."

"It's not just that, Alex." She sat up straight again. "Cam told me what happened to you ten years ago—not in detail, but enough for me to know."

Alex felt all of the colour drain out of his face. The one thing about his past he'd never wanted her to know. The scale of the humiliation he felt wiped out ten years of his life in an instant, took him right back to that moment when Cam had found him in that filthy, stinking cellar. When he dared to look at Beth again, her face was as white as his felt and her expression was one of complete horror.

"Oh, God, I never meant—"

"I don't want your pity, Beth, and if that's all there is left—"

"Shh." She touched her finger to his lips to silence him. "Not pity, never that. Love… and admiration for a man of incredible strength and courage." She laid her palm against his cheek, her other hand holding his. For long moments, she simply looked at him, and then all he saw was love and want and need. She leaned closer, her hand on his cheek coaxing his head to the right place for his mouth to receive her kiss, a gentle touching of lips to tell him what he meant to her. "I wish I'd been here for you then. I wasn't, and there's nothing I can do about that, no matter how much I wish it. What I can do something about is the future—I can be here for you for as long as you want me. Please want me."

His free hand reached up, covered hers and brought it to his mouth so that he could press a kiss to her palm, as she had done so many times for him. This woman—his woman—was nothing short of a miracle. He would never know what he'd done to deserve her, but whatever it was, he hoped he could keep on doing it for the rest of his life. When he spoke, his voice was raw with emotion.

"You're here now, that's all that matters." He curved his hand around the back of her head, exerting just enough pressure to draw her close enough for a further, longer kiss. "I love you, Beth Harrison. So damn much, the thought of losing you kills me. I've wanted you since the day I met you, and I'll never stop wanting you—never."

Alex was settled back into bed after a frustratingly gentle amble around the physiotherapy department. The specialist was pleased with the way his recovery was progressing, but for Alex it wasn't progressing nearly fast enough. He needed to get back home and be with Beth. He had no intention of being away so long that she got used to managing without him. Even though they'd discussed their relationship and their feelings at length, he was prepared to work on convincing her that he was still worth keeping around.

Cam was due to arrive straight from London any moment, for his first visit since Beth had let slip that the other man had told her about what had happened ten years ago. Alex had made a point of asking him to get there early for a quiet chat before Beth arrived. He let his friend make himself comfortable in the visitor's armchair before speaking.

"Why did you tell her?" Alex knew he didn't need to

elaborate any further.

Cam squared his shoulders. "I'm sorry, but I had to, Alex," he said quietly. "She wouldn't take no for an answer. You know, you really need to train your sub better."

Alex took in the tentative wry grin on his old friend's face. He knew Cam wasn't happy about having talked to Beth. Alex also knew how much he valued their friendship. "You've nothing to apologise for, Cam. You were right. I should have talked to her. She said she wished she'd been there for me. Can you believe that?"

"Of course I believe it. That's exactly what she said to me. She's Beth—she couldn't be any other way. I told you: she loves you."

Starting to feel a little more at ease, Alex allowed himself a small wry grin. "Where is she?"

"Right here," a female voice, as clear as a bell, announced. "Is this a private party, or can anyone join in?"

Beth was standing in the doorway. Although not all the shadows had gone, with her usual lovely smile back in place, she'd lost the haunted look he'd seen far too often over the last few days.

"Beth!" Cam jumped up to offer her his seat. "Come and sit down."

"It's okay, Cam, she'll sit here." Alex patted the bed beside him. When Beth perched delicately on the edge, he turned towards her, timing it just right, so that the kiss she intended for his cheek landed squarely on his mouth.

Cam groaned. "Come on, guys, get a room! Do you have any idea how nauseating it is for a blissfully single man to watch you two get all loved up? I'll have indigestion for a month!"

"Ignore him, sweet, he's just jealous."

"Maybe we should do some matchmaking," Beth suggested mischievously.

This time, Cam's eyes rolled. "Heaven preserve me! Just for that, I'd make you walk back to Winterleigh, except he'd try to beat the crap out of me."

The three of them talked a while longer, as only three people bound by one single, terrifying experience could talk. If any good could be said to have come from that incident, it was that it further cemented the friendship between the two men, strengthened the love between Beth and Alex, and created an unbreakable bond between all three.

Eventually, Cam stood and rolled his shoulders. "Right. I'm going to get the car and bring it around to the front. Anything to get me out of here while you two do the kissy-kissy thing." His face creased in a comically over-the-top grimace.

"You're just jealous, Cam!" Alex hurled the comment at his friend, and received a silent but cheerfully and expressively obscene parting gesture in return.

Once his friend had gone, Alex turned to Beth, his expression becoming serious once more. "There's something I have to ask you, love. The things you saw, the things I did—"

"Shh." She placed a finger on his lips. "I know it was self-defence. I know you did it to protect both of us. What terrified me most was the possibility of you being hurt. When I saw the blood..." Her voice trailed off, eyes fixed on the area where he'd been wounded.

"It looked worse than it was, sweetheart."

Her face spoke volumes about the degree of her scepticism. He could understand her point of view, but relative to the experiences that had already left their mark on him, the gunshot wound was next to nothing.

Her breath came out in a huge sigh. "I wish I didn't have to go home. I hate being without you."

"It won't be for much longer, I promise." He kissed her fingers. "I'm going to get out of here just as soon as I can."

As he watched Beth, felt the small, comforting movement of her thumb over the back of his hand, a sense of soul-deep rightness swept over Alex. This was how his life was meant to be, shared with this unique woman.

It was how Beth's life was meant to be, too, and the radiance of her slow, gentle smile told him that she wasn't about to argue. She was home.

Contrary to statistics and the forecast, there was a white Christmas that year.

It was Beth and Alex's first Christmas together. The events of autumn were behind them now, though not forgotten, and since then there had been many changes in both their lives.

The way things turned out, for all practical purposes,

Beth had moved out of her apartment the night her ankle was injured in the mugging. She'd returned to her former home for the sole purpose of collecting her belongings and arrange for larger items to be transported to Winterleigh, all of which she'd done without a hint of regret. Nor had she been back to the office, for one very significant reason—there was no office for her to go back to.

Oh, the building was still there and so was the business, but the latter no longer belonged to the man walking hand-in-hand beside her through the snow. Alex, just about fully recovered from the lingering effects of his wound, had sold Paduan Ventures and even given up the lease on his London apartment. He was now deciding what to do with the rest of his life—besides supporting Beth in her new career as a writer.

Alex had finally managed to persuade her to let him read her novel. He'd provided some constructive criticism and then encouraged her to submit it to a suitable publisher; the news had finally come about ten days prior to this wonderful Christmas Day that her manuscript had been accepted for publication.

That had been Beth's second-best Christmas present. The first had been an early one—Alex's release from hospital, a little premature in the doctor's opinion, but Alex had insisted.

At least it had given Beth the opportunity to boss the big, bad Dom around while she supervised his recuperation… and to fall even more deeply in love with him. He'd been every bit the difficult patient she expected him to be, but she'd managed to keep him in line with promises of what he could do to her when he was fully recovered. A somewhat rash decision on her part, since she'd barely been able to sit down for three days, once he'd regained his strength. She smiled, hugging the memories to her, like a warm blanket.

"What are you grinning at, Beth? It's bloody freezing out here! I don't know how you managed to talk me into this route march."

"I seem to remember that this route march was your idea, Master," she reminded him. "Let's go for a brisk walk, you said. It'll blow the cobwebs away, you said."

"Did I say that? Are you sure I said that?"

He was teasing her. *Again.* Over the last few weeks, since he'd sold the business and moved to Winterleigh full-time, since they'd settled into the routine of being a couple, he'd been more relaxed and playful than she'd ever seen him, as if the weight of the world had been lifted from his shoulders. Unless they were *playing*, of course. Then he was every inch the Dom—her Master. At those times, she just melted with wanting him.

She'd also succeeded in persuading Alex to return to the counsellor, to deal once and for all with the demons from his past. Beth had sat beside him through every session, holding back the tears as Alex had gone into the details of his ordeal, passing her love and her strength to him through the simple act of touch, and on more than one night, she'd held him while he wept in her arms. The tears had helped to cleanse his soul, and then one night, after what had turned out to be his last session, instead of the tears, he had kissed her and made love to her with heart-breaking tenderness. While the memories—of both the IED incident and the kidnapping—would never truly leave him, they'd become something he'd learned how to manage. The bad days were fewer in number now.

"Oh, I'm absolutely sure."

He shrugged. "Whatever. You didn't answer my question." He'd switched on the Dom tone, his sure-fire way to get what he wanted from her.

"I was thinking of when you got your own back on me for making sure you rested when you came out of hospital, Master."

He laughed, the sound one of pure joy. "And if you tell me you didn't enjoy it, I won't give you more of the same when we get back home."

Eyes narrowed, Beth shot him one of her looks while trying to ignore the desperate need curling into life low in her belly. As always, she fumed at the ease with which he turned her on, while at the same time loving it. It was all part of their game. He'd decided that they would be spending most of the festive season enjoying each other in a variety of ways, and on New Year's Eve, he was planning to take her to Club Aegis for the first time. Beth was thrilled at the prospect.

"Here we are."

Alex had brought her to a secluded clearing in the woods that formed part of the grounds of Winterleigh. He turned to face her. Gloves removed, he framed her frozen face with toasty warm hands, his gaze intense as he lowered his head to kiss her. It was a kiss that claimed ownership of everything that she was, everything she would ever be, and in that claiming, she knew that he was giving everything he was to her.

"I love you, my sweet sub," he declared with a controlled, powerful passion. "I don't tell you that often enough."

"You don't need to say the words, Master. Your actions tell me that every day."

And they did. Beth knew without doubt that she was loved, protected and cherished beyond measure. She also knew she loved and trusted this man with all her heart, all her soul and all her life. He owned her, yet she felt freer than she could ever have imagined possible.

"Do they tell you how much you mean to me, sweetheart?"

She kissed his palm—an act that had come to symbolise her total devotion to him. And she knew exactly how much she meant to him. This man had risked his own life to save hers.

In the weeks that followed that terrifying incident, the truth had emerged about Ewan Underwood and the motivation behind his actions. The tragic event of his younger brother's death while under Alex's command had sent Ewan completely off the rails. In the years between Jimmy's death and the incident at Winterleigh, he'd been in and out of prison, each sentence providing him with the opportunity to pick up the skills and contacts he'd needed to exact his revenge. His desire for vengeance had taken over his life and ultimately robbed him of it.

"As much as you mean to me, Master."

He kissed her again, this time wrapping his arms around her to hold her hard up against his body. "I brought you here today for a reason, Beth. In spring this clearing is particularly beautiful—it's my favourite place on the entire estate—but I couldn't wait till spring. Not for this. This is too important and too urgent."

He released her, freeing one hand to delve into the pocket of his winter-weight parka. What he brought out remained hidden beneath clenched fingers.

"Beth Harrison, a man could wait his entire lifetime and never find a woman like you. I consider myself lucky beyond all any man could hope for, that you chose me to love."

Beth's smile radiated all she felt for this special, unique man. He was wrong about one thing, though. "As if I had any choice. You are an irresistible force, Master."

"In that case, you'll know that this is not a question." His grin clearly communicated his satisfaction with her assessment. The fingers of his clasped hand slowly opened, revealing a platinum and diamond solitaire engagement ring.

"Marry me."

AVAILABLE IN THE CLUB AEGIS SERIES

THE VELVET RIBBON
A former SAS officer has it all—except the one woman he wants more than life itself. Fate brings them together, but with someone from his past conspiring to destroy first his business and then his life, he must stop his unknown enemy before his woman becomes a target.

A WANTING HEART
When their paths cross at a family wedding, the ex-Royal Navy officer and the woman who ended their relationship three years ago can't fight the attraction that still binds them together. This time around, though, circumstances are very different—and so are they.

LOVE IS DANGER
Having witnessed his friends' happiness, an ex-SAS security expert and lifelong loner opens himself up to the prospect of a committed relationship. He falls for a woman he finds stranded in a broken-down car, but when she's injured in an incident connected with his work, his overprotective nature comes between them, with devastating consequences for both of them.

PASSION'S LAST PROMISE
Assigned to protect the genius behind a project of national importance, a former Royal Military Police officer must keep him safe while battling her attraction to him. He goes missing when a temporary transfer takes her away from him, and she must put her life on the line to save his.

WINTER'S FIRE
A former Royal Marines Commando must team up with his commanding officer's maddening assistant, to investigate the disappearance of a politician's daughter during a vacation at an exclusive resort.

COMING SOON

NO GOING BACK

Captivated by the stunning events manager at the hotel where a family wedding is being arranged, a jaded security expert must come to terms with the beautiful woman's secrets, when the past collides with the present and puts both their lives in jeopardy.

History isn't always carved in stone...

Since losing the woman who owned his heart and shared his soul over a decade ago, Sir Guy Somerton has dedicated himself to his work and the defence of the country he loves.

Maddie Scott's job as the events manager at a country house hotel revolves around happiness, celebration and organisation—worlds away from her previous life, where one false move could have meant instant death... if she was lucky.

When his niece asks him to accompany her on a visit to a potential venue for her forthcoming wedding, Guy doesn't expect to meet a woman who reignites a fire he's long believed extinguished, but for Maddie, the encounter presents her with an impossible situation and a temptation she can't resist.

A single word unleashes devastating secrets from the past, but then a far more dangerous threat comes calling, one that could tear Maddie and Guy apart forever...

ABOUT THE AUTHOR

When Christie Adams, author of contemporary steamy romance, isn't completely absorbed in the writing process, she's probably thinking about it—either the book she's currently working on, or one of the dozen other stories she'll have percolating away at the back of her mind.

In addition to writing, she also loves investing time in reading a good book, or browsing the internet in search of cute videos of puppies, a pastime that often helps with writer's block—or so she claims. On those rare occasions when she can tear herself away from the computer, she has a weakness for James Bond movies and romantic comedies.

Good chocolate is also one of her passions in life, often accompanied by a glass of her favourite tipple, English sparkling wine. And if she can be persuaded to abandon her writing for a while, she finds that chocolate, wine and a good movie on TV is an excellent way to pass a winter's evening.

To find out more about Christie and her books, please visit her website (http://christieadamsauthor.com/) or email her at christie@christieadamsauthor.com.

Printed in Great Britain
by Amazon

40822627R00218